Sea Road to Neverland

Steven L. Rowe

Archway Publishing books may be ordered through booksellers or by contacting:

Archway Publishing
1663 Liberty Drive
Bloomington, IN 47403
www.archwaypublishing.com
1 (888) 242-5904

Because of the dynamic nature of the Internet, any web addresses or links contained in this book may have changed since publication and may no longer be valid. The views expressed in this work are solely those of the author and do not necessarily reflect the views of the publisher, and the publisher hereby disclaims any responsibility for them.

Any people depicted in stock imagery provided by Thinkstock are models, and such images are being for illustrative purposes only.
Certain stock imagery © Thinkstock.

ISBN: 978-1-4808-2600-7 (sc)
ISBN: 978-1-4808-2601-4 (hc)
ISBN: 978-1-4808-2602-1 (e)

Library of Congress Control Number: 2016900990

Print information available on the last page.

Archway Publishing rev. date: 2/24/2016

Chapter 1

A Matter of Honor

Eager hands had cleared the common room of the tavern in Tortuga of furnishings to give the two men ample room to fight. Tables and benches had been shoved against the walls, piled up in a careless fashion that made the proprietor silently groan with dismay.

His display of consternation was silent because he understood the temperament of his clientele. Pirates, smugglers, thieves, unhung murderers, and other assorted cutthroats crowded around the open area at the center of the room. They were not the sort to appreciate any slights pointed out by him with regard to their behavior. To criticize their handling of his furnishings was to invite those same chairs and benches to be shattered as a response to his boldness, perhaps across the balding dome of his skull.

Muttered bets and shouted oaths of encouragement rumbled in a low thunder that foretold the storm of violence that was to come. There was already a clear favorite. Most of those willing to wager their stolen coins felt certain who the victor would be.

The barkeep and the doxies who served the rum and ale crowded together behind the heavy wooden bar for safety. This was supposed to be an affair of honor between two sailors. Everyone who worked in the Bent Cutlass knew that such an affair could quickly dissolve into an all-out brawl that would result in smashed furniture and broken bones at the least.

Barney Goodtipple, owner, proprietor, and dispenser of strong drink, had been in the position of having to rebuild his grogshop from the walls out more than once. Buccaneers were notorious for their rough ideas of amusement and their careless handling of the property of others—almost as much as they were known for the free hand with which they spent their ill-gotten gold.

If Barney had to purchase new tables, chairs, and tankards once every few months, it still left him a handsome profit from gentlemen such as the two preparing to settle matters between them with a contest of strength, cunning, speed, and cold steel. Besides, those same brigands brought in chairs, tables, and other such necessary items from stolen cargoes, which they sold at bargain prices simply to empty their holds.

Sizing up the two combatants, Barney leaned cautiously over the polished expanse of wood and whispered hoarsely, "A doubloon on the skinny fellow."

The wager was eagerly taken by a grim-faced man wearing a dirty frock coat that marked him as a leader among the rough brigands. His chin appeared almost blue with the thick black bristles pushing out for their rendezvous with the razor. The man drank black rum, was hard faced, and had a low, commanding voice. He had been called "Flint" by one of the men getting ready to fight; the others, clearly of his crew, simply called him "Captain" and were quick to jump to his commands.

Most of the bets were being placed in favor of a tall, broad-shouldered young corsair with a bland pale face. He was an eloquent speaker in his way, even though his accent was that of the West Country, and his words were not those of an educated man. Flint and his crew were offering to take all wagers against this man, their champion, yet only a few among the other customers were taking them up on their offer.

One who did was a genial-looking, soft-spoken Irishman,

a bit rotund and yet still with an air of danger about him. The spectacles that he wore low on his round red nose made him appear harmless and a bit silly, while the cutlass on his hip and the crowd of daggers and pistols in his belt told another tale entirely—a pirate, as most there were, though no friend to Flint or any of his men.

He had entered not long before the insults had begun to flow, and he sat apart from all others, enjoying his rum and the entertaining sights found in an establishment like the Bent Cutlass. The wenches who served out the rum and ale were especially fine, and the customers displayed among them excellent examples of buccaneers and smugglers for those eager to see such creatures in their natural habitat.

The Irishman had silently measured both the fighters with a keen eye when their cross words and threats had first been exchanged. He thought hard before holding up a small pouch and jangling it to attract the attention of one of Flint's men.

Barney Goodtipple saw the wager placed and decided that he might venture a second gold coin on the cadaverous fellow as well. In height, that man was a match for the first, of about the same age as well. He wore a serviceable rapier at his hip and had a well-used dagger under his belt, and his emaciated form held a confident stance. His face was handsome and proud, swarthy in coloring and a touch imperious, with a thick fall of long black hair that hung in tightly curled columns, perhaps more fitting on a wench than a man who sailed under the black flag. The piercing blue eyes might have recalled the color of forget-me-nots—had there been any of a poetic nature among that rough crew—beautifully blue and hinting at a soul-deep sadness forever unspoken. But not even the genial-looking Irishman had that much of a poet within him, even though the Irish were known for their lyrical way with words.

Like his opponent, the thin man was well spoken, though he picked his words with the diction of a man amply supplied with education. Such an accent seemed out of place in the Bent Cutlass—indeed, anywhere in Tortuga.

The broad-built man had been part of the crew who arrived with Captain Flint and was the only one of them who spoke to Flint like an equal. If Barney had guessed, he might have thought he was the mate or quartermaster under Flint. Such men were as much in charge of a vessel in the sweet trade as the captain himself—sometimes even more. There was a bitter rivalry between those two, if the barkeep was any judge, though neither seemed ready to try conclusions with the other.

The thin man had come in alone, a sailor on the beach as the saying had it, and seeking a ship, from the look of him. While his garments were neat and clean, they were also ragged and threadbare. Long out of style, his clothes appeared to have been looted from a trunk that had been forgotten for a hundred years. He had ordered wine, careful with the few coins in his pouch, and only began to speak to those around him after a second mug had loosened his reserve.

A captivating speaker, he told remarkable tales of his past. As a reward for his skill as a raconteur, some of those listening to him had been glad to supply him with more wine and of a better Spanish vintage than the man had afforded himself. There had even been a platter of roast pork and potatoes for him, provided by Barney, when the storyteller made slight mention of the meals he had missed in the last few days. The proprietor of the Bent Cutlass knew that such a teller of tales increased the sales of wine, ale, and rum in his establishment even more than the sight of a plump bosom or a well-turned ankle.

Those around him listened with increasing attentiveness as he told of his time sailing under Blackbeard, especially when he spoke of the last battle that the legendary pirate fought. With his educated turn of speech and neat manners, the fellow seemed an unlikely choice to have served with Blackbeard. Yet, as he spoke of how he, once Blackbeard's bosun, had been the only one of the crew to escape capture that dark day, his words were delivered in such a fashion as to be absolutely convincing.

He told of having survived the day by slipping over the side—after dispatching the man he faced—when the giant pirate had been slain and the battle had been lost. None there saw aught amiss with such an action, counting it as an intelligent act. If anything, they admired him the more for his discretion in that hopeless situation.

He recounted swimming underwater to safety among the reeds that lined the inlet where Blackbeard's sloop had been anchored. From there, he had watched with disgust as his captain's head was hung under the bowsprit of the sloop commanded by the victorious Maynard and his men.

"Bad form, I would have to say. It is one thing to kill a man, even to cut off his head in the heat of battle. After all, that is to be expected in this trade that we follow if we do not have the power to slay those who attack us. But to hang a man's head like a trophy afterward exposed to wind and weather and flies, and then parade it through Bath Town shows a certain lack of propriety that I simply cannot tolerate."

By then, the voice of the thin man had risen under the influence of the wine he had consumed and in response to the general din of the common room. His audience had called a time or two for the men gathered around Flint and his quartermaster to hush their tones so that they could hear better. At that same time, the broad, blunt man had been speaking as well, telling the story of an improbable entanglement he had found himself in with regard to the daughter of a Spanish nobleman.

The vocal conflict between the two men became obvious to both of them, and each raised his voice to be heard. As one became increasingly annoyed with the other, comments were added to their tales that had no bearing on their stories, only on the character of the man attempting to interrupt.

The matter came to a head when the thin man paused for a sip of his wine just as the broad-built man thundered out, "He'd no more know the truth than he would the name o' his own father."

As insults went, that one seemed a pale and listless thing, the sort that preceded a casual dismissal of a tale between friends and not much more. For all that, it stung the thin man where more pungent words had not. In a quick flash of anger, he hurled the contents of his mug into the broad pale face of his rival.

In all truth, there were but the dregs of the wine left, only a few drops that moistened a stained and much-mended shirt—wine that was lost amid the ale that already wetted the quartermaster's chin and chest. It was not the wine so much as the contempt of the gesture that fired anger to meet rage and set the two on the path to violence.

"Ho there, Barbecue," Flint called out in a falsely jovial tone. "Let this ragged popinjay give us a bit o' entertainment afore ye carve him up. Make room, lads. Make room. We'll have us a proper dance floor fer these two ter dance their jig. An' rules as well, ter make this an interestin' amusement."

Flint studied Barbecue a moment, thinking on what pleased his quartermaster, or, more correctly, what would displease him the most.

"We'll keep this a friendly fight—that be my decision," he said with a slow, vicious smile. "Daggers only, just ter the drawin' o' first blood, with the winner bein' him what shows the color of t'other's blood first."

The Irishman might have been the only one to note the slight wince from the thinner of the two combatants when Flint had made his pronouncement—an insignificant tightening around the lips, a touch of increased pallor to cheeks already pale, and sharp white teeth that ground together with an audible click.

"There is an unusual dislike in this one for the sight of his own blood, it seems to me," the Irishman said to himself. "That will fire him as much as his bruised pride, perhaps even more, or I'm a Dutchman."

With that thought in mind, the jovial fellow jingled another small pouch and displayed the gold within to another piratical patron who displayed interest in wagering on the outcome in favor of Flint's man.

Barbecue was protesting loudly and profanely about the restrictions that his own captain had set.

"I be hardly warmed to such an affair until a bit of blood be showed," he complained. "Why, a pinking or two be what brings me to my best. Let this beanpole have a touch o' luck and call him the winner on that account? T'ain't fair nor proper, says I! Lay on with our blades until one can't stand, that be the way to settle matter twixt us, as always has been!"

"Fair, my cocker?" Flint said. "Proper, says ye? Ye've slit many a gullet in yer day—I grants ye that, Silver, an' blood fair brings on a frenzy in ye, from yer veins or any other's. We'll measure who be the quicker wit an' the faster blade to settle between ye, and that be my last word on the matter!"

The thin man looked down his nose at Flint and spoke.

"Your last word on the matter? Do you think that your word can bind me? This dull ox from your crew deserves to have his tripe introduced to the night air. Why should your last word decide my actions?"

Flint showed his collection of blackened and broken teeth in a grimace that some might have considered a smile. His right thumb drew back the edge of his grimy coat and rested on the butt of a worn flintlock thrust into his belt.

"And there be a mate o' this one right aside it," the blue-chinned pirate said, chuckling, "so as ye both can have a taste o' fire and lead iffen ye ignores my words. You too, Barbecue. Iffen ye slips once I calls a winner."

"Ah, I see," the slender fellow replied, seemingly unruffled. He might have been at the meeting of a London debating society for all the emotion he displayed. Only a devilish glimmer of angry light in his blue eyes gave a hint that he felt anything at all.

"You present an argument that I am unable to refute, and so I shall acquiesce to your decision. I give my word that I will not continue once first blood is drawn."

He eyed Barbecue with cold disdain. "Unless your man refuses to accept his defeat," he added as a codicil.

Flint laughed with a hacking sort of sound that put one in mind of a dying man—not a man dying from poor food or sickness or simple old age, no—a man coming to his end because of the cruelty of his fellow man, aided and urged on by the insertion of a cutlass to his vitals. That was the kind of laugh Flint had, and it brought equally cruel laughter from his men.

"Ol' Barbecue, he knows what will come his way iffen he don't lay up his blade when I calls winner, and no mistake o' it."

The Irishman decided that Flint was hoping that the burly man would indeed forget himself, giving the pirate captain an excuse to use one of his pistols. He also judged that Flint was concerned about the opinion of the rest of his crew, so there had to be a clear disregard for the rules before Flint would feel safe in ridding himself of the rival.

"I agree to the terms of this duel, then. Let us prepare forthwith," the slim man said haughtily, speaking as if he had been the one dictating the rules of the fight and not Captain Flint.

In concert with his words, the fellow drew off his baldric and hung it carefully over the back of a chair that stood by itself near the door to the tavern. He took pains to ensure that the scabbard of his rapier tilted toward the open space where the fight was to occur, ready for his hand if he had occasion to need it. He followed the belt with his worn and faded doublet and folded it as neatly as if it had been fine and new.

In response, Barbecue pulled the cutlass from his belt and carelessly tossed it over his shoulder. The naked blade was snatched from the air by a dark-visaged rogue with shifty eyes.

"Thankee, Black Dog," Barbecue said, without looking around.

In a mockery of the thin man's care for his shabby finery, Flint's man pulled off his stained and dirty shirt and threw it behind him with the same care he had displayed for his cutlass. The garment was snatched out of the air by the same furtive man who had caught the sword.

The chest that was revealed was broad, muscular, and hairy. A map of scars crisscrossed the pale expanse of skin, showing that the quartermaster had no fear of taking a cut. That he was still alive suggested that those who had wounded him in the past had not survived to tell the tale.

The plump Irishman poured half a tankard of ale down his throat. It appeared that, just as the broad-chested man had boasted, he fought his best once blood began to flow. The Irishman fished in the pocket of his waistcoat until he retrieved the last coins he carried. Holding them up, he soon had a taker for that wager as well.

He knew it was a risk, placing all the money he had on the thin stranger. It might mean that the ale in his mug was the last he would taste that night. Or he might win enough for a truly memorable drunk before stumbling back to his duty and the captain he dreaded. By the nature of his Irish soul, he was willing to take such a gamble and not only because of the winnings he might take with him. It appealed to him to give support to the man who, at first glance, seemed to be the underdog in the contest. Barbecue was a pirate with high standing among his mates. Even his captain recognized how formidable he was. That Flint had not already rid himself of that obvious contender for command of their ship proved what a dangerous character this quartermaster must be.

Blackbeard's former bosun, for all the handsome cruelty of his features, for all his fine speech and education, for all the evidence shown by his well-used sword and dagger, did not seem to have much of a chance against a brigand like Barbecue, even in a contest that would end when first blood was drawn.

The Irishman grinned at that thought. He had seen, often

enough, that first blood and heart's blood could be the same thing. The bland quartermaster undoubtedly knew that and was prepared to strike to the heart to end the affair in his favor. The question that had not yet been answered was if the thin stranger understood that fact as well.

Both men had their daggers in hand—fittingly, one broad bladed for Barbecue, the other long, slender, and gleaming with a razor's edge for the thin man.

"Be ye ready, my fine cockerels? Aye? The let the feathers fly, me jolly lads, and have at it!"

Barbecue leaped forward with a lunge and slash that would have sundered shirt, flesh, and ribs had it connected. The thin fellow fluidly slid out of the way of that rush, riposting smoothly with his own thin blade. His opponent twisted to the side, and the blade that would have sliced his shoulder to the bone only managed to harvest the tip of Barbecue's tarred pigtail.

Flint had called it a dance floor in jest, seeking to annoy both his own shipmate and the stranger. In truth, it soon seemed very much like a dance as the two men lunged, sidestepped, whirled, and made sweeping gestures with their arms to strike and to avoid being struck.

Barbecue was fast for a man of his bulk, fast for near any man. His thin opponent was perhaps even faster by a hair, managing to avoid the sharp tip of the knife that continued to seek his flesh by the scantest of margins.

It was an elaborate, deadly dance, which went on for several minutes. The thin man had beads of sweat on his forehead that plastered down his long black curls. Barbecue had perspiration running in streams down his broad chest. His pale face was red with exertion, and his breath came in violent explosions.

One of Flint's men, a villainous cutthroat with curiously flat, dead eyes, had put a hand to his own slim blade. The back of the slender fellow was to him now and again and presented a tempting target. It was clear he wanted his shipmate, Barbecue, to emerge the victor and thought to aid him in an obvious fashion. He had his dirk halfway from its sheath before the Irishman spoke calmly from behind him.

"It's Pew that they called you, were it not? Aye? Well, friend Pew, if it is thoughts of giving aid to your big compatriot you're having, I advise you against such an action. Little Timmy Thunder would take it amiss."

The Irishman had more than sweet reason and polite words on his side. The vicious-looking Pew suddenly paled as he felt the wide mouth of a short-barreled pistol grinding hard against the small of his back. That would be the Little Timmy Thunder the bespectacled Irishman spoke of. The soft, friendly voice seemed so at odds with the threat presented by the barrel of the flintlock that even a hardened murderer like Pew shivered.

If ever there was a man ready to smilingly commit cold-blooded murder—and have no hard feelings about it—that Irishman seemed the man. The blade that Pew had half-drawn slid back into its leather scabbard. Pew kept his hands carefully away from the other weapons that festooned his sash so as to not provoke the Irishman or his friend, Little Timmy Thunder.

The two combatants had not been using just their knives against each other. Fists and feet had been a part of the battle as well to hold, trip, or slow their opponent. In avoiding Barbecue's steel, the thin man had laid himself open to several punishing blows to the ribs from his opponent's free hand. His shirt hid the growing bruises from sight, so that only those few in the audience who were thoughtful men guessed at the pain he felt. It was the Irishman who best guessed what his champion was suffering, and he began to regret the wagers he had made.

The quartermaster grew angry, and with his anger came a berserk strength. His keen blade whistled as it cleaved the air in an attempt to reach flesh. Once the knife came close to opening the neck of his thin opponent, ripping through the dingy foam of lace at the throat of his shirt. Another time it sliced deep though the ruffles at his wrist, barely missing the flesh and bone above the hand. Had Barbecue connected as he had intended, the educated brigand would have held both his spoon and fork in his left hand for the rest of his life. If he had any life left to him.

The howls and cheers of the onlookers had grown to a thunderous roar. Barney Goodtipple and his barmaids had climbed atop the bar to watch the fight, joined by half a dozen of the shorter patrons. In their excitement, they leaped up and down, unmindful of the strain they were putting on the abused wood.

Flint's crew and the other brigands who frequented the Bent Cutlass had been joined by a score of villainous passersby who were attracted by the commotion. The sound of a good fight always brought customers to the Bent Cutlass, though Barney was of no mind to fill tankards at that moment and miss the sight of such an excellent scrap.

For a fight that had been in progress so long, the ending came with surprising suddenness. Barbecue was menacing his slender opponent with his superior strength and reach in one moment, and, in the next, the big man had slammed down on the planks hard enough to make sawdust jump from the cracks.

The one-time bosun of *Queen Anne's Revenge* had whirled in close to the blade of his opponent, bending back at the waist to allow the steel to pass over him by a scant inch. As he came up again behind his foe, he kicked hard, striking the quartermaster at the back of his knee with enough force to knock that pin entirely out from under him and drop the big man flat on his back.

In a flash, the cruelly handsome man was atop his foe, one foot jammed in an armpit to keep the knife-hand pushed away, the other under Barbecue's chin. The tip of his long, slender dagger hovered over the inside of his enemy's thigh. At the first sign of struggle, that blade would drive deep, and Barbecue knew that all too well.

"I know my father's name quite well," the thin man said conversationally, trying to hide his panting. "I could name him for you, just whisper that name into your thick hairy ear. If I were to do so, however, I would be obliged to end your life before you could betray that knowledge to another. And I would feel the need to kill you if I disclosed my reason for that as well."

The slender man looked around at all those who had witnessed the battle. Those who had been cheering or groaning the outcome fell silent, stung by the cold force of his stare. Those who stood in the inner circle drew back, for the first time willing to relinquish their position to those who had previously been trying to push forward.

"I am completely familiar with the concept of truth as well, such as the undeniable truth that I could draw first blood from this vein in your leg, and you would be dead before I could collect my belongings."

He turned his cold blue eyes on Captain Flint.

"Or the truth that your captain would be happy to see me do just such a thing, which is a truth you already comprehend, I suspect."

"Aye, aye," agreed Barbecue, sweating because of the fact that his life was entirely in the hands of one who had no cause to think kindly of him, and there was not a thing he could do about it.

With that knowledge before him, Barbecue let the knife fall from his hand.

"What saves you this night is the simple fact that it would be bad form to take advantage when I hold you so helpless. What I could do and what is the proper thing to do are two very different things."

The thin fellow suddenly flipped his dagger into the air, caught it so that the blade was point downward in his fist, and thrust, driving the steel into the worn floorboards along the *outside* of Barbecue's left leg, the keen edge slitting the fabric and lightly cutting the flesh beneath. In the silence that followed, the leg of the dirty canvas breeches darkened as blood stained it from the shallow cut.

"Is there any question as to who the winner of this affair has been?" he inquired, working his blade free from the wood with care not to scratch Barbecue a second time. First blood only had been the rule he agreed to. It would be bad form to violate his word through carelessness.

"Ye be the champion this night, and no mistaking it," Flint declared, with some reluctance.

For all that the pirate captain had enjoyed seeing his quartermaster bested in the tavern fight, he was out a good number of coins. The same could be said for many of his crew. Much of their losses had gone to that grinning ape of an Irishman from Red Michael Conner's crew. Bad enough to lose that much gold to anyone—but to a member of Captain Conner's crew? It was shame they would have to bear until they had a chance to meet their rivals on the open sea.

Flint shook his head in disgust and harshly told his lads to pay up without delay or argument. No man of the *Jolly Roger* would ever be able to say that Captain Flint and his crew did not pay their debts.

The thin victor sprang to his feet with a vigor that belied the violent exertion he had just undergone.

"I find that I am in need of fresh air after such a brisk business as this," he remarked coolly, slipping his dagger into its resting place. "Captain Flint, I bid you and your men a good evening."

When he turned, he was surprised to see a smiling red-cheeked Irishman with his baldric slung over one shoulder, holding out his doublet to aid him in putting it on.

"A glorious bit of work, young sir, and it is pleased I am to have witnessed such a display of skill. Would you be minding if I walked with you for a time and perhaps put to you a proposition as well?"

The Irishman had abandoned his plan of getting gloriously drunk thanks to the gold he had won. He could see possibilities in the victor of the fight and did not want to miss an opportunity.

Rum, he reluctantly decided, would simply have to wait until another time.

The black-haired man cocked a thin, aristocratic black eyebrow and considered the Irishman. There seemed no mockery in him, nor did he appear to hide a sinister motive. There could be no thought of robbery, for the winner of the duel had nothing of value to his name save for the clothes on his back, the sword at his hip, and the dagger in his belt. Items like that argued against robbery from even the most desperate.

"That is agreeable to me, Mister …?

"Smee, sir. Mr. Smee. A bosun, a thing what we shares in common from your words before that unpleasantness with the bully Barbecue. Where you once served Blackbeard and *Queen Anne's Revenge* in that capacity, I now serves aboard the *Jolly Roger*, Red Michael Conner, her captain."

The pair exited the Bent Cutlass together. Flint watched them go, speculating what the bosun from the *Jolly Roger* might want with the cadaverous stranger. Barbecue was doing his own speculating, wondering the best way to deal with this new enemy should the two of them cross paths again. He was unused to losing in a contest of that nature and even more unused to the feeling that his opponent had aroused in him. Fear.

Mr. Smee and his new companion walked for a while along the waterfront of the pirate stronghold on Tortuga. Even that late at night, the area was brightly lit with lanterns and torches. Grogshops and taverns were crowded with carousing buccaneers and their doxies. Warehouses holding stolen goods gathered from across the Caribbean were under heavy guard. A dozen ships lined the quay, ranging from a battered ketch to an elegant French frigate with gleaming brass guns arrayed on two gun decks.

It was the Irishman who finally broke the silence. Though he did not know it, it was another victory for his companion who had been determined to force Smee to speak his mind rather than asking any question of him.

"What might I be after calling you, sir?"

"James," was the flat reply.

"James what?"

"Just James. That name was given to me by my mother, and it is all that I have from her," James said, in a quiet, controlled voice.

"Ah," Smee said, thinking hard on what to say next. "What then of your father?"

James was silent for so long that Smee began to think he did not intend to answer. Perhaps this had been a bad idea after all. Smee was on the point of giving it up as a poor choice when James finally spoke.

"My father made it clear that he wanted nothing from me and had nothing to give to me. I have no use for the name he might have provided for me. I will not use the family name of my mother either, for I intend to become infamous in my career and will not have her memory tainted even remotely by my deeds."

This was not the first time the man had considered the impracticality of living his life with only a single name—and a name that was as common as the one his loving mother had given him in the bargain. It was becoming clear to him that he would need to adopt a name to replace the one he had rejected. Some name that would be as uniquely his as James was completely common.

"Ah, I see," Smee said, though in truth he did not. "So, it's Jimmy, then, is it?"

"No, it is James, never Jimmy; nor will I answer to Jim either, lest it be with my blade!" he replied, with the sort of cold anger that would send a chill through the most hardened of buccaneers.

Smee thought a bit on that and on the vehement way his companion had said it. Perhaps this father that James had been disowned by, and had thus disowned, had called him Jim and Jimmy in his younger days. Fathers tended to diminish their sons in that fashion until their sons proved their own worth. If that were so, it might be the reason for the dislike that James showed for those friendly names.

"James, though, it seems so formal," Smee protested. "Not friendly in the least. It's sure that you have friends. What, then, do your friends call you?"

James unbent a bit, seeing that the Irishman meant no harm and spoke with him on the most friendly of terms and in such an open fashion.

"Jas. Those few who are close to me sometimes call me Jas."

Smee smiled broadly at that admission.

"Well met, then, Jas. Smee, as I've said afore now. Just Smee, for I don't much care for the names my parents gave to me, either of them. Smee to my friends, and Smee to my enemies as well, until one of my friends here has words with them."

With that said, Smee patted the cutlass on his hip with his left hand, touching knife hilts and pistol butts sticking up from his belt with his right like he was tousling the hair on so many adorable little tykes all in a row.

"Well met, Mr. Smee," James said, offering his hand.

"Well met, indeed, sir," Smee replied, pumping the offered hand with enthusiasm.

James found it pleasing to his vanity that the Irishman readily recognized the high quality that was native to him. A pirate he might be, a brigand and a villain, but a villain of a superior sort—a scoundrel with breeding and education rather than a common cutthroat like Flint or his quartermaster, a man who attempted to act in good form no matter what situation confronted him.

"Indeed, it is wholly pleased I am to make the acquaintance of a man of your caliber, James," Smee continued, releasing the hand he had been shaking so vigorously.

"We have need of men, and you are a man indeed. I saw that right off. Now, here we are, sir, here at the *Jolly Roger*. And a finer ship never sailed under the black flag!"

The part of the ship revealed by torchlight did not live up to Smee's boast. What paint that could be seen was peeling. Bare wood showed where damaged areas had been repaired with new planks. Patches of mismatched paint suggested that wood had been pilfered from other ships. The mouths of half a dozen black iron cannons frowned at the rail, streaks of rust clear even in the uncertain light. The rail leaned outward drunkenly in two places, and the sails were filthy gray and patched with whatever scrap had come to hand.

"Oh, she needs a spot of paint and a touch of polish, that be true enough, but the *Jolly Roger* is still a fine brig—and a fast one too. She just ain't seen the proper care she requires since ol' Red Conner had that little dispute with Tommy Two-Toes, the quartermaster. Shot Tommy right in the brisket, Red Michael did, and heaved him over the side while he was still gaping in surprise."

Smee pushed up his spectacles with one finger, squinted at the ship, and shook his head, letting the spectacles slide down again.

"What we needs aboard the *Jolly Roger* is a new quartermaster, and I'm thinking you might just be the proper gentleman to occupy that position."

The brigantine did not look impressive. To the thin man, however, she showed promise. Ships he had planned to command in the past had all come to sorry ends before he could put his campaigns into action.

Sam Bellamy had been too stubborn to listen to reason when a nor'easter had blown up off Cape Cod, driving both his *Whydah* and *Mary Anne*, another ship in his pirate fleet, to wreck and ruin. *Queen Anne's Revenge* had been lost because of the secret schemes of Blackbeard to rid himself of excess crew and keep more of the loot for himself. The sloop *Adventure* had been taken by Maynard and his mercenary crew because of Blackbeard's carelessness in the enemies he made and the bearded pirate's fondness for black rum.

This brigantine, the *Jolly Roger*, ill cared for as she currently appeared, might be the very ship he was seeking. Becoming her quartermaster was a first step he had employed before. This time, he would have to act more swiftly.

Chapter 2

Captain Red Michael Conner

A sleepy guard sat on a barrel by the head of the gangplank leading onto the *Jolly Roger*, his head drooping down as he dozed. The fellow had massive arms and handsome features in the Mediterranean mold. A curiosity about him was the pair of heavy silver coins he wore dangling from his earlobes.

As soon as Smee put one foot on the gangplank, the man was instantly alert and on his feet, a long stiletto appearing in his hand with the unsettling suddenness of a conjurer's trick.

"Ah, Meester Smee," he muttered in a thick accent, relaxing and making the knife disappear again. "Issa early for you to re-turna. Oh ho, I see. You has a new hand for the *il capitano* to meet, *si*."

"Aye, Cecco, a new hand. The *Jolly Roger* has been without a quartermaster for too long to my way of thinking. Mr. James here has the qualities we are in need of, and no mistake of it. Why, you should have seen the neat way that he handled Barbecue."

That brought the darkly handsome sailor fully awake, just when he was settling down on his barrel to doze again.

"Ah-hah-hah? Theesa one? He bested Flint's *quartiermastro*, eh? Eet has verra bloody, mebbe? Theesa Barbecue, he dies verra hard, I have the hope?"

Smee shook his head sadly, sending his spectacles lurching from side to side across his round face.

"Ah, me. More's the pity, but no," he said, settling his spectacles back in place with a blunt finger. "Cap'n Flint said it were to be just a fight to first blood, and no more than that. Mr. James here, he played with ol' Barbecue for quite some time afore knocking him from his feet and pinking him, thoughtful-like, on the leg. Ain't something Flint's man will be forgetting any time soon, and you may lay to that, Cecco."

"Ah. Atsa good. Thatta one, he'sa no good, him. Too much of himself inside is 'at how you say?"

James looked at Cecco, the merest curl of a sneer wrinkling his mouth. He did not wish to begin his time aboard the *Jolly Roger* by giving needless offense to an established member of that crew, no matter how ignorant that man might be. It would be, after all, bad form to start in such a fashion. The position that Smee had proposed was desirous to a man without a farthing to his name. Even more so to a man with deeper plans for the future that he would not be divulging to anyone. It was difficult for James to subdue his natural inclination to display his obvious superiority over such an untutored lout as this Cecco. Only by keeping the ultimate prize to be gained by his scheme foremost in his mind was he able to find the impetus to curb his normal instinct.

"You mean that the blustering buffoon is full of himself?" he said to Cecco.

"Ah, si, si, Senore James!"

The slender man allowed himself a pleased smile at the show of respect.

"Yes, he most certainly was a puffed-up toad, though I have taken him down a peg or two, I should think."

James looked at Cecco a moment, considering the accent that marked his words.

"You are from Liguria, am I correct?"

"Si, si," Cecco replied excitedly. "You know theesa place? Just outside the glorious Genoa, in a leetle village, there I am born. Mebbe there I go back sommaday."

James smiled with a politeness that he could not bring himself to feel for the hulking Italian. Rather than speak the words that came to mind, he merely commented that he recognized the accent even though he had yet to have the pleasure of visiting Genoa or the environs around it. He could see no reason why he should explain how he had come by his knowledge of accents from that part of the Mediterranean, for that episode from his past would have no bearing on his future.

"Atsa good anyway. Mebbe later, we can share some vino, and I tella you about when I escaped from the *carcere di Goa*. Hah, what I do to the *governatore* there, they not gonna be forgetting much soon, no!"

Smee guided his new acquaintance away from the voluble watchman, turning their steps toward the rear of the brig and the companionway that led down into the stern of the ship to the captain's cabin.

"Oh, that Cecco—he's a choice one, so he is," Smee chuckled. "Always going on about that little prank he played on the fellow who was in charge of that prison when he escaped."

The bosun dropped his voice to a conspiratorial whisper.

"Don't let on as I've told you," he continued, "but he had himself a bit of fun breaking out. Wrote his name large with the point of a knife right in the governor's back."

Smee laughed again, almost an unseemly giggle.

"I heard tell that Cecco, not being so educated as you and me, misspelled it!"

The Irishman laughed again, a more proper, hearty laugh as a pirate should laugh.

"Oh, he'll talk your ear off over that, Jas," Smee chortled, wiping tears of mirth from his eyes.

He did not notice his companion stiffen at the casual use of his name.

"Talk it off or cut it off?" James inquired, acid in his tone.

"Took his measure straight off, did you?" Smee said happily. "Aye, he is a quick one with a blade, that Cecco, especially when he feels like he has been insulted."

He did not notice the displeasure James displayed at his familiarity—or he chose to ignore it as unimportant.

As they reached the companionway, a squat, bald-headed seaman stomped up the ladder and out on the deck. His skin was as brown as a walnut and nearly as wrinkled. One big ear flapped with three heavy rings of gold. It gave him a disconcertingly unbalanced appearance, for the other ear had been cropped off close to the side of his head, leaving only a grisly hole on that side.

"Ahoy, Jacob. Too many prunes again?" Smee inquired amiably.

Jacob growled a greeting to Smee and glanced curiously at James before marching resolutely toward the bow and the darkness there. James wondered if Smee's friendly heartiness was wearing thin with at least one member of the crew.

"Jacob there didn't think too much of Cecco's tale and told him so to his face, you see," Smee remarked, using a forefinger to waggle his own ear on the side where Jacob was lacking one.

If James was in any way shocked or amused upon learning of such an action by Cecco, he declined to show it. Given that his past history had included voyaging with the infamous Blackbeard, that might be easily understood.

Edward Teach—to use the name Blackbeard claimed as his proper one—had been known to be a notorious prankster. James had been in his captain's cabin when Blackbeard had drawn his pistols under the table, blown out the lantern, and then loosed both barrels at random. It had been the sailing master, Israel Hands, who had taken the brunt of that witty joke, one of the pistol balls smashing his knee and giving him a lurching limp for the rest of his life. It could just as easily have been the bosun instead of the sailing master, for Blackbeard had not cared which man he shot. Reminding his men of why he should be feared and respected had been his goal—nothing more serious than that.

To find himself aboard a ship where such pleasant jokes were played from time to time came as no surprise to James. A cropped ear or a missing finger was counted as nothing so long as the jest was sufficiently humorous. In a place like Tortuga, such a merry crew was the rule rather than the exception. What they would do to one another as a jest to pass an idle moment was but a mild indication of how they would treat the crew of a prize when they were in deadly earnest.

But the next person they encountered belowdecks did prove to be a surprise to James.

Curled up on a salt-stained bit of carpet before the door that led to the stern cabin was a boy. A very handsome boy he was too, perhaps twelve years old, though somewhat thin and small for that age.

Asleep as he was, he displayed a most winning countenance, being blond of hair and fair of skin. The sun had given him a constellation of freckles across rosy cheeks and his snub of a nose. His mouth was open a tiny bit, showing strong white teeth. There was a small gap between the upper front pair so that his sleeping breath whistled on the exhalation like a mouse squeaking. A slight smile curled one corner of his lips as if he were lost in pleasant dreams of fire and blood and murder—for Jas could think of no better dreams for a boy who sailed aboard a vessel like the *Jolly Roger.*

Smee looked at the sleeping boy and sighed. It was the kind of sound that a fond uncle might make on observing his sleeping nephew, content with how the boy was in repose and with just a touch of melancholy at the thought that the boy could not remain so young and innocent for all his days.

James immediately looked upon the child with suspicion, for all that the lad had not even opened his eyes, much less said a single word. Such a tender, familial affection was not right and fitting for a pirate like Smee.

Perhaps when a pirate retired from the sweet trade he might take a wife and produce offspring to dandle on his knee and look upon with such insipid warmth. James could not imagine wanting such a thing for himself, but he had heard there were those who sailed under the black flag who sometimes spoke of such a distant day in their future. Usually such longings emerged when the rum was gone and the wind did not blow and the weevils fought the rats for the last of the ship's biscuits.

The sleeping boy reminded James of his own brothers. Fair of skin and hair like this lad they were, so very innocent to the eyes of those who did not know what experienced devils they were beneath their adolescent facades. James had known them for what they truly were, though his father would never acknowledge their wickedness even when they displayed it openly before him.

James was the black sheep of the family, in looks and in manner. His deeds always merited reprobation rather than admiration, even those deeds that had been performed by his brothers. No matter who stole the jam or put a mousetrap beside the butler's shoes at night, it was James who got the blame and the punishment for the exploit.

Seeing this tyke asleep in such a blameless manner made James distrustful from the first. He viewed all boys as dangerous and deceitful, and, in his experience, boys as who displayed such innocence were the most dangerous of all.

This sour attitude was a result of his unfortunate familiarity with such creatures when he had been much younger. Younger— that was how James always thought of his past self. Never as a boy—he never recalled being a boy as other boys were—but as a younger *man*, for even before his schooling he had been called a young man, and he had been treated like a young man, even to his punishments. He was serious, intelligent, and always attempting to do what he understood to be the proper thing. Even if his understanding was not always perfect, he was always displaying good form, just as he had been instructed from his earliest memories. Cutting capers or playing ball or catching frogs and other such unfortunate creatures that commonly fell into the cruel, uncaring hands of boys the world around was not for James.

Thus, he could have no feelings for boys in general save those of suspicion and distrust. When he encountered one that engendered fond feelings in a grown man who should have remembered his own boyhood and been wary, his mistrust was redoubled.

"Tuck," Smee whispered gently. "Tuck, m'lad, is the cap'n awake?"

The boy opened his eyes, wide eyes that were an even paler shade of blue than those of James. For a moment, he looked about as if fearful of a blow and then relaxed upon seeing that it was Smee bending over him. In that brief moment of honest terror that Tuck showed upon waking, James could almost have forgotten his misgivings about a youth with such an apparent lack of guile.

Almost.

"Oh, Mr. Smee! It be you! Ye gave me a turn, so you did, sir," the boy uttered in a low voice, relief evident in his tone. "The cap'n? Aye, awake, I think. He stays up all hours when we is in port. Drinks and plots and looks over his charts and sich things as that. He ain't tol' me orf to my bunk yet, so I reckon him awake, sir."

Smee made a shooing gesture to tell the boy to move away from the door and then knocked briskly.

Tuck looked up at James and gave him a tentative smile. For his part, James did no more than nod to acknowledge that the boy existed. That seemed enough, for Tuck grinned broadly at the newcomer aboard the *Jolly Roger*.

The roar that came in response to Smee's knock might have come from a drunken walrus or perhaps a bear with a toothache. The bosun was not alarmed by such a bestial sound, swinging wide the cabin door and striding right in.

"Time to meet the cap'n, James," was all he said.

The stern cabin was filled with crates, chests, and barrels. Most had been plundered of their contents and then partially filled with empty bottles, soiled garments, broken weapons, and rotting detritus from a score of old meals. There was a massive table littered with more empty bottles. The scarred wood groaned under stacks of plates—pewter, silver, and even gold—all covered in scraps of food, chewed bones, and the newly hatched offspring of a few hundred flies. Because the *Jolly Roger* was at anchor in a calm harbor, the windows of the cabin were all open wide, allowing the effluvia from the filthy room to escape and be replaced by the far more pleasant odor of low tide and rotting fish.

Sitting behind the table was a man who could only be the captain of the pirate brigantine, Red Michael Conner. The filthy hulk could have been no one else, as no one else would have remained in that stinking space for more than a few minutes.

His massive shape draped in torn, tattered, and stained finery taken from a dozen different Spanish galleons, Red Michael leaned back in a colossal chair that creaked distressingly under his weight. The hair across the top of his head was thin despite the youth of his face, and it grew thick down his jowls and into a ginger beard about a finger's length long.

The sight of him put James in mind of an Irish mocking version of the obese Tudor king, Henry the Eighth. The smell of him gave thought to a herd of swine.

"Here, Cap'n. I found us just the man we needs aboard the *Jolly Roger*," Smee said happily, ignoring the black look Captain Conner sent his way. "This ol' ship ain't been the same since Quartermaster Two-Toes … err, left us sudden-like."

"Aye, the men ha' been lax in th'r duties," Conner allowed, eyeing the newcomer with suspicion.

"Well, Cap'n, I was over at the Bent Cutlass, having a tankard just to keep me warm what with this damp air and all, when I beheld a sight what give me great pleasure and also showed an answer to the ship's need."

Red Michael lifted up a bottle half full of raw rum, belched out a cloud of fumes that killed a dozen flies, and poured the deep amber liquid down his gullet, making a gesture that clearly told Smee to get on with it and not waste time.

"This here gentleman not only bested Flint's quartermaster in a first-blood duel, he was bosun for Blackbeard himself, even to the end."

"Mmmph?" Captain Conner asked eloquently while finishing his rum.

James stepped forward to address the massive pirate captain. As he had observed Smee doing, he breathed only through his mouth, which gave an odd quality to his voice.

"All true, Captain Conner, and much more as well. What your esteemed bosun has not yet learned is that I was also quartermaster for Captain Bellamy until he ignored my advice and ran his *Whydah* aground during a storm off the coast near Wellfleet. Three of us alone survived that wreck—with another seven from Bellamy's *Mary Anne,* which suffered the same fate for following too close. Saving for the ship's carpenters from both vessels, who pled that they were forced men, all the other survivors were hanged as pirates except young John Julian, the redskin, and he was sold as a slave. I, alone, of all of them escaped wreck, storm, and trial."

Red Michael wiped the rum from his chin with the back of a grubby sleeve.

"Seems t' me that yer either a lucky man or a Jonah," he belched. "Which be it?"

Still breathing through his mouth, James composed himself before answering with his customary pride.

"Blackbeard would have never lost his *Queen Anne's Revenge* had he heeded my advice, though I think it has become obvious that he planned to rid himself of that great vessel in an attempt to leave piracy behind. Later, when he decided that the sweet trade was the only life for him, my advice would have preserved his life when Maynard made his attack on Blackbeard's sloop, *Adventure*. Bellamy also ignored my words and lost his ship, his treasure, and his life. That I survived captains who made poor choices only shows my fine qualities, nothing more than that."

The account that James gave of his association with Black Sam Bellamy and Edward Teach was mostly true. Any lack in his brief words was with regard to his own schemes and not those of his deceased captains.

Leaning forward suddenly, the captain planted both broad hands on the table, spilling bottles and plates. Small black eyes in blubbery pits over a rum-reddened nose regarded James thoughtfully, right and left.

As Captain Conner stared hard at the man that Smee had brought before him in an attempt to judge his worth by the evidence of his eyes alone, James came to understand how the grotesque buccaneer came by the sobriquet of "Red." Those ginger whiskers were not enough to justify such an alias. But those massive hands gave the true explanation.

Every thick finger and both thumbs wore at least one ring, and nearly all of them carried at least one stone that was the color of fresh blood. On the right pinky was a silver ring with tiny skulls and scrolls and a round carnelian like a drop of fresh blood in the center. The ring finger and index finger of that hand also had their rings—one of silver and the other gold—each with a blood ruby the size of a man's thumb tip set into it. The pointer had three yellow bands with speckles of blood-red carnelian on each, and the thumb had a thick, silver band with a strip of crimson ruby as red as a fresh wound.

The left hand was much like the right, drops and blots of blood-colored gems on nearly every digit. The left pinky was an exception, for that ring was entirely of silver and carved into the shape of a grinning skull wearing a captain's tri-corner hat over a curled periwig with crossed cutlasses below. Conner's massive fingers required rings of such size that James could have worn only the captain's pinky rings on his own hand.

Looking at the array of crimson jewelry, James found that he lusted after one of them and one alone—the one on the smallest of Connor's fingers. It was the pure silver ring—that was the one he longed to see on his own hand. Veiling the thought in his mind, he looked up into Captain Conner's eyes.

He vowed to himself that someday that ring would be his. As would that stern cabin, properly cleaned and appointed, and the whole of the *Jolly Roger* and the crew she carried. Captain Red Michael Conner was unworthy of any of what he had.

This was the captain he had been seeking since he had chosen piracy as his path to infamy. Sam Bellamy had been too stubborn. Blackbeard had been too crafty, with a dozen plans of his own always at odds with the schemes James tried to put into effect. In coming to Tortuga, he had been seeking another vessel to ship on where he could eventually seize command and begin the reign of terror that would make his name known and feared throughout the world. In Captain Red Michael Conner, he found the perfect man to supplant and so to begin his design to gain revenge on all those in the world who had rejected him as unworthy, who viewed the circumstances of his birth as a mark against him that nothing could ever erase.

All those thoughts were in his mind as he met the gaze of Red Michael. Such was the superiority of James that not a single one of those thoughts showed in the periwinkle blue orbs that looked without a waver into the bloodshot eyes of the pirate captain.

"There be a familiar look to you," Red Michael slurred at last, squinting his piggish eyes to focus through the rum. "Boy! You lazy scut, get in here! Them pi'tures of them ol' kings, where be they? Find them, you worthless numbskull, and be quick about it!"

Tuck scurried in at the summons and proceeded to dig through the shambles that filled the cabin. He found a portrait and held it up, only to be roundly cursed by Captain Conner for finding the wrong one.

James noted that the painting Tuck uncovered had been punctured by pistol balls and thrown knives. Evidently, Michael Conner had no liking for kings or their portraits—a common attitude among those who sailed under the skull and crossbones, if truth be told. Some claimed a fondness for king and country but only so long as they were at a great distance from both their king and their country.

Three more paintings that had been treated with similar disrespect were pulled from the detritus and discarded before the boy found the one his captain demanded. A smallish thing, done by an artist of indifferent skill, it showed Charles the Second with a grim expression on his face, as if he had been contemplating the singular lack of skill of the painter trying to capture his likeness.

"There, there, y'see, Smee? That be what this rogue looks like! He could be the by-blow o' one of them royal Stuarts!"

With his eyes squeezed shut in laughter, Red Conner did not see the dangerous look that crossed James's face for an instant or the tiny spots of flaming red that appeared in those blue eyes. If James had had a pistol in his belt at that moment, he would have put a hole through the fat freebooter and damned the consequences.

Smee laughed weakly along with his captain, knowing that such mirth was a good policy whenever Red Michael laughed. There was a thoughtful look in his eyes—which did not share laughter with his mouth—as he compared the amateurish painting to the elegant, if somewhat shabby, man standing beside him.

"He pleases me, Smee, so I'll give him a go as quartermaster," Conner said at last. "Get the trash out of Tom Two-Toes's cabin, and let our new quartermaster settle in. Like enough, you'll have that cabin back for storing rubbish in a week or two, but maybe this rascal can have this tub halfway clean 'for I pitches him over to feed the fish!"

With that, Captain Conner exploded into laughter again, as if he had displayed great wit.

Picking up his rum bottle, the obese brigand tilted back his head to let rum flow down his throat, only to discover that the bottle was empty.

"Tuck! Tuck, damn yer eyes, where's the rum! Fetch it quick, you scum, or I'll …"

He drew back his ring-laden hand to strike, and Smee cried out in alarm.

"Cap'n, no!"

There was stark fear in Smee's voice as he blurted out those words.

Conner looked at the bosun in anger for a moment and then considered his upraised hand and the boy cowering before him. His face paled as if he had been about to do something as foolish as checking the gunpowder in a cask by the light of an open candle.

"Aye. You have the right of it, Smee—not while we're in port. His nightmares would serve us ill here," he muttered nervously, lowering his hand slowly. "Stop yer sniveling, you cowardly runt, and fetch me my rum. Then off with you, all of you. I needs to think on our next prize."

Dismissed by the great tub of lard, Smee and James left the cabin while Tuck rummaged for another rum bottle. There was nothing that would ever get James to like the ship's boy, and certainly, he would never have the sort of affection for him that Smee displayed. From the moment when Red Michael had raised his hand to strike, however, James felt sympathy for the lad. Aye, sympathy and a desire to see Red Michael dead for reasons other than his own lust for the *Jolly Roger*, her crew under his own command, and that silver ring on his hand.

Captain Red Michael Conner had displayed terribly bad form

in his threat. James could tell that Tuck had felt a blow from that hand many times before. Even Smee's words confirmed that, but what the bosun said also hinted at something else, something that puzzled the new quartermaster of the *Jolly Roger*.

There was a mystery behind the fear that Smee displayed when Conner had raised his hand to the boy. It was more than just alarm for Tuck's safety, that was certain. James observed that Red Michael himself had felt dread when he realized what he had nearly done, and it had not come from revulsion at nearly having struck the boy.

If James was any judge, that fat greasy dog enjoyed brutalizing Tuck verbally and was only refrained from doing so physically because they were in port. Why that should matter to Red Michael was something that James knew to be important, although until he discovered the secret, he would not know *why* it was important.

"Here you go, Jas, er, ah, Quartermaster James. Your cabin," Smee babbled pleasantly. "Reckon as how it ain't fittin' for me to refer to you all familiar-like now that you are quartermaster."

James was pleased that Smee had come to that conclusion on his own. It saved him the trouble of impressing on the bosun the need to show respect for those of higher rank. It also prevented the hard feelings that such a lesson might have brought out in the otherwise good-natured Mr. Smee.

Aboard a vessel sailing on the account, as the *Jolly Roger* was, discipline could be nonexistent, or it could be as strict as aboard a ship of the line with a martinet in command. In James's view, even a pirate crew functioned better when only one man was captain rather than all men having an equal voice. That also meant that the ship's officers had their hierarchy that had to be respected by all aboard, from captain to cabin boy. From what he had seen, Red Michael Conner enforced respect for his position of command, and Tuck showed every indication that he understood his place aboard the *Jolly Roger* as well.

Smee fumbled with a handful of keys until he found the one

that unlocked the small door and swung it open. As an after-thought, he took the key off his ring and handed it to James.

"It was so unexpected when Tommy Two-Toes, er, left us, that all his belongs were left behind, Mr. James," Smee explained, lighting a candle from the hallway lantern and placing it on a tiny desk in the little closet of a room.

"Seems only right that whatever is here is yours now, seeing as how you are taking over Tommy's duties. Don't rightly know that his clothes will fit your frame, him being more like the cap'n in build, but there be instruments, pens, parchment, and pistols all through there, so I figures you'll find much of what you need."

James looked around the dusty, cobwebby cubical dubiously. It was larger than anything he had had aboard the *Whydah*, *Queen Anne's Revenge,* or *Adventure*. It was also nearly as filthy and crowded with debris as Captain Conner's cabin, so the dis-pute between quartermaster and captain could not have been over cleanliness. A particularly vicious arachnid the size of a teacup scuttled out from behind the moldy pillow on the narrow folding bunk. The creature braced itself in a position of threatening defi-ance, daring James to enter its domain.

"Mr. Smee, these quarters will do once they had been properly cleaned," the new quartermaster said, whipping his rapier from its scabbard and lunging expertly.

The defiant spider expired, skewered like a specimen in a naturalist's collection.

"That will require daylight and the assistance of some of the crew," he continued, pulling a tattered remnant of a handkerchief from his sleeve.

He used the bit of rag to clean the spider off his blade and folded the tiny corpse into the stained cloth.

"For this night, all I will require is a hammock and a place on deck, preferably where the sea breeze can reach me and drive away the stench of the port."

"Aye, Mr. James," Smee replied, amazed at the display of skill, speed, and nerve required to dispatch one of those deadly jumping spiders in the uncertain light of a single flickering candle.

"I knows of just the place, and there ain't many of the crew aboard tonight, so you won't even be bothered by their snoring."

James allowed a slight smile to turn up the corners of his haughty features. There were many things aboard the *Jolly Roger* that bothered him, but they were all things that he could put to rights in time. The snoring of sleeping crew members was the last thing that would be troubling him that night or any of the nights to come.

James rested well that night, troubled only by a brief dream of a glittering star that he desperately yearned to find. It was an old dream, the only dream he ever recalled having. When he awoke briefly in the darkness on deck, the star was still gleaming in his mind. He took the dream as a good omen for the future.

Chapter 3

Aboard the *Jolly Roger*

The new quartermaster of the *Jolly Roger* looked around with great satisfaction. He stood proudly in the waist of a vessel much altered because of his influence. A month under a firm hand guided by a keen mind had changed the brigantine for the better in his opinion.

For all his faults, most of which James was perfectly willing to claim, none could say that the quartermaster of the *Jolly Roger* lacked self-assurance.

He felt the most pride when he thought of the changes that had been wrought on Captain Red Michael Conner's grimy cabin.

That chamber had lost its sty-like facade and had been re-turned to the glory held before the blubbery Conner had taken command of the *Jolly Roger*. At first, James had undertaken the work with assistance only from young Tuck. Smee aided their cause by keeping the captain engaged on deck with various trivial matters relating to the course they should be following. While Red Michael was thus occupied and distracted, James and Tuck gathered the worst of the garbage and dumped it out the stern windows and into the sea.

It was a nasty trick to play on the fishes, even though there were culinary delights for those finny creatures among the trash.

The fish found bones that had not been picked clean of meat; rinds, seeds, and peelings from exotic fruits; and, most bountiful of all, the grubs and maggots that had thought themselves safe and secure among the debris while they waited to mature and bring forth another generation of flying vermin.

Rats that had nested amid the litter were likewise evicted, mostly chased out for a long swim by the broom wielded by Tuck. Some escaped into the hold to join the colony of rodents that always could be found in the dim corners of a vessel, no matter how clean it was kept.

Michael Conner had not showed gratitude for the transformation at first. On returning to his cabin to find the boxes, chests, and casks that had once filled the room bobbing in the wake of the brig, his face went red with anger. He raged and bellowed that the new quartermaster was overstepping his authority. He threatened to whip young Tuck with his belt until the boy howled—punishment for aiding in the desecration of midden the captain had made of the chamber. He yowled and carried on as if he had been robbed of something of great value until Smee arrived with several bottles of rum under his arm. The bosun knew the best way to treat the captain's sense of loss.

Rum served to calm the captain's nerves and quiet his bellowing. The exquisite logic and supernal tact of James helped Captain Conner to accept that his cabin was but the first and most important enhancement to be made to the *Jolly Roger*. Filthy, ill-kept ships flying the skull and crossbones were as common as fleas on a dog's back in the Caribbean—or lice in Red Michael's bedding. A vessel that displayed care and discipline would cause great consternation when the black flag was hoisted to the masthead.

Every merchant captain feared the ferocity of the dirty, unkempt, disorderly buccaneers who were the terror of the Spanish Main. How much more would they be affrighted when they saw a ship as neat as an admiral's gig hoist that dreaded banner to declare itself? How much quicker would most sailors be to surrender for fear of incurring the wrath of such supreme scoundrels who took meticulous care of their vessels, who showed such deep pride in themselves that they kept fresh paint on the hull and holy-stoned the decks without the cat to tickle them, and yet, who still followed the sweet trade with cutlass and pistol?

It may have been the copious amounts of rum that Smee brought along, and it may have been the honeyed words that James was infernally inspired to pour into Red Michael's thick and hairy ear. Whatever the reason, the pirate was taken by the idea, even if it meant that his comfortable wallow had to be transformed into a proper cabin for a proper captain.

Changing Red Michael into a proper captain was beyond the abilities even of a genius like James. The man had been born to be a pirate, and a pirate was all he would ever be. There was no improving on what nature had made him—even if he had desired such an improvement, which he did not. The best James could do, with the aid of Smee and Tuck, was to see that their captain had a clean coat that fit his corpulent figure and a dashing hat to hide his thinning ginger hair. That and his inborn talent for drunken violence were all he needed to lead the crew of the *Jolly Roger*.

When he had a moment to think about it, James realized that he did not want to make Red Michael into anything more than he had been born to be. His goal remained to supplant Captain Conner one fine day. There was no need or value in helping Conner be a better pirate or a better man, since either would make removing him all the more difficult when the time came.

Transforming the *Jolly Roger* and her crew, on the other hand, fit in completely with the future that James envisioned for himself. To that end, he set to work with a will, making himself known to the collection of scoundrels and cutthroats that had gathered together to compose the crew of the *Jolly Roger*.

The new quartermaster had no intention of ingratiating himself with those men. As he viewed the matter, he was far above them in breeding and education. And even if he did follow the same trade, his reasons for sailing under the black flag differed from those of men like Smee and Cecco, who only sought gold from the easiest source.

James could never be friends to such men as Bill Jukes or Skylight or Cookson, for there was too great a gulf between such common clay and himself. He could command them, however, and he could give them reasons aplenty to obey his commands without hesitation.

For a start, he was wise enough not to demand too much of the crew. A little work every day with scraper and brush and mop—that was enough at the beginning. To that, he added words of praise when it served him best and threats when threats served better than praise. By the time the brig was ready to sail from Tortuga, she already looked fiercer than when James had first clapped eyes upon her. After another four weeks at sea, she was as fine as ever she had been.

Instead of peeling paint and bare wood, the hull now displayed a fresh coat of red and black. Even the gilt work gleamed, from the gruesome gold skull that served as a figurehead to the carved wooden scrolling around the stern windows of Red Michael's cabin. Course by course, the sails had been taken down, mended, and scrubbed before being hoisted again. This treatment changed them from a dingy gray to as close to white as they had even been.

By James's efforts, the crew of the *Jolly Roger* had been transformed as well, though that was accomplished in a more subtle fashion. Aye, they still spent their idle hours at cards and dice or singing rude songs accompanied by Cookson's guitar and Cecco's squeeze-box. They were still lazy, quarrelsome, and quick to anger, and they still played violent pranks on one another without a thought of the consequences. And they were still as bloodthirsty as they had even been.

The changes wrought by the quartermaster seemed minor things, almost too small to notice. It came in the form of shirts washed and breeches changed at least once a week. It was displayed in chins shaved as often as breeches were changed; in hair that was cut short to deprive lice of their ancestral homes; and in the vigorous use of a comb and a bit of twine to tie that hair in a neat queue rather than letting it fly free in the wind. It came, in short, as a display of pride in personal appearance. This change was one that James had wrought by personal example rather than by lashing the crew with his tongue or the cat, as would have been his right as quartermaster.

Before they left Tortuga, James had already cleaned out the cubbyhole that was to be his cabin, laying aside the weapons he deemed useful and bundling up the garments and knickknacks that the late Tommy Two-Toes had left behind. These latter items James traded ashore, gathering up a proper wardrobe of ruffled shirts and knee pants, silver-buckled shoes, and stockings to fit his taste. It was not a large collection of clothing, for what he took ashore had little value. But the garments he stowed aboard were of proper fit and fine condition, which counted more to him than the number and variety of pieces in his wardrobe.

The quartermaster strode the polished deck in his clean doublet and ruffled shirt, looking very dangerous and very fine. That struck a spark in the men who scrubbed that deck with holystones in their hands, and they thought they could do better than their ragged shirts that had more holes than cloth, which were as often as not stained with rum, salt water, and the blood of the men who had owned those shirts before them.

Bill Jukes was first, and he came on deck one morning wearing a clean bright-blue waistcoat he had taken from the slop chest to replace the rag he had been wearing for weeks. Jukes had not sought out a shirt, for he did not want all his tattoos hidden from sight and admiration. Knee breeches of a bottle green had replaced the tatters his belt had held up the day before, though he still scorned shoes of any sort and stockings as well.

It might have seemed surprising that such a rough character as the much-tattooed Jukes would be the first to respond to the example set by the new quartermaster, but there was a reason that he was the first to imitate the wearing of clean attire.

A pirate of many years standing, Jukes had sailed on other vessels before the *Jolly Roger*. Among them had been Flint's *Walrus*, so Jukes knew blue-chinned Captain Flint, Barbecue, Pew, and Black Dog and all the rest of that villainous crew as if they were his own vicious brothers. It was aboard the *Walrus* that Jukes had been whipped by Flint himself, more than three dozen strokes with the cat, because of Jukes's refusal to relinquish a trove of gold coins he had snatched fairly from a dying Portuguese aboard a ship they had taken, looted, and burned to the waterline.

Any man who could best Flint's cunning quartermaster and put the fear into Barbecue in the bargain was a man to be admired. As Bill Jukes viewed such matters, the proper way to show that admiration was through imitation. It might be that some of the qualities that James had displayed could be found in the style of garments he wore—or so Jukes fervently hoped.

One by one, the majority of the crew cast off their rags and tatters and availed themselves of what the slop chest held. More than that, they showed care and concern for their garments; especially when they realized that the chest where the common clothes were stored was nearly empty. Until such time as they looted another ship, they would have only such finery as they had already claimed to strut around in. And since there was nothing new to replace what had been soiled, they had to resort to washing their clothes, a task that few were familiar with.

While James preferred to keep a distance between himself and the other members of the crew, even he could not remain an island unto himself. He came to know each of the crewmen and many of their quirks.

He discovered that Starkey had been, oddly enough, an usher at a prestigious public school in England. Even if not so grand an institution as the one James had attended until his expulsion,

"Gentleman" Starkey, as he was sometimes called, still had a delicate way about him, especially when engaged in murder.

Dusk, the gigantic African with filed teeth, changed his name every time he changed ships. He was happy to boast that the name given him by his mother was still used to frighten disobedient children along the jungle river where he had been born.

The old, near-sighted freebooter who went by the name of Skylights claimed to have gone to sea as a boy under the command of the great Henry Morgan himself, who was as close to being a patron saint of the sweet trade as any pirate could ever hope to be.

It was Morgan who christened the boy "Skylights" after his raid on Porto Bello. When confronted with a massive, locked barrier that kept them out of the treasure vaults, the boy had wiggled through a narrow window in the roof. He pistoled two Spaniards standing beside a small cannon loaded with canister before raising the bar and pulling the door's bolts to let Morgan and his followers in.

There was also Noodler, who had been born with deformed arms and had those same arms cruelly twisted and broken when he fell into the hands of the Inquisition. Despite those injuries, he had managed to escape the fires of the auto-da-fé and return to his life at sea, though when his mangled arms finally healed, his hands were so off from those of normal men that they appeared to be backward. He still managed to perform his duties aboard the *Jolly Roger* and fought with such an odd style because of his twisted forearms that few men could stand against him.

There was Foggerty, from the eastern most reaches of France, and Mullins and Turley and many others, each with his own story. Some were strange and fascinating; some were sorry and mundane. It was one of James's strengths that he could remember all that he learned about the men of the *Jolly Roger*, from the least to the greatest among them.

The greatest, at least in his own mind, was Captain Red Michael Conner, though his past was the most dreary of them all.

Born among the pickpockets, thieves, drunkards, and cutthroats of Port Royal, young Michael might have been just another shiftless thief had not Mother Nature taken a hand.

Just before noon on the seventh of June, as rotund little Mike was contemplating a pair of sailors who were already deep in their cups, prospective victims for his nimble fingers, the island of Jamaica shook with a mighty earthquake that sent the inhabitants fleeing and left a third of Port Royal beneath the waves. Homeless and orphaned, Michael Conner was forced to find what employment he could just to survive.

Sweeping and cleaning taverns in Kingston allowed the boy to keep in contact with shady acquaintances of his smuggler father. Among those men was one who had managed to lay hands on a small ship that had been left ownerless and adrift after the earthquake. Seeking to have an occupation that would allow him to avoid the noose and still provide plenty of gold, George Macintosh obtained a royal commission as a privateer and was seeking hardy men for his crew.

Young Michael signed on as cabin boy with "Lord George" Macintosh aboard his brigantine *Calabash*. With little experience as a privateer and a large ego, Lord George sought out Spaniards to loot and sink, usually to discover that his prize contained tobacco or plantains or leather or, worst of all, crude knickknacks made by the native slaves of the Spanish Empire.

Being singularly unsuccessful as a privateer and stubbornly refusing his crew the slight change required for them to enter into more lucrative piracy, Lord George was retired from his position as captain, and the mate took his place as commander of the brigantine. Captain Paul Baker was generous enough to provide his former captain with a proper pirate's pension even though Lord George had refused to turn pirate.

Set ashore on his own private island, which even included a single palm tree, the deposed George was provided all he would ever need: a bottle of rum, a flask of water, a pistol with a single charge of shot, and a hearty fare-thee-well. Thus marooned, Lord George was forgotten by the time his tiny island was below the horizon.

Captain Baker never put on airs nor claimed to be anything but a bloody-handed pirate. He renamed *Calabash* as the *Jolly Roger* and had the mundane figurehead of a chaste maiden replaced with a large wooden skull that was painted gold. His success at the sweet trade was not great, though it was enough to keep him firmly in the captain's cabin.

As was common with pirates who are not retired by their fellows, Captain Baker fell in battle. To be precise, he tripped over a cowering passenger while boarding a prize that had surrendered without firing a shot when the black flag was first raised. Stumbling into the sea, Baker discovered that swimming when his belly held a full cargo of rum, and his belt a similar cargo of pistols, daggers, and cutlasses, was an impossibility—and especially impossible for a man who had never assayed to swim a single stroke in his entire life.

Thus it was that the crew held a vote and made Sidney Tolliver their captain. But Tolliver had the misfortune of being recognized as a pirate whilst quenching his thirst at a tavern in Kingston, and he was led off to pay his respects to the admiralty court and dance the hempen jig. After Tolliver's untimely end with his neck in a noose, Jasper Sykes was made captain. And after him, Hangdog Haskell took command of the *Jolly Roger*.

The *Jolly Roger* proved to be a lucky ship for Michael Conner, if not for the long string of captains who commanded her under the black flag. Through all the captains and all the years, Michael Conner served aboard the brig and learned all the skills needed to be both a sailor and a pirate. Never in the forefront nor ever in the rear for any adventure, Conner bided his time and advanced in rank by virtue of longevity rather than merit.

When, in the fullness of time, he reached the position of mate aboard the *Jolly Roger*, he discovered that he had an ambition to become her captain. Once ambition reared its head, it was not long before Captain Kendrick—who had raised Conner to mate thinking him to be the least likely to cause trouble—found himself sharing an island with Lord George, who was very poor company to the new resident of that speck of land, having used his pistol as was expected of him many years before.

Captain Red Michael Conner proved to be surprisingly successful in the sweet trade. An unexpected boldness marked his exploits once he assumed command of the *Jolly Roger*. Having developed a favored tactic, he used it often and to great effect.

Striking in the late afternoon, he would sail out of the setting sun to attack and board a vessel. Seizing treasure and cargo, he would leave behind fire and death, fleeing with the wind filling his sails while any escorting ships were still trying to come to a favorable position. No matter how closely pursued into the thickening dusk, the *Jolly Roger* invariably found herself on an empty sea the next morning, all signs of enemy vessels vanished like the dawn mists.

In the month that he had been aboard, James had heard several anecdotes of a similar nature, but he had yet to see such action taken by his new captain. Some of the men seemed mystified by the events and ascribed inexplicable powers to Red Michael. Others, like Smee, seemed to understand, though they were loath to speak of it; it was as if it shamed them deeply. For his part, the new quartermaster was intrigued to see what he would learn when they finally found a prize worthy of their efforts.

"Ho, Mr. James," Smee called out from the companionway behind the quartermaster. "Cap'n wants you in his cabin. Says we're going after a rich prize."

Many of the hands around James perked up their ears at Smee's words. Cruel smiles displayed broken and rotting teeth while callused hands caressed the hilts of knives and the worn butts of pistols tucked into many sashes. The mutterings said that it was time and past time for the captain to bring gold onto the deck of the *Jolly Roger.*

James strode quickly to Red Michael's cabin. As he entered, he could not help but allow a slight smile to play across his lips. No longer a garbage dump, that cabin seemed surprisingly roomy even with the girth of Captain Conner spilling over the side of his heavy chair. The table was clear except for a chart, the inevitable bottle of rum, and a single plate with the remains of a boiled chicken still on it.

James knew that Tuck would nip into the cabin as soon as the captain left even for a moment. The boy had his orders from the quartermaster to allow no plate nor cup to remain behind once the captain had finished his meal. Since Red Michael Conner drank his rum straight from the bottle, that proved no inconvenience to the fat pirate at all.

Another order from James had Tuck gathering up the empty rum bottles to be stowed away for other uses. Now that the cabin had been cleaned and scrubbed down, Red Michael, captain though he might be, was not going to turn it back into his personal midden again. The fleas and lice might still have their place with Red Michael, but those pets were confined to the stern cabin through the liberal use of lye and vinegar all around Captain Conner's quarters.

"Quartermaster; Bosun," Captain Conner greeted them with a snarl. "Time we got down to proper business."

"Time indeed, Cap'n," Smee agreed. "The men are not happy that we've sailed so long without taking a prize. Cook didn't stow that much vittles aboard, as you know, and we haven't had a single chance to take on supplies from a prize yet, on account of not seeing a single ship to lay board-to-board with."

"They're all fools, and you're a fool, Smee, to let them bark so. Well, I've got something for those dogs."

Red Michael stabbed a thick finger onto the chart, the ring on that finger reflecting crimson streaks from its jewel.

"Isla de Tres Palmas," he announced with a passable Spanish accent.

Smee gasped in surprise, and even James was so stunned that his mouth hung open most unbecomingly for a moment. That Spanish fortification was well known for the strength of its walls and the power of its guns. It was also known as a miserable rock with a mangrove swamp on two sides, a small harbor, and not much else. The Spanish crown kept a garrison there to keep other European powers from doing so. If not for the springs of clear water, there would have been no interest in the small island at all, for it had nothing to otherwise recommend it.

"If I may be so bold, Captain Conner," James said, recovering from his astonishment, "What might there be at such a place to interest us? And how, given the strength of the garrison, are we to get the prize?"

Red Michael tilted back his flabby head and poured rum down his throat, ignoring the question until the bottle ran dry. He slammed it down with enough force to rattle the plate on the table and make the chicken bones dance. Tuck slipped in quietly, discretely placed a fresh bottle of rum within easy reach, and retreated with the empty bottle before Captain Conner could cuff his ear.

"The best prize of all, Quartermaster. Gold. Spanish gold, wrung out of the natives on the mainland, minted on the mainland, and being readied to ship back to Spain for their greedy king."

Captain Conner laughed and wiped his rum-wet mouth with the back of a hairy hand. He enjoyed making his new quartermaster wait for his answers.

"There be a galleon there what was sailing for Spain when she sprung a bad leak. Her captain put into the nearest Spanish port, that being Isla de Tres Palmas," he explained with an unpleasant smile. "Ain't much happens from one end of the Caribbean to the other that ain't known in Tortuga right quick. I spread enough coin around to make sure such tales are carried to me first."

Smee grinned in admiration of his captain. James made note of that stratagem as well. It might serve him well someday. Knowing where a rich prize could be found was important intelligence, that was certain. Gaining the information before other freebooters was even more important. Many vessels sailed under the black flag of piracy. There was more to the sweet trade than simply knowing where gold could be found. The Spaniards had gold aplenty on the mainland. They also had soldiers—and ships and cannons enough to sink an entire fleet.

Even the remote island fortress of Isla de Tres Palmas could mount enough guns to blow the *Jolly Roger* out of the water and a score more like her in the bargain. There had to be more to the captain's scheme than that. James waited quietly for Red Michael to continue while Smee laboriously came to the realization of the dangers in a bold frontal assault on such a stronghold.

"Cap'n, might it not have been better to give us your plan in Tortuga? There are not more than eighty souls aboard with us. We could have joined up with some other vessel so as to have enough men to properly do the job and live to tell the tale."

"Who would we have joined with, Smee? Flint and his *Walrus*? Black Jack Kennedy and those Irish dogs of his aboard *Green Hills*?

Red Conner laughed disdainfully, though James was not certain whether it was at the bosun or the thought of joining forces with Flint or Kennedy.

For his own part, Smee appeared to take no offense either at that laughter or his captain's disparaging remarks about his countrymen.

"What this takes is thought, Mr. Smee, not more men. Daring. Wits and courage. I been thinking this out since we sailed, and I have a plan."

The captain pushed the cork out of the bottle with a thick thumb and took a long swallow of raw rum.

"Simplicity itself, me hearties! We land a party under cover of darkness here at the far end of the island." He pointed to the swamp marked at the south end of the island. "They sneak up on the fort from the landward side, scale the wall, and spike the guns afore dawn. The *Jolly Roger* sails in at first light, smashes the galleon with a broadside, boards, and snatches the doubloons, and then off we go!"

The quartermaster looked closely at the chart spread over the table and rubbed his long chin with the back of his thumb. The nail rasped on the close stubble that darkened his swarthy skin.

"Simple, Captain, save for one detail. What of the shore party? Are they to enter the fortress, spike the guns, and be ready to board either the galleon or the *Jolly Roger* without being seen by the guards? The Spanish tend to be sleepy that early in the morning, but I wager that not all of them are that sleepy."

Red Michael showed his teeth in a jagged, unpleasant smile.

"Mr. Quartermaster, how the men you take ashore meet up with us again will be a problem for you to solve."

Perhaps Captain Conner expected James to protest or to propose a different plan. If so, the new quartermaster of the *Jolly Roger* surprised his captain by merely nodding as if such faith in him was entirely natural and to be expected by a man of his abilities.

"I'll pick the men to go with me," James said. "If that is agreeable to you, Captain," he added.

Captain Conner just repeated his nasty smile and made a grand gesture of acceptance of his quartermaster's proposal.

"Any man, save for Smee. I will need him aboard with me. And Dietz. We'll need our gunner, if I know Spaniards."

"Aye, Captain," James said absently, his keen mind already mulling over the best men to take with him.

Dismissed by Red Michael, who had serious drinking to do,

Smee and James went back up on deck. Those men not engaged in pressing duties, which is to say the majority of the crew, crowded around their bosun and quartermaster to learn about the next prize the *Jolly Roger* would sail after.

There were some complaints that they would be launching an effort on land rather than attacking ships at sea. There were also those who viewed it as a better chance for loot, since it was seldom that they found much in the way of gold aboard the ships they took, relying mainly on the sale of stolen cargo for their coins. Some showed dismay on hearing the name Isla de Tres Palmas. Others seemed relieved that their captain would begin his assault at dawn, as if his habit of late afternoon piracy disturbed them in some unspoken fashion. The details of the treasure were of far more interest to men like Gentleman Starkey and Bill Jukes than the part they would have to play to claim their share of the booty.

That helped the quartermaster decide who he wanted beside him on that desperate venture. Jukes, for certain, and Starkey. Dusk, Cookson, Noodler, and Jacob would also be required for the job. And Cecco too, with his stilettos, would be a useful man in the small hours before dawn.

Resorting to the knowledge he had gained over the last few weeks, James decided on a dozen men for the endeavor. He viewed this as an opportunity to test the mettle of those hands that he wanted to be the core of his personal crew of loyal men—men who could be counted on, when the time came, to side with him over Red Michael for control of the *Jolly Roger*. His demonstration of intellect and skill ashore on Isla de Tres Palmas would be a vital first step in cementing their loyalty to him. James thought that he could safely trust twelve carefully chosen men to support him without word reaching the captain. Besides, more than a dozen would only add to their risk of being discovered while ashore on this foray. Red Michael had hinted that he expected a larger force from the *Jolly Roger* for the raid. It would please the quartermaster to demonstrate his ability while using a much smaller group of picked men.

"Planning and daring," Captain Conner had said. It was easy to see that there was need of careful planning for his part in his captain's scheme. For one thing, based on experience, James wanted no firearms ashore with his men. He had seen the accidental discharge of a pistol ruin more than one careful plan when stealth was required.

Another point was being ready to spike the guns. The normal procedure of a small iron wedge or nail being pounded into the touchhole would be impossible. The ring of a hammer against soft iron on the first cannon would awaken even the sleepiest of guards and have the whole garrison down around their ears in short order. What they needed was to be able to disable the guns for a short time, just long enough for the *Jolly Roger* to slip in and slip out with the treasure.

The old brigand Skylight inadvertently provided the answer, picking at his few remaining teeth with a wooden splinter.

A bit of wood like that, thought James.

He had Carver, the ship's carpenter, lathe down several dozen thin bits of wood as long as his hand, and little thicker than a gentleman's toothpick. Each man in the raiding party would carry several, along with a small block of cloth-wrapped wood to force them down the touchholes of the Spanish cannons. Properly and, more importantly, *silently* pressed into place, those slender bits of wood would make it impossible for the guns to be fired until the wood was picked clear.

While the guns would not be damaged, which James thought to be a pity, at least they would be in no condition to be used against the *Jolly Roger* for as long as an hour after the alarm sounded. That temporary delay would have to be enough.

The noon sighting had put them at a point where they would arrive off the easternmost point of the fortress island soon after sunset. The shadow of the island itself would cloak the brig on her approach. There would be no lights shown aboard the *Jolly Roger* that night beyond a single shaded lantern needed to see the binnacle.

Even the ship's cook, LaSalle, had the fire in the galley banked so that there was not a wink of light to be seen from the brigantine. The evening meal was cold biscuits and dry cheese, washed down with watered rum. James himself mixed the dosage for each man, for he did not want them too merry for the business ahead.

Tuck carried food and drink around to all hands at LaSalle's command while those worthies that the quartermaster had chosen checked the edges on their knives and cutlasses. Much to the dismay of Mr. Smee, James requisitioned a dozen belaying pins for the men under his command. He also had a dozen monkey-fist knots tied into short, thick lengths of rope, each knot having a heavy musket ball at its core.

With the shadows growing long, the lookout gestured to the west, straight ahead on the course Captain Conner had set.

"Island ahead," Foggerty called down in a harsh whisper.

That was the loudest sound the Alsatian could make. The French navy had tried to hang him once over a charge of murder, without notable success. His strained voice and that livid scar around his bull neck gave testimony that an old rope was no match for his powerful muscles. It could be said that he did not talk much about that episode, but then again, given the nature of that injury, Foggerty did not speak much at all.

"Make ready the longboat," James hissed to those gathered around him. "No one talks above a whisper from here on out, or I will see that they talk no more at all."

He stroked the handle of his slender dagger by way of reminding his picked crew that he meant what he said. They knew all too well how sound could carry at night and were doubly resolved to be as silent as possible.

With little noise, the dozen men lowered the boat into the sea and, as silent as shadows, slipped over the side to find their places. James went last, nodding once in farewell to Smee.

Tuck was there, close behind the bosun. James tried to look stern as the boy waved and mouthed the words "good luck." Somehow, he found himself nodding in acknowledgement, which seemed to please the ship's boy as it had before.

Chapter 4

Isla del Tres Palmas

Standing in mud and brackish water up to his knees was not something that James was fond of in the least. Doing so during the dark of night, with clouds obscuring what little moonlight there was, rated even lower in his estimation. Swarms of biting flies and mosquitoes added nothing to the pleasure of the experience.

Transferring from the *Jolly Roger* to the edge of the mangrove swamp had been accomplished with little fuss. James and his handpicked crew of brigands had loaded into the longboat as silently as possible. Under the whispered directions of the quartermaster, they had manned the oars and carefully rowed to the first of the trees. One by one, they had slipped over the side, finding their footing in the swallow water.

Once James had his men ready, he gave three hard tugs on the light cord that was attached to the stern of the longboat. At the far end of that line, aboard the brig, Smee felt the line jerk and signaled half a dozen of the crew to pull away with a will, drawing the longboat back to the *Jolly Roger*. While the quartermaster arranged his raiders for their order of march, Smee had the boat loaded back aboard.

In a few moments, James and his men heard the faint squeak of block and tackle and the distant flutter of canvas filling with wind as the sails were set. The brigantine moved off into the night, a dark bulk that melted into the tropical gloom. They were alone, thirteen men on an island inhabited only by enemies.

The quartermaster assigned Dusk to lead the way. Born and raised in the jungles of Africa, the massive killer seemed to have the senses of a hunting cat as he moved in complete silence through the water between the trees. At the order of his commander, Dusk wore a rope tied around his waist. Six feet of that rope led back to a knot that Bill Jukes held tight in one hand. Like the huge black pirate, Jukes had a rope around his own waist, the free end being held by Cecco, whose rope was held by Starkey, whose rope was held by Noodler, and so on all the way back to James, who had no rope of his own as he was the last one in the long line.

Under no circumstances was anyone to release the rope. This James had impressed on them in the strongest of terms. If they did not hang tight to those ropes and reach the landward wall of the fortress together, there was a strong likelihood that before the next setting of the sun the Spaniards would see them all hung together with tight ropes tied around their necks rather than their waists.

Dusk, having both of his hands free, carried a slender staff, the end wrapped in several layers of canvas. With that pole, he alternately felt in the water ahead of him and then in the air above, seeking roots, rocks, low-hanging branches, vines, and other obstacles to their progress. In that fashion, he found a path through the mangroves, avoiding deep pools and tangles of sunken limbs broken off by the summer storms. Jerks on his rope silently warned those behind him of dangers, two quick tugs meaning below the water and three tugs indicating an obstacle above.

The men following along in his wake like beads on a string did not move as noiselessly as Dusk. Splashes and stifled curses marked their passage as they slipped and floundered through the miasmal gloom. To James, the commotion they made seemed loud enough to alarm the distant sentries. He had to remind himself time and again that it was only his nerves that made the slight sounds seem so loud.

As proof of that, there were frogs serenading their amphibian ladies and insects humming and chirping their nightly chorus seemed undisturbed by the passage of the raiding party through their territory. Turtles, snakes, and other unseen creatures splashed and slithered in the darkness without fear of the intruders.

Waves lapping at the boles of the mangroves and chuckling evilly among the twisted roots made no louder sounds than the clumsiest members of the group that James commanded.

Among all those normal sounds of the night, the few additional splashes provided by James and his party would not be noticed, even by the sharpest ears. And their muffled profanities seemed little different from the irritated cries of the birds disturbed on their nests by the normal creatures that prowled through the swamp by night.

All this James told to himself, and he hoped that it was all true.

At one point, Jukes tripped on a root that Dusk had not found and was dragged through the noxious water for several paces before the colossal pirate leading the way recognized the extra weight tugging at his waist. Despite getting a mouthful of the foul, brackish water, Bill Jukes never loosed his grip on the rope. Cecco almost tripped over Jukes and muttered a pungent oath in his native tongue, yet he remembered the quartermaster's threat and kept his voice pitched low, even when Starkey ran into him and sent him sprawling over Jukes.

That tangle assured James that he had made the correct decision in not allowing pistols or muskets among the weapons the expedition carried. If ever there was a muddle that would get a flintlock to fire when it was most unwanted, it was the tangle that followed after Jukes tripped. Had there been any such weapons among them, surely one would have discharged and alerted the Spaniards—either that or their powder would have been thoroughly wetted and rendered useless. Better to depend on stout wood, weighted rope, and cold steel, all of which would function no matter how many dunkings they underwent that night. The temper of the men survived the mishap as well as their weapons did, though James was certain that the unfortunate Spanish soldiers they encountered would regret, if only briefly, the suffering the pirates endured to reach the fortress unseen.

Having enjoyed the life of a buccaneer for many years, the experience of wading through a treacherous swamp in the blackest part of the night was nothing new to the quartermaster. Since the day when he had been forced to leave his school, forced to say a hurried farewell to his mother, and forced to leave behind even his family name, James had experienced a variety of unique situations that would never have troubled the life of a proper gentleman. Of course, as his brothers had always been eager to point out at every opportunity, James had never displayed what their father had considered to be the qualities of a proper gentleman.

James also understood quite well the havoc that would be wrought upon his garments—many would have to be discarded if he lived to see the morrow. Of course, such a loss would be more than compensated for by the return he would receive for his labors. It was much more profitable to let his mind dwell on the golden reward he could expect than to fret over the discomfort of the moment, the danger in the near future, or even the unfair and unchangeable events of his tragic past.

Each of the men in the raiding party kept to his own thoughts during the miserable slog through the mangroves. As was the nature of such men, most of their thoughts revolved around gold even as the thoughts of their quartermaster did. Worry about what was to come before they had the gold in their hands was not for such bravos of those handpicked men from the *Jolly Roger*. While they knew that any of them might fail and fall during the battle that they were certain to face, to each mind it was always the other fellow who might breathe his last.

That failing, if failing it was, infected even James, despite his superior education and knowledge of the mortality of man.

Without any sight of the moon and stars, it was difficult to guess how long they spent stumbling through the black water, slapping at the bite of mosquitoes, and keeping their profanities locked behind clenched teeth. What seemed an endless march finally came to an end just as tempers frayed nearly to the breaking point.

Dusk held up a hand in warning to those behind him, and they realized in surprise that they could see the gesture. His massive figure showed as a black silhouette against a gray background beyond the frame of the last of the mangrove trees. Moving cautiously forward, the party stumbled up and onto dry ground, a few dozen yards from the looming wall of the fortress.

Dark figures crouched in front of a dark background, James was certain that they would have been unseen even if an idle soldier was to look over the parapet during his sleepy patrol. Even so, he had no intention of letting his men remain in such an exposed position for long.

At his whispered command, each man divested himself of his rope, and the lengths were expertly knotted together into a single length of hemp. For this next job, the nimble Dick Brown would lead. At home among the yards as he was on the deck, Dick scaled the rough stone wall with the rope trailing behind him as easily as a monkey running up a tree.

The slender pirate paused below the lip of the parapet, listening for the scuff of a boot on stone or the sleepy breathing of a stationary sentry. Not a sound came to his ears. As slow as the rising of the moon, his head came over the top of the stone wall, his eyes seeking any movement or sign of danger. All was still and empty.

It had been their hope that the rearward walls of the fortress would be deserted at that hour of the night. Despite such a hope, the quartermaster was not the man to take chances, and he had instructed Dick Brown to take no risks at all. After making the rope fast to a railing post so that his companions could make the climb with more ease, Dick scuttled in a low crouch to one end of the walkway and then the other, peering into the gloom for any glimpse of a sentry.

Seeking trouble, Dick found some close at hand. Leaning against a support pole for the thatched shelter at the right-hand side of the walkway was a gaunt soldier, his head drooping forward on his chest. The crested helmet he should have been wearing had settled between his feet, and his pike rested against his shoulder. The rhythmic whistle of air through his nostrils showed that he was asleep.

Dick Brown made certain that the soldier would sleep a long time, using the belaying pin he carried with expert care above and slightly behind the man's right ear. A forceful blow, it would have tumbled the man over with a clatter of steel armor had Brown not grasped the soldier's sleeve with his free hand even as he struck the blow.

A frantic gesture brought Starkey and Teyne to Dick's side, where they aided their slender companion in removing the stunned soldier from view. Starkey was all for heaving the fellow over the wall and being rid of him. James allowed his annoyance to show in his voice as he stopped Starkey even as Starkey was hoisting the soldier up to roll him over.

"Did you think of the noise that will come if he lands on the rocks below?" James asked acidly. "You might as well ring a bell, Mr. Starkey, and call the Spaniards to capture us."

The quartermaster shook his head in disgust. There was still much work to be done with these dunderheads before he could trust them to complete a task without his guidance.

"Just stow him in the shadows where no one will trip on him," the quartermaster whispered, a sigh of loathing implicit in his tone. "And put that helmet on your own head, Mr. Starkey.

It might fool one of these soldiers long enough for you to do him before he can do for you."

The commander of the garrison must have been confident in the safety of his command, for the raiders discovered only five more nodding sentries as they advanced to where the main battery was arrayed to cover the harbor. Three of those drowsy sentinels were dealt with in a fashion similar to that which Dick Brown had used. A belaying pin or weighted knot made their sleep much deeper, and they were laid aside to awake later in confusion with aching heads.

The last two had been standing close together, talking to each other to stave off sleep. Those two had been removed in a more permanent fashion, since they still wore their iron helmets, which made the use of monkey fist or belaying pin impossible.

James and Jukes took out one, while Dusk and Cecco did in the other.

Jukes grabbed an arm and slapped a broad palm over the soldier's mouth while James did the honors with his dagger, stabbing down through the armhole of the armor on the left side to reach the heart.

The massive black pirate grabbed the other soldier before he could react, pulling his head back brutally while Cecco made a single neat slash with his stiletto, a deep cut that did not remain neat for very long.

"The cannons, lads—fix them as I explained. And make no noise if you value all of our lives!" hissed James when the last of the soldiers had stopped twitching.

Jukes ran quietly to the first of the long cannons on the left of the row. Cecco stopped five guns down and began there. Cookson plunged the first of his wooden rods into the touchhole of the cannon five to the right of the one Cecco started with. And so it went for the thirty culverins, with James having half his men free to be led down to the smaller guns closer to the harbor.

The process was the same on all the cannons, large and small:

The wooden dowel was inserted into the touchhole as far as it could go and then broken off with an inch protruding above the iron. Using the padded wooden block, the rod was pressed down into the hole and squeezed into the narrow chamber until the touchhole was entirely blocked.

A nail, filed blunt, was used to further compress the wood into a compact mass that could not be seen on casual inspection. Only when the gunners tried to charge the touchhole would they discover the blockage.

Foggerty nudged the quartermaster as the work was completed and pointed to the flagpole. It was the highest point on the fortress, indeed, on the entire island. The gold ball at the top of the long pole gleamed with a deep orange fire as the first rays of the rising sun painted the tip with ruddy light.

"Come, men. We must find someplace near the docks to hide until the *Jolly Roger* arrives," James said in an urgent whisper. "Soon enough the sergeant of the guard will rouse himself and wonder where his men are. We must find cover before the Spaniards find those guards we removed."

Quietly and quickly, James and his dozen raiders slipped out through the open gates of the fortress. There was a single high tower where a sentry watched for enemy ships, and they had neither cause nor means to deal with that lone sentinel. His attention was usually focused on the sea, but they did not want to chance that he might glance back at the fort while thinking of the warm bed waiting for him and thereby spy strangers where no strangers had any right to be.

Where the island was not mangrove swamp, it was rock. The fortress had been built upon the highest point of that rock, where a spring had struggled up from the depths of the earth to provide cool, clear water to an island that was too small to have a source of water otherwise. There, the three lonely palms that gave the island its name still grew, jealously guarded from harm by the *comandante* of the garrison.

The harbor that the fortress overlooked was located between two low arms of rock that formed a triangle, the broad end against the Isla de Tres Palmas, while the broken point of the triangle provided a deep-water entrance to the enclosed lagoon. That narrow entrance was amply protected by the thirty massive bronze culverins of ancient and ornate design. Any ship attempting to force an entrance could be driven off by the might of those guns—or sunk if the captain of such a vessel was suicidally stubborn.

Within that protected harbor, a massive Spanish galleon sat at anchor. There were other smaller vessels in the harbor as well, most of them tied to the docks. The ornate galleon, like a pampered bull pastured among sheep, drew too much water to safely come close to the docks. The galleon had to remain aloof in the middle of that triangular expanse of water while the flock of smaller vessels seemed to huddle together as far from the ornate and dangerous bull as they possibly could.

The galleon was a thing of beauty, covered in gilt scrollwork and brightly painted. The white sails had been gathered into neat bundles along the yardarms, and the rigging was in perfect repair. A single light gleamed at the waist, up toward the high forecastle. Men had been left aboard to stand guard, though likely only a handful at the most.

The galleon rode deep in the water. Given the amount of time that must have passed since she had come seeking a safe harbor with the leak that drove her there, it could only mean that her hull had been repaired and her cargo of gold loaded aboard once again. They had arrived just in time to catch the mighty vessel still at anchor. In another day or two, her crew would have been aboard and she would have already set sail for the distant port of Cadiz.

The bell in the watchtower began ringing stridently before James and his men were halfway down the road that led to the cluttered docks. Squinting into the darkness that lay beyond the entrance to the harbor, the quartermaster could make out the white sails of an approaching vessel. It could only be the *Jolly*

Roger, striking at the earliest moment of dawn. It seemed that Captain Red Michael was eager to load his brig with gold—perhaps too eager for the good of the men he had sent ashore.

"What'll we do?" Harris squawked in alarm.

"We make for the docks and steal a speedy ketch, of course," James replied coolly, drawing his rapier and dagger.

"How d'ya knows there be a ketch fer us to steal?" demanded Bill Jukes, his own blades already in his hands.

"This is not the first time I have been outnumbered in a Spanish port," replied James frostily. "There is *always* a ketch when you are in a situation like this."

Jukes snickered Harris, Cookson, Starkey, Jacob, and Teyne snorted laugher through their noses in an attempt to muffle the noise, while Jacob, Noodler, and Mullins fought to keep their mirth silent. Only Dusk, Cecco, and Foggerty did not laugh at the remark from their quartermaster.

James was puzzled for a moment as to why his simple statement of fact, based as it was on his experience in Spanish ports, had elicited such a response. Reviewing his words in his head, he realized the inadvertent joke he had made. And he understood why there had been three who did not laugh, for English was not the language that they had learned first in life. Such humor worked best on those who knew the subtleties of the language the joke was told in.

While it had not been his intention to be humorous, James decided to allow himself a slight smile as if pleased that his witty thrust had struck the mark.

"Come, my brave lads; blades out and be ready," James said in a low voice. "There are sure to be some soldiers in our path. We have no time to dally with them. Strike, and strike without mercy!"

The small band hurried on, coming to stone warehouses and wooden sheds. A maze of fishing nets had been laid over drying racks, and small boats were overturned and waiting for repair.

There were stacks of crab pots and other such items used to supply the garrison with their main source of food.

Boats tied to the quay that could be seen between the sheds and warehouses. They were small boats for the most part—rowboats for fishing in the lagoon, longboats from the galleon, and the gaily painted gig that the commander of the fortress used to greet important visitors to the island.

And there was a ketch, rigged out for deep-water fishing beyond the lagoon, just as James had expected to find.

It was not in the best of repair, having been used mostly by soldiers who had little understanding of ships or the sea. Even furled, the patches on the sails showed that they had been stitched on by an inexpert hand. Repairs to the railing had been made with crudely cut lengths of timber tied on with odds and ends of cord. From stem to stern, she was filthy and stank of fish that had lain too long in the hot sun.

"There's always a ketch," chortled Bill Jukes.

At that moment, more than a dozen Spanish soldiers burst from an empty warehouse where they had been sleeping instead of patrolling. Awakened by the alarm bell, they had hoped to reach their assigned duty stations before an officer noticed that they were not where they were supposed to be. Among them was an old sergeant, fat, gray-bearded, and wise to every possible ploy that a soldier could use to avoid hard work.

On seeing James and his men, the sergeant immediately recognized them for what they were. With the galleon in plain sight over the shoulders of the pirates, the sergeant also was able to make a leap of logic to discover the reason such brigands were there on Isla de Tres Palmas when the sun was still so low in the east. Here was hard work that no soldier could avoid, no matter how many tricks he knew. Nor would any good soldier of Spain seek to avoid such a duty.

"Pare ellos, matarlos!" he roared. "Capturar esos perros piratas!"

"I ain't sure what 'e said, but I don't think I likes it none," Noodler remarked, holding two long knives at angles that seemed awkward because of his deformed forearms.

"Whatta he say, I know," replied Cecco grimly. "Issa not for to be liked by us, no! We keel them all much quick, si!"

The quartermaster, being a man of wide and varied education, understood exactly what the sergeant was demanding of his men. He also understood that it would not be long before more soldiers came marching down from the fortress to defend the docks against a possible landing from the approaching vessel. His men would have little time both to fight those Spanish dogs already on the quay and to ready the ketch so that they could flee before a larger pack of vicious hounds descended upon them.

The pirates had two advantages over the soldiers. One was surprise, as the drowsy Spaniards had not thought to find enemies so close when they had burst out from where they had been sleeping. Second, before gathering to share a bottle and doze their watch away, they had left their muskets at their posts. James and his men faced them armed on equal terms.

"At them, lads!" James called out, suiting his words to action by whipping around his rapier and engaging the first of the soldiers.

"Jukes, Cookson, Starkey, Teyne, get to that ketch and hoist the sails. Get her ready to cast off while we deal with these Spanish scum!"

If they were reluctant to miss out on the fray, the named men did not show their dismay. Indeed, they obeyed the quartermaster's command with alacrity. No doubt they were so assured of the martial superiority of their companions that they were untroubled by the thought of leaving them to face almost twice their number in Spanish soldiers.

The battle proved to be almost equal odds. James and his remaining men were limber and fast, and while the Spaniards were encumbered with helmets and armor, the metal protected their vitals from the blades the pirates held. At close quarters, the soldiers met the cutlasses and dirks of the buccaneers with swords and daggers of their own. Agile, the raiders from the *Jolly Roger* could strike and dodge, cut, thrust, and whirl away from the lumbering soldiers of Spain. At the same time, the armor that slowed the Spaniards also preserved their lives, for it was difficult for the pirates to land a telling blow on an unprotected spot without risking a lethal riposte.

Cecco, supremely skillful with the deadly blades he carried, scored the first kill, flipping one stiletto into the throat of a skinny guardsman who was attempting to circle around behind Mullins. Dusk, through sheer brute power, beat down the blade of the next soldier and sent his helmet skipping across the dock with his head still inside. The strange twist to Noodler's arms befuddled the first of his opponents, allowing the pirate to slip the point of his cutlass under the left arm of yet another soldier.

The fight did not go all in favor of the pirates by any means. One of the Spaniards sliced a deep wound in Mullins's left arm. Another pair flanked Harris while he was dueling with yet a third and ran him through left to right and right to left. Foggerty took a slash down his face from forehead to chin that left him with only one good eye.

James proved to be magnificent with his blades—the rapier for offense and the dagger in his left hand to fend off attacks.

He had learned to fence at Eton, where he had learned so many other useful things. Because of what was common rumor about his background in those days, he often had to pit his fledgling skill against two or even three boys who were his senior in years if not in ability. Those lessons in the unfairness of combat had stood him well in the time since, never more valiantly than on the docks of Isla de Tres Palmas.

Ah, if only his father could have seen him at that moment. No doubt, the man would have disapproved of the reasons that his disgraced and disowned son fought, but even he would have had to admire the skill with which an English sword stood against Spanish steel. Slash, parry, thrust and thrust, parry again, and riposte, fending off three blades at once.

How his blade sang in the early morning air with joy at being wielded by a cool wit, a keen eye, and a firm wrist! A moving net of gleaming steel baffled the blades of his foes and left two opponents gasping their last breathes on the stones even as three more crowded in to replace the two already disposed of.

It was a noble, even epic, effort from James, though his cause was not a noble one. His rapier and dagger formed a wall of deadly steel thorns that kept back five of the Spaniards while Cecco dispatched another, and Dusk, aided by Jacob, took down two more. The curls of his long black hair flying wildly, James was at last in his element, the place in all the world where he was at his very best, and he moved naturally and without thought in the very best of form.

His every move was true, without deception or even a hint of malice. What he did with his sword was what had to be done—and done in the purest of intent. It was a battle against odds in which he never took unfair advantage, pitting only his superb skill against those who sought to match their ability against his.

For the moment, the only motive James had was to complete that deadly dance as it should properly be done, without thought to anything but the terrible beauty of mind, body, and steel acting together in a contest where only one man could be the winner.

It was not bad form on the part of James to see it as a battle that only he could survive. It was, because of the unconscious purity of the moment, the very best form possible. He did not even note that his mouth told the others to get the wounded aboard and prepare to cast off or that they obeyed him with frantic haste. He did not see Dick Brown pause too long and meet his end on Spanish steel. He did not even feel triumph as another soldier and then yet another fell to the inevitable sharp sting of his blade.

It might have gone on until the Spaniards were all dead or

scattered in defeat but for the actions of the fat old sergeant. He recognized a supreme swordsman when he saw one, dispatching his soldiers one after another. One thing he was certain of in a case like that: a swordsman was much less a threat without his sword.

Sergeant Pacheco had been many things in his career. A thief, a murderer, and many things even worse that had been cloaked by his service to his king. He was not, however, a coward, nor was he slow to act when danger threatened.

Dropping his own blade, Pacheco swept up an empty barrel and hurled it with all the considerable strength of his rotund body. The ungainly missile struck James and swept him from his feet, the sword and dagger flying from his hands.

Dropped thus suddenly from the dizzying height to which the perfection of his swordplay had lifted him, James was momentarily as any other mortal man bereft of his weapons in the face of several armed enemies: dismayed and uncertain.

It was not right; it was not fair; it was not *good form*!

No, James thought sadly in that moment of paralyzing shock, he could not even charge that. What could a common solider know of good form? Even a sergeant? And certainly a Spanish sergeant had to be excused, for there was no way such a man could know about such things, and thus he could not be blamed for violating conventions that he did not even know existed. What was there for him to do except take what had come his way with as good a grace as possible and try to survive by any means?

At least the barrel, in rebounding from James, had scattered the remaining Spaniards for a moment. In scrambling to his feet, James looked around for his sword and dagger or for anything he could use as a weapon.

The rapier lay beyond his reach, almost at the feet of one soldier. The dagger was gone from sight, probably lost in the dark water of the harbor. Something else then as a weapon, or his adventures would come to a finish on that dock, on that early morning or at the end of a Spanish rope very soon afterward.

The thought that he might never get his revenge on the world inspired James in his swift assessment of the possible weapons around him. Close beside him was a drying rack for fishing nets with one net draped in folds over it. Not of much use to the quartermaster. A pair of oars? Perhaps he could use one like a short staff? No, they were too flimsy and too light. A fisherman's gaff hook? No, it … but wait … perhaps, yes!

James snatched up the gaff with a graceful step and a twist, dodging the thrust of the first of the soldiers to attempt to avenge the fellows he had killed. With his left hand, James twirled the gaff and struck, thrusting the butt against the soldier's skull just under the edge of his helmet. As the Spaniard stumbled, James struck again, another harder thrust that sent the helmet flying and left the soldier reeling to the edge of the dock.

Gravity and a spot of grease lent their aid to the cause of the pirate. The soldier went over the edge and was dragged below the murky water of the harbor by the weight of his breast and back armor.

And then there were four.

Four against one—for all of the surviving men from the *Jolly Roger*'s shore party were awaiting their quartermaster to join them aboard the ketch. Even if James was in no position to see it, they could all plainly mark the score of soldiers who were quick-marching down from the fortress, pikes on shoulders or long muskets in their hands, giving them only a few moments before they must cast off or face either death or capture and the noose.

James knew only that he had to fight if he wanted to live. A gaff hook was not a fearsome weapon to a man in armor and helm, so James would have to give the three soldiers and their sergeant good cause to fear the man if not the tool.

Quarterstaff play was something else he had learned at his school, even if that had been more of a game than his endeavors with the rapier. Whirls and reverses, sudden jabs mixed with a leg sweep, and angled strokes guided swords harmlessly away without striking flesh or wood. Once the hook caught a sleeve and the flesh beneath, James yanked the man in close and used a knee up under the edge of the armor in what was considered good form in such a brutal, lopsided contest. He thrust the man aside to spew out his last meal where he would not be underfoot.

That move almost proved his end, for Sergeant Pacheco came in with his sword raised for a stroke that would have split James from crown to brisket. A quick twist brought the gaff up to block, the old wood cracking as the steel bit into it. It was sturdy enough to hold back the blade, though just barely. James slipped away with a piece of the broken gaff in each hand and a prayer of thanks to whoever had crafted that worn tool.

A short length of splintered wooden pole in his left hand, the iron hook and a foot of wood in his right. Even in that moment of stress, James saw that the gaff had been made from an old boat-hook, the fending spike and the hook both filed down to needle points. It was perhaps more of a weapon than he had originally thought.

James knocked aside the sword diving for his vitals with the length of wood in his left hand and thrust with the spiked hook, a lunge straight into the throat of Sergeant Pacheco. Twisting the man about with the spike, he placed the dying man between himself and the other three soldiers. One went to the left, one went to the right, and the third, back on his feet after depositing his dinner on the stones, stopped in his tracks, baffled by indecision.

There was no such moment of vacillation for James, who struck left with his wooden rod and leaped right, digging the hook into the soldier's arm to spin him around. That ploy had worked so well by accident that he would use it again to good purpose.

Once again, he had a Spaniard between him and his remaining foes, now two in number. A foot delivered with enthusiasm to the fundament of the wounded soldier tore the hook free of his arm and catapulted him into the arms of a companion. The other soldier, dodging to one side, left himself open to a solid thwack across the nose with the heavy iron back of the gaff hook.

Much though he would have liked to remain and provide a proper finish to the fray, James could see that his men had already cast off all lines. He could heard the pounding of running feet and feel the planks of the pier tremble under his muddy shoes.

With a jauntiness that he was too weary to truly feel, James bid farewell to those of his opponents who were still able to hear his words. He sprang hard upon the armored back of a soldier who sought to rise and then leaped from the dock, reaching for the receding rail of the ketch.

Bill Jukes leaned far out and caught the quartermaster around the wrist, overbalancing himself until Cecco and Dusk pulled both of them to safety.

"My thanks to you, Mr. Jukes," James panted, getting his feet under him on the deck. "And to you as well, Dusk, Cecco. I shall not forget."

"Like we won't forget that fight, b'God," gasped Jukes in admiration. "Never saw the like in all my days. Yer a devil with a sword, Mr. James, but I've not see your like in all my days with a hook like that."

"Si, is much true," Cecco agreed. "With the sword, you are *supremo*, si! With that hook, *da parte di tutti i santi*, never have I seena theese before. Truly, you are Meester James of the Hook, a dangerous man what I am be proud to know!"

James waved them back to their duties, noticing that he still retained the broken part of the gaff hook. It was an old, ugly, and very rusty piece of iron, even uglier with fresh ruddy stains on its sharp points.

The quartermaster could find another sword and dagger to replace those he had lost. He had done so more than once since leaving England and leaving his favorite sword behind. That would have left his father seething with anger, James realized with faint satisfaction.

This hook, though, was something special for all its common and brutal look. It could be polished and cleaned. Carver could fit a new, short shaft to it, designed as James would like it to be for best use.

A sword at his hip, a dagger in his belt, and this hook where his left hand could grasp it quickly—there were possibilities in that, great possibilities as he saw it, just as there were possibilities in the name that Cecco had casually given him.

James of the Hook? No, not that, though something alone that line. James the Hook? It still did not flow smoothly from the tongue; it did not have the appropriate panache. James Hook? Yes, that would do.

James Hook, pirate.

That had a fine ring to it. As his nom de guerre—and he understood that he was at war with the world—"Hook" had a fine and fearsome sound. And someday, not too far in the future, the newly self-christened James Hook promised himself, the name would sound even grander when prefaced it with the title of captain.

Chapter 5

The Galleon of Gold

As the sun came up huge and orange, causing the fortress to appear as naught but a featureless and ominous black silhouette, Red Michael gave the order that took the *Jolly Roger* into the mouth of the harbor of Isla de Tres Palmas. He issued his command not in faith but in fatalism.

The new quartermaster had proven himself aboard the brig as far as the running of the ship was concerned. But Captain Conner had only the man's word on his ability in a fight. Smee might have been impressed with outcome of the duel at the Bent Cutlass, but the captain of the *Jolly Roger* did not hold the opinion of his bosun in high regard. Smee was no more than a fool in the view of Michael Conner—a useful fool at times, especially when keeping the crew in line, yet still no more than a fool.

The stolid German who served as gun captain, Dieter Trommler, stood amidships by one of the loaded starboard guns. In his phlegmatic fashion, he had overseen the loading of all the cannons in the ship's battery. Solid shot for the portside guns, chain on the starboard. He had already fixed the elevation of the starboard guns as well, for the orders had been to sweep the decks of the galleon and bring down her masts. The port guns were in reserve in case the quartermaster failed in his endeavors—or to use as a waterline salute to the galleon after she had been looted.

Red Michael drained the flat-bottomed bottle of rum he held and hitched up the enormous belt that held his gut in check while supporting his cutlass, a brace of pistols, and a knife nearly large enough to be counted as a second sword. Needless to say, the leather of that belt was very stout leather indeed.

Tuck caught the empty bottle that his captain casually tossed aside. With a battle in the offing, he would need to go below very soon. One of the many rules Captain Conner laid on the boy was that he never expose himself to danger. Another was that he always had a bottle of rum ready for his captain. Tuck often ran afoul of one rule or another in attempting to obey Red Michael Conner.

"Are you miserable dogs ready to be unleashed?" Red Michael shouted to the men gathered around him on the poop deck. "Are you ready to teach these Spanish lubbers another lesson?"

"Aye!" came the roaring response from more than three score of throats.

The villainous crew of the *Jolly Roger* waved boarding axes, pikes, and cutlasses aloft. If there were any sailors aboard the galleon, there could be no question as to their fate at the hands of that murderous rabble. Cruelty for cruelty's own sake was a part of their nature to the very core.

"Aye, aye, Cap'n," Smee said with enthusiasm, waving the blade he affectionately called Johnny Corkscrew.

The bosun's belt was crowded with his closest friends, from Little Timmy Thunder and his brother Big Tommy Thunder—a flintlock longer than Smee's own forearm—to the worn, old, knob-by-headed bit of blackthorn he referred to as Bobby Shillelagh. They were the only family Smee laid any claim to, and he was as proud as any father when they did the work he wanted them to do.

Smee was one of the few among those blackguards who would crack a skull or slit a throat without animosity toward his victim.

All in the way of business, as he thought it, and no offense meant at all.

The boarding party was crowded together on the poop because the galleon was so high-sided even at the waist that only from the stern of the brig were they high enough to lay the boarding planks from ship to ship. The carpenter had already removed a section of the poop rail to make that operation easier, and the long boarding planks with their iron spikes at the end to bite into wood were raised and ready to be dropped down on the enemy deck.

The approach was the chancy part and near to every man aboard the brig felt the tension. Captain Conner swigged his rum while others either gave thought to prayers they had once known as youngsters or considered their response to the orders that might be given if the heavy guns of the fortress opened fire on them.

As the *Jolly Roger* surged ahead with all sails billowing in the morning breeze, the pirates could hear the distant clangor of the alarm bell in the tower, and they could see the tiny white-and-silver figures of distant Spanish soldiers boiling out of their barracks like enraged ants. The gunners ran to their guns and began loading. Squads of musketeers and pikemen formed up under the shouted commands of officers in striped pantaloons and polished steel breastplates. Crested steel helmets glinted in the shadows.

All occurred as might be expected when a Spanish harbor was invaded by a vessel boldly flying the skull and crossbones. All, that is, except for the roar of cannon fire.

Shoving his immense bulk through the press of men like a broad-beamed man-of-war breasting the waves, Red Michael forced a path to the starboard rail and clapped his spyglass to his eye. The many rings on his fingers flashed crimson and gold as the first rays of the morning sun crested the fortress and struck down into the harbor. The sight that met his eye caused him to give out a great bellowing laugh of genuine humor.

Spanish gunners were running to Spanish sergeants, who in

turn ran to Spanish officers to report that the guns could not be fired. The quartermaster had done his duty well it seemed. The shore party under his command must have also avoided detection, since the Spaniards had been caught unaware when the *Jolly Roger* sailed into the harbor.

The guns were spiked as had been planned. The galleon lay at anchor as had been hoped. She rode deep in the water, displaying that her holds were full of a weighty cargo. That fickle wench, Dame Fortune, smiled fully on Red Michael Conner that day, and he was not about to waste her favor while it held.

"Bring us about, you lubber!" Red Michael shouted to the man at the wheel.

"You scurvy monkeys, prepare to take in sail!" was the shout for the benefit of the men aloft. That was followed with another bellow directed amidships: "Dietz, you Dutch donkey, fire a proper salute to the dons!"

"Deutsch, nicht Neiderlandisch, du fettes schwein," the gunner muttered without rancor as he brought the linstock down to the touchhole of the cannon as the gun came into line with the masts of the galleon.

Attempting to acquaint Red Michael Conner with the difference between Holland and his homeland of neighboring Hannover had proven fruitless. In part, that was because Dieter lacked the experience with the English language to properly explain the difference. A larger part was because Red Michael simply did not care about such details.

The cannon belched flame and smoke, spitting out a whirling mass of tangled iron links. As the *Jolly Roger* drove through the cloud of white smoke, the mizzenmast of the galleon folded gently, like an old man bowing too deeply, and then collapsed over the side.

At the command of the gun captain, the rest of the starboard cannons fired, raking the deck and rigging with iron. Wood splintered and flew in whistling fragments, lines lashed out as they were cut, and yards crashed down as the tackle that held them was shattered.

There were no casualties among the watch aboard the galleon, for that handful of sailors were experienced hands and had known what was coming from the moment they saw the black flag streaming from the mast of the brigantine bearing down on them. With that knowledge, those courageous seamen had scrambled over to the starboard side well before the cannonade came in from the port. They piled into the small rowing boat that had been tied alongside the galleon as their ship trembled under the assault from the pirate's vessel. As soon as two men untangled themselves enough to reach the oars, they had the boat moving at a smart clip for the docks.

At sea, they would have fought for their ship with a hundred sailors and Spanish soldiers at their back, showing all the courage of cornered rats. In the harbor of Isla de Tres Palmas, it was the duty of the comandante and his troops to defend their ship. They had no intention of placing themselves between the soldiers of their king and those that it was the sworn duty of those soldiers to attack, so they rowed all the faster to get out of the line of fire.

"Let go grapples, and heave away," shouted Captain Conner as the *Jolly Roger* drifted up to gently kiss the ornate side of the towering galleon.

Men on the forecastle whirled grappling irons on lengths of chain and let them fly upward to snag the rail of the galleon. Other men hauled on the lines tied to the chains, bringing their little brig snug against the side of the Spanish behemoth.

Smee quietly directed a pair of men close beside him to throw their own grapples and snug down the lines. That accomplished, the ships were almost touching, with canvas-swaddled timbers holding the two hulls apart by little more than a yard.

"Boarders away, Mr. Smee!" roared Red Michael.

"Aye, sir! Boarders away! Drop the planks and board, lads! Search out the loot, and do for any who stands in your way!"

Captain Michael Conner was content to let his men board the prize while he remained aboard the *Jolly Roger*. If there was any resistance, Red Michael could see no reason to expose himself to danger. That was why a captain sailed with a crew, as he saw things. Their purpose was to take the risks that made him rich.

The bosun, on the other hand, preferred to watch over his men as they went about their duty. He sought to make certain that they did not, purely by accident, of course, allow a handful or two of doubloons to fall into their sashes before all the booty was transferred and they were well away.

The punishment for such "accidents" being what it was, Mr. Smee thought it best to keep a weather eye on the crew for their own good. Marooning was an unpleasant end for a man suffering from just a touch of simple greed. The additional penalties Red Michael enjoyed inflicting on those given such a sentence made Smee determined to prevent any member of the crew from being so foolish as to tempt such a fate.

Under the guidance of the bosun, the boarders from the *Jolly Roger* quickly assured themselves that there was not another soul aboard the galleon. After that, they got down to the serious labor of hauling heavy chests, sacks, and ingots of gold up from the hold. It was hard and hot work, but the men went at it with a will—and with a song on their lips as well.

Well might they sing, for it had been many a voyage since they had last taken a prize with so little risk and never a haul as rich as this. Mr. Smee aboard the galleon and Red Michael aboard the *Jolly Roger* directed the men in stowing the treasure. The bars were stacked in the hold of the brigantine, and the chests were piled amidships to allow all hands the pleasure of viewing the heap of wealth.

It should not be thought that Captain Conner was so enraptured by the glitter of gold that he forgot to keep a sharp eye on the fortress and the antics of the Spaniards there. Nor was Mr. Smee so remiss in his duties that he failed to observe how the brig sat deeper and deeper in the water as the harvest of gold filled the hold.

Red Michael measured the passage of time by how the fortress came out of its own shadow and revealed details that had been hidden by the rising sun. Its ominous black walls became plastered and whitewashed stone. Even from where they sat in the harbor, Captain Conner could see patches where the plaster had been weakened by wind and weather, where sections had fallen away to reveal the bare stone beneath.

It seemed that the comandante did not care to spend time or gold on keeping the walls of the fortress in good repair. That, as Captain Conner knew from long experience, was common among the officers in charge of remote Spanish outposts. Whatever moneys were allotted by their king for the maintenance and repair of his remote garrisons more often than not found their way into the pockets of the most senior officers. It was a fact that buccaneers used to their advantage time and again.

"Begging your pardon, Captain, but—" Mr. Smee started to call across to Red Michael, only to be interrupted by his captain.

"Enough, Smee. Have all our dogs back in their own kennel. Strikes me as it won't be long 'fore even those Spanish lubbers get their guns cleared and in action. Though it grieves me to leave so much behind, best we show the dons our heels 'fore they be set to shoot us twixt wind and water, eh?"

"Aye, Cap'n. As you say," Smee responded, happy that he did not have to argue his case to Red Michael.

While the brigands from the *Jolly Roger* streamed back aboard their ship, Smee noted the ketch sailing boldly for the mouth of the harbor. Even without a glass, he could recognize the lean figure of the quartermaster among the men on that small craft. It was good to know that his friend had not only succeeded in his mission but that he had survived as well.

Once clear of the harbor, the brig and the ketch could meet, and the raiders could rejoin their shipmates aboard the *Jolly Roger*.

In the meantime, it was best that the lesser vessel continue with all the speed her smaller sails could provide. Even with her belly full of gold, the *Jolly Roger* would have no trouble catching up to James and the ketch he had commandeered.

Alf Mason scurried across the boarding plank last, a pair of massive gold candelabras in his arms. Smee signaled for the planks to be raised before the man was entirely aboard, causing him to be pitched on his face as the boarding planks swung up and free of the galleon. A moment later, the lines holding the *Jolly Roger* tight to her victim were cut as sails were unfurled and the brigantine swept deeper into the harbor before coming around to turn her back on the fortress.

As their portside guns came to bear, Dieter fired the waterline salute that his captain had asked for. They had to leave a fortune in gold behind, for the *Jolly Roger* could only carry so much of that heavy treasure. But they did not have to make it easy for the Spanish to recover what they could not take. Like naughty boys who could not eat all the pies they tried to steal, Captain Conner and his men did not leave anything behind for others to enjoy, preferring instead to destroy what they could not have for themselves.

Solid shot punched into the hull of the galleon as she rocked, the German gun captain timing each shot so that the target was rolling away when the next iron ball struck. His care allowed each succeeding shot to smash through under the waterline. The water of the harbor flooded into the lower decks of the galleon. Without a soul aboard to man the pumps or attempt to patch the leaks Dieter caused, the ornate giant was visibly listing before the *Jolly Roger* passed between the rocks that marked the mouth of the harbor.

"Let the dons dredge their gold up from the deep," Red Michael crowed derisively. "They needs to work for their booty same as the rest of us!"

As if in parting salute, one of the long guns of the fortress spoke, the massive iron sphere passing yards to their right. A second gun saluted the departing pirates, landing with a splash that wetted a few of the men at the port rail. While they cried out in derision, three more culverin belched out their futile message of anger, demonstrating only that Spanish gunnery was still nothing to be feared at a distance. Each cannon shot fell close to the brig, though none so close as to give any man aboard her a single qualm.

Red Michael had searched the harbor for any sign of a Spanish ship that might give them trouble as they fled. There had been no craft large enough to be a threat among the collection of small vessels. The ketch that James had absconded with was the next in size to the galleon they had looted, so there was nothing to fear unless they had the bad fortune to run into a *guardacostas* of New Spain approaching the island unexpectedly.

The sea beyond the harbor proved to be clear of vessels except for the ketch that lingered just beyond the range of the guns of the fort. In short order, the *Jolly Roger* matched course and speed to the smaller craft, and James led his remaining men aboard the brig—just ten of them where there had been twelve with him before. No one questioned the loss of two men, accounting such deaths as merely a normal peril of the life outside the law that they chose to lead.

At the command of the captain, the brig came around to a course that would return them to Tortuga and to all the vices that could be found on that small island. Behind them, the ketch lost way without a hand on her tiller. A thread of smoke curled up from the vessel, soon becoming a thick column.

Just as Red Michael had sunk the galleon when he could take no more from her, so too had the quartermaster set a small fire that would devour the ketch. Some might regard it as a waste. James preferred to think of it as furthering the reputation enjoyed by those who plied the sweet trade, especially that of James Hook.

They needed their status as murderers, arsonists, and thieves to make their prey cower before them without any show of resistance. If every ship gave resistance when they approached with their black flag raised to display their intention, piracy would soon be as much hard labor as honest work and perhaps even more dangerous. Better for all involved that merchantmen feared pirates and surrendered without a fight.

"Well, Mr. James, it seems that you know more than just how to clean a ship," Red Michael greeted his quartermaster grudgingly. "Only lost two hands—better than I had hoped."

"Aye, Captain. All went as planned ashore until the Spanish lookout saw the *Jolly Roger* sailing in so bold. Still, we managed our business successfully enough. Is it too much to hope that you can say the same?"

With a smile that contained a large measure of sneer, the corpulent pirate captain stepped to one side so that the quartermaster and his men could see the heap of chests and sacks, doubloons spilling from ruptured canvas.

"Odds bobs, hammer and tongs!" the quartermaster cried in amazement, seeing the size of the prize Captain Red Michael Conner had hauled aboard the *Jolly Roger* in such a short time.

While that seemed like a strange exclamation of surprise to many who heard it, there was a good reason for such words coming to the lips of the quartermaster of the *Jolly Roger*. For James, who made every effort to be as unlike other men as he could manage, it was simply another display of his will and determination.

Any common fool could swear by saints he did not believe in or use the ordinary profanities and plebeian oaths that were heard in every tavern. In fact, common fools did just that every day and every night, for little reason or no reason at all.

James had determined that such crude expressions would never pass his lips, yet recognized at the same time that every man had need from time to time to articulate his strong emotions with words of little actual meaning.

Rather than use rude terms for bodily functions, call for

divine judgment that he had no power to decree, or use any of the other vile terms generally thrown around at such moments, James had trained himself to use other phrases for those moments when anger, fear, or, as in this instance, wonder caused his mouth to act before his marvelous brain could intervene.

The bosun, Mr. Smee, was quite taken with such expressions, seeing in them evidence that his friend James was a man of a very different stripe than most who sailed under the skull and cross-bones—a fellow of education and finer sentiments, much as the bosun thought himself to be.

The rest of the crew, from cook to captain, thought that such words merely offered further proof that their quartermaster was the oddest duck among the typically odd crew of the pirate brigantine.

"A good haul for the work, eh, Quartermaster?" Captain Conner asked jovially, working the cork out from another bottle of rum.

"Remarkably good, Captain," James replied.

"And that doesn't take into account the ingots we've stored away in the hold either," added Smee proudly. "All because of your good work Jas … er, that is to say, *Mr.* James."

"No, Mr. Smee. No, not I alone," the quartermaster said in a honeyed voice designed to carry to the entire crew crowded close around. "I merely led these brave men. Dusk deserves as much praise as I, and Cecco as well. We could never have succeeded without the efforts of Starkey or Bill Jukes or poor Dick Brown, who scaled the wall and took down the first of the guards in silence. Poor Dick Brown fell bravely defending my back while I held off the Spaniards so my good men could prepare the ketch for our escape to rejoin the rest of our shipmates."

James looked around to see if he might be laying it on a bit too thick. No; every hand listened intently to his humble praise of the men who had accompanied him, and all thought the more of their quartermaster for the tribute he paid to those who had simply followed his orders without a serious mistake.

"It is not I, but these good stout fellows who are deserving of any praise you may wish to bestow for the successful completion of our dangerous adventure ashore."

The crew of the *Jolly Roger* raised a cheer at those noble words. Even Red Michael Conner joined in, believing, at least for that moment, that he had the best quartermaster a captain sailing under the skull and crossbones could ever wish to have. Dusk, Jukes, Cecco, and the others who had gone ashore with James cheered as well, seeing him as brave, intelligent, and humble.

Already they thought of how much they owed to the quartermaster. His words colored the events of the past few hours subtly in his favor. Already, in their own minds, they magnified his words and deeds. Soon enough, when they spoke of their adventures, it would be James who held the central position and no other. Dick Brown would be remembered, as would his companion in misfortune, Robert Harris. Perhaps those two would hold a higher place in the story of the raid on Isla de Tres Palmas than Cecco or poor Foggerty, who would wear a patch over his ruined eye for the rest of his life, but the man most spoken of would be James, the quartermaster of the *Jolly Roger*—James Hook, as all would soon refer to him.

Tales of that nature only grew in the telling, as James well knew. The seed he planted that morning on the deck of the brig would grow and grow over the coming months, of that he was certain. What fruit would come from that seed he could not say, nor whether that fruit would be sweet or bitter. Time alone would show what came of his efforts that day.

James allowed himself a slow smile, thinking on what he hoped to harvest in the future. As he had discovered years ago, while he was still at school, the world was an uncertain place at best, and the most carefully laid plans could run onto shoals even when the course seemed clear and free of dangers. Such a disaster had befallen him before and driven him from England, and such a disaster might happen again.

He had learned to lay his plans with care and always have another scheme in reserve, if not two. It was said that fortune favored the prepared, and James sought always to prepare for the disfavor of Dame Fortune.

It had been his failure to plan far enough ahead that had seen him with only the clothes on his back and a few coins in his pouch that night at the Bent Cutlass when he met Smee for the first time. He had made the mistake of thinking he had a scheme without flaws, and it had cost him nearly everything. Such events would never occur again. That was a vow he made to himself, and he intended to keep it.

With sails set and the course laid, Captain Conner told LaSalle to broach a keg of rum and serve it out to all hands. That order was met by a cheer from the men. Even James thought it a fine idea though he partook only briefly of the wild celebration that followed. With such wealth aboard, the men danced and sang and boasted of what they would do with their share once they reached Tortuga.

James had other, more immediate, desires to fulfill. The march through the mangrove swamp had left him caked to the waist in dried mud and slime. Twigs and bits of the gray moss called old man's beard were tangled in his hair. His doublet and shirt were in tatters, and they were rank with dried sweat. What he wanted most was a seawater bath and fresh garments, followed by a long sleep. The men he had led ashore were content to swill rum until they collapsed in their filthy garments. He preferred to be clean before taking the rest he so richly deserved. He needed the rum only to help calm his mind, for his body was eager for repose.

The ship's boy proved eager to assist the quartermaster, perhaps seeing such aid as his way to steer clear of Red Michael and his ever-ready fist. While James stood on the beakhead, Tuck pulled up bucket after bucket of water to sluice over the quartermaster as he scrubbed his garments clean while they were still on his body. James used his fingers to comb out the moss, bugs, and twigs from his long, curly black hair.

The cold seawater showed him aches and pains that he had ignored during the frantic action ashore and relief at being safe aboard the *Jolly Roger* once more. Yes, sleep was what he needed, far more than rum, dancing with his shipmates, or songs sung discordantly off-key.

James squeezed the water from his shirt and breeches, wincing with pain from some of the bruises he had collected. The boy had thought to bring an old blanket along, which James used to dry his long black hair, swarthy face, and strong thin hands. Much of the remaining water was patted from his garments with that blanket until it was sodden. Tuck would see that it was hung out to dry after the quartermaster was asleep.

The boy went with him back to the tiny cabin, staying in the quartermaster's shadow as James endured the congratulations of his shipmates, punctuated by hearty slaps on the back and punches to his shoulder. Once belowdecks, Tuck helped lay out the old, worn nightshirt that James preferred when he slept. It was a habit from his younger days that he still retained, a touch of civilization that he held on to despite his change in circumstances.

Suddenly weary, James sat on his narrow bunk while Tuck unbuckled his shoes, tsk-tsking over their sorry condition.

"I'll see what I can do for them while you sleep, Mr. James," Tuck said earnestly. "I'll clean them best I can and oil the leather. Might be I can make them fit for use again. Not so fine as they once was, but good enough for battle, sir."

It surprised James to find that he believed the boy to be sincere. He pulled off his doublet, examining the sorry condition it was in after the fight on the dock.

"Here, sir. Let me help you with your shirt," the boy said, still honestly wanting to be of assistance.

The tattered linen was removed, and the boy held it up and looked it over with a critical eye.

"I can sew a bit, Mr. James; so these tears can be mended. Mr. Smee taught me to use needle and thread. Not pretty—I won't claim that, sir—but, like the shoes, you can wear them aboard ship or in battle."

James bestowed a slight smile on the boy. As he was more used to cuffs and kicks from his captain than smiles from anyone, Tuck glowed with happiness at that slight show of kindness.

"This here was cut up a bit," the boy continued, holding one slit in the shirt open with his fingers. "A wonder, sir, that you weren't sliced up as well. You must be a wonder with a sword, sir."

Tuck looked at the narrow, muscular chest that the quartermaster displayed.

"Oh look, sir. Does that hurt?"

Tuck pointed to a spot low on the left side of James's ribs.

"Someone touched you, at that. I'll fetch a cloth to bind it with!"

Without waiting for a reply, the boy bolted from the tiny chamber.

With a feeling of dread, James looked down to where the boy had pointed. A thin line had been traced there by a sharp blade, sharp enough that he had not even noticed the wound. It was not deep, but it still oozed a small amount of thick, darkly purplish blood.

The room swam suddenly about him. If there was one thing that James feared, it was the proof of his own mortality in the form of seeing his own blood before him. The color of it marked him as different from other men, yet seeing it come from his own body showed that he differed from the common herd far less than he wanted to believe.

He had let the blood of other men more times than he could easily count. He had watched them falter and fail before his steel, seen the rich crimson flow from their veins as they took a fatal wound. Yet, his own blood spilled, even in a small amount, gave him dreadful evidence that he was as prone to the reaper as any other man. The tangible proof that he could falter and fail as they did aroused a fearful sickness within his breast.

When Tuck returned, he found the quartermaster collapsed in apparent slumber, the nightshirt still over the foot of the bunk. With great care not to awaken James, Tuck cleaned and bound the slight wound and struggled to pull the nightshirt over his head.

"He must have completely exhausted himself ashore," Tuck thought wonderingly, for the quartermaster showed no sign of waking, even when the boy pulled his arms through the sleeves of the nightshirt.

"What a man he is, to exert himself so for the safety of all of us."

Chapter 6

Tuck, the Ship's Boy

Roses. That was what James saw as he tried to get his eyes to focus. Golden roses, three of them, mixed with golden skulls, three of them as well. Two roses with a skull between them, and two skulls with a rose between them—and all around them dots and beads of gold and sparkling crimson gems the color of fresh-spilled blood. The color of the blood in most men's veins, at any rate.

It was a ring, a fat gold ring on a fat finger, part of a puffy, powerful left hand. There were other rings on that hand, all but one bearing a blood-red gem, and that particular ring held his eye.

That ring was smeared with blood, thick and purplish, not like the blood of an ordinary man. But that was to be expected, since James had never been ordinary, not even when he was the youngest he could remember.

It came from standing up for the ship's boy, of course. Boys were always trouble, as they had been since he was a young man of five or six years of age. Then it had been his brothers—half brothers, in truth—every bit as fair and innocent to the eye as this boy. The difference came in that Tuck was what he appeared to be to his very core: honest, earnest, and humble. His brothers had been imps from the infernal regions set loose on the world—not that anyone but James had every known them for what they truly were.

James had not expected the blow any more than he had expected the power behind his captain's slap. If Red Michael possessed such strength as that, he must be holding back when he struck the ship's boy. In true rage, that strength would have been enough to kill the child in just a few blows.

Yet Captain Conner beat the boy, and it seemed that he beat him coldly and without mercy, all for some fault that neither James nor Tuck could understand. Conner beat the boy with some purpose in mind besides cruelty and anger.

That Red Michael had reason for anger was certain, though that anger should have been directed at himself and not Tuck. It had been Red Michael who had planned to intercept the merchantman a day's voyage from Jamaica. It had been Red Michael who had ordered the prey disabled and looted, even though a pair of royal navy vessels were within sight of the battle.

Rather than flee and live to fight another day, Captain Conner had ordered the black flag run up and had attacked the heavily laden vessel, cutting down the foremast with chain shot and raking the deck with canister before closing in and boarding.

A swift attack and a brutal one, the pirates cut down any sailor who did not move aside swiftly enough. Cargo was shifted with haste, casks of rum mostly, and then a fire was lit in the hold to give those poor swabs something to think on rather than attempting to join with the English warships in pursuit.

The *Jolly Roger* fled east with every stitch of canvas her yards could hold. The frigates behind made only slow progress in closing the distance, yet it was enough to see that the pirates would be hard-pressed to lose their pursuers, even after darkness fell.

And if they did not lose the frigates by dawn, they would all be with Davie Jones or in chains before the sun set a second time. What would follow capture was well known to all of them. That dreaded short drop and a sudden stop, the hempen jig that captured pirates danced, once and only once, for the entertainment of those who considered themselves loyal and law-abiding subjects of their king.

All that could be laid to Captain Red Michael Conner. Instead of shouldering that blame, Red Michael had called a trembling Tuck on deck and slapped him from his feet and then waited until the boy stood to slap him down again. Three, four, five times he repeated the process, with Mr. Smee and the rest of the crew looking on shamefaced and never speaking a word of protest or raising a hand to defend the boy they all treated like a little brother.

At last, the quartermaster had stood all that he could. He had no fondness for Tuck for all that the boy appeared to simply and honestly worship James as a hero. No, it was not out of any soft emotion that he stepped forward to arrest Captain Conner's upraised right hand. It was not because he liked the lad, but simply because it was such incredibly bad form for the captain to strike the child in such a fashion as that and for no discernable reason as well.

Laying on the deck with blood trickling down the side of his face, James understood in a muddled fashion that Michael Conner was not beating Tuck as he had the ability to do, but merely terrorizing the boy for a reason unknown to the quartermaster. He even held the suspicion that Red Michael had not struck him as hard as he might have but had restrained his blow because he knew that his quartermaster had no understanding of what was going on.

Faint from the sight of his own blood as much as from the buffet to the side of his head, James Hook tried to get his hands and feet under himself to rise, feeling the rhythm of the waves change under the brig.

* * *

The return of the *Jolly Roger* to Tortuga was accomplished without adventure or incident of note. It was a calm and peaceful voyage, with all hands in high spirits. Considering the bounty that lay in the hold of the brig, it was no wonder that those scoundrels were full of joy and song at all times of the day and night.

The harbor of the pirate stronghold was empty of great ships when the *Jolly Roger* returned. Flint's *Walrus* and Kennedy's *Green Hills* were sailing the Spanish Main in search of prey, as were the *Black Joke*, *Bird of Paradise*, *Laughing Maiden*, and *Wolf's Fang*. All the pirate captains of note were about their unlawful business, seeking out ships to seize or towns that would be worth the effort to sack.

An unusual event that was, for it was seldom that the majority of those who sailed under the black flag were absent from Tortuga all at once. Until the early return of the *Jolly Roger*, the port was empty save for a few brave merchant ships that traded on that island. It was a rare time for the local inhabitants to draw breath and repair all the damage done by those who brought wealth to the island along with mayhem, entertainment, and destruction in uncertain quantities.

But then the *Jolly Roger* did return and return with more gold than Tortuga had seen since the days of the great Spanish treasure fleets. The alehouses and taverns brought out their very best and priced all their goods accordingly. The choicest meats and the finest wines and spirits, strong enough to drop a horse, were all available for a price. There was fresh fry bread with honey or crushed sugar, wrapped in banana leaves, and sections of delectable fresh fruit on thin wooden skewers ready to purchase for a few small coins.

The merchants put on display the best of their goods, which were often items that had been sold to them by other pirates. Garments of the best cloth, firearms decorated with silver and ivory, blades of the finest steel available in the world, as well as a hundred other items large and small that might attract the interest of a buccaneer with plenty of gold.

The wenches brought out their finest garments and the gaudy

jewelry designed to lure a man's eye to their more interesting features. The faux rubies and emeralds merely served to draw the gaze to the expanse of dusky skin displayed by low-cut bodices. With paint and powder and perfume, those doxies made their lips more kissable, their skin more smooth to the touch, and their scent as sweet as the tropical flowers that bloomed in abundance on the island.

All this and more was done for the crew of the *Jolly Roger*, as would have been done for any pirate crew who returned with such treasure. Anything that could be sold was available in exchange for their gold, and what could not be sold was rented out by the half hour. For so long as the gold lasted, Tortuga would remain a wild celebration of every vice and passion that those cutthroats might have.

Tortuga, even in the full throws of a wild saturnalia because of the influx of Spanish gold, was still just a tawdry little island filled with thieves, murderers, soiled doxies, and rum merchants all eager to part honest pirates from their ill-gotten wealth. James remembered Providence as being much the same, though on a grander scale, before Woodes Rogers had brought the law of the current weak king to the paradisiacal island of Nassau.

Before that, there had been Libertalia in Madagascar, half a world away. That pirate nation had promised freedom and equality for all those who sailed under the skull and crossbones—a voice in every decision and a share from every prize. Another illusion, another myth, like buried treasure, Libertalia had been like Tortuga, and like Providence, except that the native beer was much blander and the native wenches were much bolder and more fiery, even more than doe-eyed Spanish doxies.

James walked the cobblestone streets of the pirate haven, aloof from the carnival atmosphere about him. It was not that he lacked vices and passions of his own. He just preferred to exercise such peccadilloes in a more gentlemanly fashion than that displayed by his shipmates. What he did ashore in Tortuga, and with whom, was not done in the muddy streets or in the public room of taverns. Even in that, James remained apart and above the common buccaneers he consorted with.

Nor was the quartermaster one to lose himself completely in rum, food, and laughing wenches. He had his duties as well as his goals, and they took precedence over the base hungers of the flesh.

First, there was the matter of his wardrobe, which needed to be replenished in proper style now that he had the gold for it.

Tuck had proven good to his word, restoring the muddy, water-soaked shoes to useable condition. He had also mended the torn doublet and shirt with surprising skill. That ability could be laid to the feet of Mr. Smee, for the unconventional bosun had taught the lad the art of mending with needle and thread as a master tailor might teach an apprentice.

Even with those items salvaged, there was much lacking from the collection of garments that James aspired to own. Only a small part of his share was enough to correct that lack. Daily fittings and alterations kept the ship's boy busy running parcels back to the quartermaster's cabin aboard the *Jolly Roger* while James browsed through collections of lace-trimmed shirts, silken stockings, waistcoats, knee breeches, and broad-brimmed hats.

"Cap'n Conner, he said I weren't to leave the ship," Tuck had protested when first ordered to accompany James ashore.

"Red Michael Conner is only captain," James had replied. "He has no more say on the matter while we are in port than any other member of the crew. We are, after all, free gentlemen of fortune, not common drudges fearing a taste of the cat. Even you, boy, are free, though I can think of no finer home for you than aboard the *Jolly Roger.*"

The quartermaster could see no reason for Red Michael to command the boy to remain aboard the brig while they were in port. Tortuga held its dangers, true enough, though Captain Conner showed no concern for the boy's safety at any other time.

At most, James put the captain's order down to the bullying nature of the fat brigand.

"You know what they are calling you, sir?" asked Tuck, when he returned for the eighth time from running to the ship for the quartermaster. "On account of *that*, and your fight against the Spaniards?"

Tuck pointed to the gaff hook that hung at the quartermaster's left hip. The ship's carpenter had mounted the iron hook on a cut-down oak belaying pin and wrapped it in cord to give a proper grip, just as James had demanded of him. Since then, James had taken to wearing it on his belt just aft of where the hilt of his rapier would be once he found a replacement for the one lost on Isla de Tres Palmas.

"Eh? And what would that be, boy?"

"Hook, sir. They calls you Hook now, for what you did with that."

James glanced at the ship's boy, a hard look in his eyes.

"Hook, is it? Just Hook?"

"No, sir. They is always respectful-like, sir. It is Mr. Hook they calls you or Quartermaster Hook—both the crew and them folks ashore what repeats your tale. All 'cepting Mr. Smee, that is. He calls you James Hook, and he says it with pride and friendship, sir. Proud of you he is, Mr. Hook, and proud to be your friend too!"

Mr. Hook. As he had thought it would be. A good name. Every bit as good as the one he had left in England. Indeed, for a gentleman of fortune, as he styled himself, it was a far better name than he had been born to. The sort of nom de guerre that would inspire fear whenever it was uttered, for it was certain that he was at war with the world.

Perhaps Hook would not be a respected name, but at least he could make certain that it was feared name. Respect might be denied him by the circumstances of his birth, but there was naught he could do about those events of the past. The future remained

for him to seize. If he could not command respect, he could enforce fear on the world at the mention of the name James Hook.

"Come along, Tuck," he said, pleased with what the boy had
related to him. "You have reminded me that I still need a proper
gentleman's weapon at my hip. Time that you learn a thing or two
about good steel as well, I should think. I have not seen you with
so much as a sailor's knife, which is strange even for a ship's boy,
considering the vessel on which you serve."

Tuck's eyes grew wide at the quartermaster's words.

"You mean, I might get to handle a knife, Mr. Hook?"

Respect from Tuck, for that name at least, and from the crew
of the *Jolly Roger*. It was a start.

"Handle one? Yes, my lad, at the least. You are a member of
the crew, same as everyone else. I have not seen you spend a single copper coin of your share on sugar cane or molasses candy or
aught else. You should have all you need to buy yourself as fine a
knife as you could ever want."

The boy looked confused.

"My share, sir? Cap'n says that not getting chucked back
into the sea and getting food and a place to lay my head is all I
deserves."

James stared at Tuck for a moment, so surprised that he forgot
himself and clapped a hand to the boy's shoulder in a concerned
manner.

"No share at all? That is very bad form indeed. I shall have
words with Red Michael about this, for you are a member of our
crew just as he is, and I have seen with my own eyes the amount
of work you do."

The quartermaster spoke to Tuck as he would have any other
lowly member of the crew who had confessed that they received
nothing from the recent prize. He forgot that Tuck was a boy and,
as such, unworthy of his trust, for he spoke openly to him like he
was just another man of the crew.

In so doing, he unknowingly gave Tuck a boost to his own

sense of worth that had long been denied him. Ever since the day he had awoken to find himself aboard the *Jolly Roger*, Tuck had just been the ship's boy, sent to fetch and carry, made to peel spuds and wash pots, set to mending shirts or sails, depending on which needed the most attention, and generally being used by most and abused by a few as if he had no value and needed to earn his bread every day.

Quartermaster James Hook saw the boy as a person, as a young man with untapped talent, as a young man already valuable for all that he already did aboard ship. To a degree, the unfairness James saw heaped on Tuck by Conner made the quartermaster think of him in the same terms that he used when thinking about his past self, a very young man constantly and unfairly punished for events beyond his control.

"I will see that you have your share, Tuck, even if it comes from my own pocket," the quartermaster vowed. "Until then, you have but to ask me for an advance on what is owed you from the common fund."

He looked at the wide, shy grin that spread across Tuck's face and felt uneasy, though he did not know why that would be. It was not as if he was treating him any differently than any other man aboard the *Jolly Roger*. What he did was no more than his duty as quartermaster. He would have done as much for Jukes or Mullins, or any other hand, had one been cheated out of his fair due by the captain.

That was what he argued to himself to silence the small youthful voice deep within him that squeaked some inane blather about friendship or kindness or some other such sentimental nonsense.

"Monsieur Favager, what have you for me?" James asked, entering a small shop located between a tavern and a warehouse.

"Ah? Ah ha! It is Monsieur Hook, of which we have 'eard so very much, eh?"

The proprietor of the establishment was a small man with thick wrists and strong hands. He was a man who not only knew blades of all types, but one who practiced often with them, a man who could recognize a boastful tyro or a quiet master of the blade at a glance. In the quartermaster from the *Jolly Roger*, he saw a man of experience who would need the best sword he could find. From the common gossip already rampant in Tortuga, he knew that this James Hook could pay well. He also knew that this man of the hook was no one to cheat. An honest deal would gain him an honest profit. Anything else would carry a price he would not wish to pay.

"I fancy a rapier, Monsieur, a blade of the old style rather than a light whip like so many carry these days."

"Of course, Monsieur Hook; this I can see already. A good blade with a diamond section, *oui*? Something with strength and flexibility, a good edge, and a keen point all together! For you, I have the thing—of good Toledo steel, if you have no objection."

While Tuck looked on wide-eyed, his hero and the sword seller dickered over blades, with James feeling the weight and balance of several rapiers, testing their flexibility and edge until he found the best Monsieur Favager had to offer. To that purchase, he added a long and slender dagger and then called Tuck to his side.

"You want me to run this back to the *Jolly Roger*, sir?" the boy asked eagerly.

The thought of carrying such blades, even if only to deliver them back to the ship for the quartermaster, seemed a great adventure to the ship's boy.

"In due time, Tuck. Firstly, though, young man, it is time you were properly armed, as I promised you. Choose, and I will see that it is paid for from your share."

It took a good hour for the boy to go through all the various knives that Favager had in his stock, and it was a very pleasant hour for all involved. The shopkeeper and James compared the virtues of each blade. The Frenchman made certain to explain the flaws in the flashy blades that caught the boy's eye. He knew that the quartermaster was aware of those defects. It would serve him better to treat Hook's young companion with respect and honesty.

In the end, the pair left Favager's establishment with all parties being pleased. Favager had gold coins stamped out at a Spanish mint in Mexico. James had a rapier at his hip again and a long blade slipped under his belt just forward of his right hip. Tuck had a workmanlike knife that could serve for shipboard duties or as a weapon, his first knife ever in that part of his life that he could remember.

The two made their way back to the brig as the day came to a close. For the rest of the crew, another raucous night was beginning, filled with drinking, carousing, fighting, and chasing wenches who did not run fast or far and who laughed late into the night. Thus it had been since they had dropped anchor in Tortuga, and thus it would be while the gold lasted. Having better sense and more refined tastes, the quartermaster was more temperate with his share of the booty, investing some in clothes and weapons and some in choice viands and fine wine rather than wasting gold on the companionship of women who could not even imitate refinement and breeding.

Tortuga by day was safe enough for the ship's boy. By night, James felt that Tuck would find himself better off aboard the *Jolly Roger*. Given his own more sober and melancholy mood, Hook decided a night under the stars in a hammock gently rocking to the rhythm of the waves held more appeal that yet another night spent at the Bent Cutlass or other such boisterous drinking establishment.

As could be expected, the port echoed with laughter, song, and the shriek of happily outraged wenches for more than two months. It took that long to spend all the gold they had taken from the galleon at Isla de Tres Palmas. The men of the *Jolly Roger* drank their gold, gambled their gold, and ate their gold until there was no gold left to them, as had always been the way of pirates.

During that time, ships came in, and their crews joined in on the revelry. The sloop *Margarette,* under Captain Sauvageot with his thirty buccaneers, arrived first, adding their paltry cargo to the festivities. After him was *The Raven,* a schooner commanded by dour, puritanical Solomon Stark. While Stark remained aloof from all merrymaking, his men were not averse to sharing the wealth of their fellow pirates from the *Jolly Roger.*

The day finally came when Starkey and Smee came back to the brig with aching heads and empty pockets; when Cecco and Dusk dragged the unconscious Mullins and Teyne back to their hammocks with the certain knowledge that there was not enough coin between the four of them for a single noggin of grog; when Bill Jukes, stripped naked of recently purchased finery by those he owed money to, returned to the ship clad in naught but the tattoos that covered him from head to toe; when Dieter Trommler had to bid a sad farewell to the pair of plump, rosy-cheeked, little blonde sisters who had acquired the majority of his wealth through their services to him; and when those men who chose to remain aboard the *Jolly Roger* returned to their only true home, ready to put to sea once again in search of another fortune to squander.

Not all hands returned to the ship. A few, a very few, had taken their gold and quietly departed from Tortuga, content that their share would see them set for life and vowing to never again sail under the black flag. More had fallen in tavern brawls and drunken duels or had become prey for the cutthroats and foot-pads that lurked in the shadows of the pirate haven to prey on drunken pirates as those pirates preyed on merchant vessels.

"Nolan, Jiggers, Sandhurst, Lacombe, and Kestrel ain't come back, Mr. Hook, and they ain't gonna," Tuck reported to the quartermaster.

"Dead, are they?" James asked indifferently.

"Aye, sir. Dead—all five."

"And we have Geoffrey, Klineholt, and Smitty sailed for Jamaica?"

"Aye, Mr. Hook," the boy responded happily.

His happiness was not because of the losses to the crew, but because he had been allowed to be of further service to the quartermaster that he adored. Tuck was glad that James had won a new surname through his own courage and skill, even if he did not understand how James had come to misplace his original family name. If he had a family name, he would never be so careless with it. Tuck was pleased with every chance to address the heroic quartermaster by that new name nonetheless.

Tuck himself had no family as far as he knew and so no family name. The *Jolly Roger* was all he knew as home and the men who were her crew—despicable pirates, thieves, and murderers though they might be—were as much family as he could remember.

It never entered into Tuck's head that James Hook might not like him. The very fact that the man who was second only to Captain Conner aboard the *Jolly Roger* never raised either his voice or his hand to him proved, so far as the boy was concerned, that the quartermaster felt affection for him.

Bill Jukes, Starkey, Cecco, and most of the rest of the common hands treated him well enough, as if he were a little brother. Mr. Smee acted kindly to Tuck, teaching him various useful skills like darning socks and such with an almost fatherly interest. It was only the quartermaster, of all those aboard the brigantine, who treated him like a man, even if a young and inexperienced man.

Tuck did not give thought to the captain's behavior toward him, for the treatment Red Michael afforded the ship's boy was worse than what he would show to a worthless dog. The captain demanded his rum at all times and saw fault in much of what the boy did. Captain Conner even found reasons to punish the boy for things that he had no hand in and no possible way to control.

It was better to not think of the worst he suffered and keep his mind on those who saw him as more than an annoying mongrel—Smee and Starkey and all the others, besides the captain, with James Hook being head and shoulders above all others in his kind treatment.

Of all the men aboard the *Jolly Roger*, only two were ignorant of Tuck's admiration for the quartermaster. Red Michael Conner was one of them. The ship's boy was someone he tolerated because of the one special use he had for the boy. If not for the one thing that set Tuck apart from all other boys, Captain Conner would have tossed the youngster off the ship at the first opportunity. And he would not have waited until the *Jolly Roger* was in port to do so, no matter how the dogs in his crew might growl and bark over his decision.

The other was James himself. He had begun to think of Tuck as a man. As a young man, of course, such as he thought of his own past self. He forgot that Tuck was just a boy since Tuck did not behave as most boys James had known. Thinking of him as a man, he saw Tuck as merely doing his duty with enthusiasm. The devotion Tuck gave to James seemed to him to merely be the respect that was due from a lesser man to one so obviously his superior in shipboard rank as well as breeding, experience in the world, and education.

The *Jolly Roger* was stocked with rum, viands, powder, and shot under the supervision of her quartermaster and the benign neglect of her captain. Mr. Smee found a dozen scarred, ugly, larcenous recruits to replace the men who had retired from the pirate life or otherwise been lost to the dangers of Tortuga. They joined with the nearly eighty bleary-eyed, penniless, satiated buccaneers who straggled aboard the brigantine to voyage once again in search of cargos to loot.

Refitted and resupplied with the best food, weapons, and equipment Tortuga had to offer, the brig sailed out in search of prey, passing a battered *Walrus* as that vessel limped in to port after a hard and dangerous three months at sea that had given them only a meager return. Captain Flint and his men would be sorely annoyed when they discovered the long celebration they had missed. The depleted supplies of rum and food on Tortuga would not please them either. Nor would they be happy to discover that the majority of wenches would be unavailable for a few weeks, needing to rest and recover from two months of merrymaking with the drunken crew of the *Jolly Roger*.

The captain set their course for the waters north of Jamaica. In a temper even surlier than was his usual, Red Michael spent most of his days and night drinking rum. Sometimes he was on deck, peering at the horizon through his spyglass; sometimes he remained in his cabin. The bottle was never far from his hand, on deck or below.

Young Tuck busied himself in pursuits that kept him out of Captain Conner's sight as much as possible. In that endeavor, Smee and the quartermaster assisted their young shipmate by assigning him duties that kept the boy far from the obese pirate captain. When Red Conner hollered for his rum, Smee would fetch it himself or Hook—how he relished his adopted surname— would have one of the more menacing of the crew deliver it to the ranting captain.

Dusk's scarred visage or that of sinister Cecco was sure to quiet Red Michael's angry bellows for a time. At his heart, the captain was a bully. As Hook well knew, all bullies were cowards who hid their failings behind bluster and brutality directed at those weaker than they were. The men that Hook sent with the captain's rum were not the sort to be bullied by someone like Red Michael Conner.

The lookout sighted a ship late on the fourth day, which brightened the captain's mood immensely. He had been expecting a fat merchantman on that course the day before. Seeing that it was only running late restored his meager faith in the sources he paid for information on likely prizes.

The man aloft slid down a line to report directly to the captain, whispering all that he observed rather than shouting it down from his post above. That would have given James cause to wonder, had he observed it. A moment later, the lookout was scrambling back to his post while Red Michael shouted for all hands to prepare for battle.

James Hook led the boarding party that day, leaving Smee aboard with Red Michael and the gun crew under Dietz. A few telling shots from the gunner convinced the captain of the merchantman to strike his sails. The boarding party led by Hook moved swiftly, ruthlessly cutting down any man who did not move back promptly enough. The vessel was stripped clean of valuables, and the booty was taken back to the *Jolly Roger.*

It was while the pirates were looting their prize that the distant thunder of a cannon shot was heard. Hook immediately sprang to the rail of the merchantman. There, far in the distance, were two vessels with all sails spread. The quartermaster could see the British colors at the masthead of each of the approaching vessels.

They were Royal Navy frigates, eager to come to grips with the small pirate vessel. The ships must have been seen by the lookout before Hook ever boarded the prize, yet no warning had been given. James looked across to where Red Michael stood on the deck of the brig, a broad, nasty smile on his coarse features as he peered at the frigates through his spyglass.

"Best you hurry along, Mr. Hook," Conner called over to him without concern. "There be company coming hard, and they ain't the sort we wants to entertain."

"He should have mentioned them ships earlier," a sailor named Magillicuddy opined sourly to the quartermaster. "Likes to taunt them, he does. One day that will cost us all dear."

Taunt them? A lone pirate vessel taunting warships of the crown? It sounded like insanity of the sort that was never repeated. Yet James had learned that Red Michael favored striking as he had done that afternoon, without concern about other ships that might give pursuit. The *Jolly Roger* was infamous for such brazen attacks, just as she was for disappearing into the night no matter how closely she was followed. Hook was curious to see what trick Red Michael used to baffle those on his trail.

James snarled to the men around him to finish and get aboard the brig, though they needed no encouragement to speed the transfer of cargo over to their ship. With Mullins and Jacob at his back, the quartermaster went below to search the captain's cabin himself, discovering a small quantity of gold and silver and a few bottles of an excellent vintage of French wine.

On the way topside, he smashed a couple of lanterns in the corridor leading to the hold. The spreading fire would give the crew of the ship something to occupy their time rather than joining in the chase after the pirates that had robbed them.

Just as James Hook crossed over to the *Jolly Roger*—the last member of the boarding party to return, just as he had been the first to cross over—the pirate brig heeled away from her prey and fled before the wind. The frigates were still beyond effective cannon range, though the closer of the pair did assay a shot now and again with her bow chasers to check the distance.

Red Michael shouted for the ship's boy to bring him rum, calling Tuck by name and demanding his presence. Knowing that he must appear when so summoned by the captain, Tuck popped up from belowdecks, a large, flat-bottomed green bottle in his hand.

The captain roughly snatched the bottle from the lad, drank deep, and slapped the boy with the back of his hand.

"Stand up, you little scut," Red Michael sneered.

When Tuck did as ordered, another slap from a flabby hand knocked him to the deck again. Mr. Smee and other members of the crew not actively engaged in trimming the sails and stowing the booty stood around, grimacing in disgust yet not voicing a protest as Red Michael slapped the boy down again and again, demanding he stand so that he could be slapped again.

When the quartermaster got over his surprise at those vile actions, and when he saw that not one of the crew was going to voice a protest, he stepped forward himself, only to be stretched out on the deck by a casual blow from the back of the captain's hand.

Tuck looked over at James. There was no disappointment on his face at the failure of his hero. Instead, Hook saw gratitude there, as well as resignation. No one else had ever stepped forward to protest the treatment he received from Captain Conner. He could not blame the quartermaster for failing against Red Michael.

Tuck might forgive James for his failure, but James did not forgive himself. He was unused to being struck in such a fashion, especially with such speed and force. That he had underestimated Red Michael betrayed a fault within himself that he seldom acknowledged. Too proud of his own abilities, he seldom thought that there might be unexpected qualities in those he held in contempt.

He returned the look Tuck gave him, attempting to reassure the youngster without saying anything to further incur the wrath of Captain Conner. Tuck's eyes seemed to shine with a sapphire light in the gloom of dusk, unshed tears making them seem larger and more liquid than usual. It must have been a trick of the last light of day, Hook thought to himself. There could be no other natural explanation for such an unusual glow.

"Now, Mr. Hook, you just step easy here," Smee whispered urgently in his ear as the quartermaster tried to get his feet under him to stand. "Captain, he's got a good reason for all this, cruel though it seems. I'll explain later."

Hook might have demanded an explanation at that moment if Red Michael had not commanded that Smee take Tuck below right at that moment and lock the boy in the tiny chamber that served as his room.

"Mr. *Hook*," Red Michael said derisively—if James found the name "Hook" pleasing, Captain Conner did not and made every effort to let his quartermaster know it—"Stand watch beside the helmsman this evening. There be much you yet need to learn aboard the *Jolly Roger*. Not the least being never question my orders or my action, as you value your life."

Chapter 7

The Mystery of Tuck

The squall seemed to come out of nowhere. Although his head was still muzzy from the slap Red Michael had given him, James was certain that the sky had been clear before the sun sank in the west. Nothing more than a few high, thin clouds, like scraps of blanket worn too thin to hold together any more. Nothing that would build into a storm.

Yet the wind had unquestionably increased, and the sea heaved beneath the hull. The *Jolly Roger* rocked violently. Lightning crawled across the sky, revealing thick, heavy clouds that should not have been there. The lightning showed that the pair of British frigates still followed after the brigantine.

Those Royal Navy captains were willing to risk their men aloft and had spread even more sail, dangerous with a storm coming on hard like that. The quartermaster was equally willing to risk some of the crew to spread out every bit of canvas the yards could carry, all with the view of keeping the gap between the *Jolly Roger* and those warships from closing any faster.

Captain Conner had gone below as if he did not have a care in the world. From his attitude, it might as well have been a pair of sailboats behind them rather than two ships that each carried a weight of iron enough to smash the *Jolly Roger* to pieces and enough marines to overwhelm any resistance the pirates might make against a boarding.

There must be something that the captain knew that he had not bothered to mention to his new quartermaster. Hook could see that the new hands on deck were nervous to the point of uselessness, while those who had been with the ship before he had come aboard were calm, if shamefaced.

The strange storm that had blown up so suddenly might work in their favor, if they could put some distance between themselves and the frigates so close behind. The quartermaster hung onto a line as the brig staggered through the waves, straining to see the vessels behind them. A sheet of lightning clearly revealed one British ship and gave hints of the second as a dark shadow almost lost in the swirl of cloud, spray, and rain.

The bosun stumbled aft, lurching from one safe hold to the next until he was able to anchor himself close beside the man he considered his close friend.

"I've seen storms like this," Smee said with a nervous imitation of joviality. "The *Jolly Roger* will weather this well enough; I can guarantee."

The quartermaster looked at the bosun with clear disdain.

"What is it you know, Mr. Smee?" he asked, cold anger thick in his voice.

The rotund Irishman looked around as if Red Michael might be hiding his immense bulk behind the mainmast.

"Later, Jas … er, that is, Mr. Hook," he said in a voice too low for the helmsman to overhear. "This storm will be gone soon enough, and then we can talk."

Aye, Smee knew more than he had told, that was certain. It was also a certainty that James should have been informed of those hidden facts long ago—if not by Smee, then by Captain Conner himself. There was more need for honesty and trust aboard a ship sailing in the sweet trade than on a merchantman or navy frigate, especially among those who held a crew of cutthroats, layabouts, and ne'er-do-wells together as an effective fighting force.

The quartermaster would have forced the issue then and there, but Smee did not wait, instead hurrying forward to call orders to the men aloft.

"You all know what to do," Smee shouted. "Be ready on my command and lively. You all know what might happen if you are too slow."

Hook realized that every one of the men in the rigging that night was one of the old hands aboard. None of the new men had been sent up there to tend the sails in the storm. Like the quartermaster, those new men had no idea what was coming.

Lightning forked and flared a brilliant white and purple over the brig. Watching astern, James saw the closest frigate lit as if in daylight for an instant, and then she was gone in a purple-tinged darkness. Half-blinded by the stroke of lightning, he felt the brig lurch and twist under his shoes. The wind seemed to pause, like a giant between breaths.

"Strike all sail!" Smee bellowed. "Get that canvas down, and watch your grip!"

Strike the sails? With those navy lads panting so eagerly at their heels?

Hook opened his mouth to shout a counter-order when the brig heeled suddenly underfoot. The rocking of the deck changed rhythm abruptly, and the quartermaster stumbled, as did half the men on deck, including the helmsman.

Hook staggered to the wheel and laid hold as Murphy, the helmsman, found his footing. As the man took his place again, the quartermaster looked at the binnacle and berated the man for being so far off the course that had been set for him.

"Never you mind the quartermaster, Murphy," Smee said with a wink and a strained grin. "He don't know what's what yet. You just bring us back to the course the captain set as the wind allows."

The bosun hollered to the men aloft to get the sails furled neat and proper, with just the jib set to catch the wind.

That was the first time Hook had seen Smee take charge with a firm hand, the first time the bosun had brushed aside the words of James Hook with commands of his own. Of all the unlikely events of that evening, Smee dismissing the quartermaster in that fashion was the most surprising of all.

"Come below, Mr. Hook. Time you were told about young Tuck and why he is so special to Red Michael," Smee said. "A bottle of rum will be needed for this task. Thirsty work it will be and uncanny as well. Rum solves both thirst and disbelief, I've found."

Hook started to protest about the frigates behind them and the storm swirling overhead. Either would be enough to have one of them on deck. Both together demanded such attention. Automatically, he looked astern to see how close the nearest of the British ships were and was amazed to see empty ocean.

He was amazed because there was no sign of either pursuing vessel on the dark sparkling waves. He was also amazed because he could see far out across the water in bright moonlight. Looking up at the low, threatening clouds, James found them to be gone. Not merely breaking up unexpectedly but gone entirely.

The bright moon was nearly three-quarters full and beamed down whitely through a sky that displayed only a few glowing wisps of clouds that moved leisurely toward the black horizon. The stars gleamed like diamond clips against the velvet black of the sky. Nowhere did he see the slightest sign of the storm that had sent lightning forking down around the yards and had blown foam from the waves across the deck.

Come to that, the waves themselves showed no sign that there had been a squall blowing up just a few moments before. They rolled, calm and serene, in endless smooth billows under the moonlight, as restful an ocean view as any seaman could ever wish for.

"Odds bobs, hammer and tongs. It's not possible," James muttered to himself.

The storm had come up with unbelievable speed, and it had vanished even quicker. And with the storm had gone two of His Majesty's finest warships, vanished without a trace. Smee said that he would explain, though James could think of no account that the Irish bosun could make to explain what he had witnessed.

The bosun was waiting in Hook's tiny cabin. The rum was already open, and a tankard sat on the tiny table, half full of the dark liquor. Smee held a similar mug with an equal amount of rum in it. James had the thought that Smee had already downed his first ration of rum and refilled his cup—all the better to relate the story Hook needed to hear.

Feeling that he needed to be equally lubricated to hear the tale, James took up his tankard and drained the rum in one long swallow. Molasses mixed with fire slid down his gullet and exploded in a ball of heat in his belly. It was a jolt harsh enough to make him gasp and cough a moment while Smee looked on smiling.

"It *is* a fine, smooth rum, isn't it, Jas?"

The scowl Hook gave the bosun made Smee rethink his familiar attitude toward the quartermaster.

"I guess it all started when our lookout spotted some wreckage in the open ocean. That was while Captain Kendrick commanded the *Jolly Roger*, not long before Red Michael marooned Kendrick and took the captain's cabin for himself."

Smee absently raised his mug to his lips and drank like a thirsty laborer on a hot day. From the sweat on his brow and the uncomfortable way he squirmed as he started his tale, perhaps it was hot work at that. The rum had no more apparent effect on him than water would have—it wet his whistle and soothed his thirst and no more than that.

"It was a strangle collection of ornate railing, barrels, gratings, and other such loose items, all lashed together with odd lengths of rope and swaddled in canvas. Sprawled atop that raft was a lone figure, the same lad who you know as Tuck."

Hook took a swallow of rum in a more restrained fashion than he had displayed before, a thoughtful look in his eyes.

"You say that as if Tuck is not the proper given name for that young man."

Smee pushed his spectacles up with a finger and then shook his head to settle them comfortably, with the result that the glass disks slid down to the end of his bulbous nose once again.

"Well, ah, Mr. Hook, I can't rightly say as to that. You see, after we brought the boy aboard and gave him water, when he came to his senses, he didn't know a thing about who he was or how he got on that pile of timbers and barrels—not a single blessed thing about his past. This name, Tuck, is what Cap'n Kendrick gave him, on account of the boy reminding poor Kendrick of a lad he had known when he was growing up."

James tugged at the thin black mustache he had allowed to grow while in Tortuga. While he still preferred to keep his chin well shaven, the thought of a carefully groomed mustache appealed to him. It would give him a dashingly sinister air. He found that the mustache also gave his fingers something to do while he was mulling over weighty thoughts, as on that night.

"Tuck has no memory of his past at all?"

"Well," Smee temporized, "that might be stating things too harshly. I've sat with the lad many a night after Red Michael beat the poor boy. What he says in his nightmares makes me think that maybe he does remember things but only in his darkest dreams."

The bosun poured more rum into his mug, noted that the bottle was nearly empty, and swallowed down the last few swigs that would have overflowed the rim of the mug.

"I think," he advised his companion, "you might find sitting by young Tuck's bedside the next time Cap'n Conner raises his hand to the boy an educating experience, Jas. It might be that a man of your keen insight and education may make something of the ramblings he mutters while tormented by nightmares."

"That still does not explain the way Red Michael treats Tuck, most especially the way he was punishing the young man this night, all for no reason. It does not explain that squall, either, or what happened to those two frigates pursuing us."

Smee looked into his mug of rum as if it held the words he needed. James thought that the bosun was going to swallow the entire dose down again to gain courage to speak. Instead, the Irishman shook his head resolutely and set the brimming mug back on the tiny table.

"There is an explanation, Jas, hard though it may be for an educated man like yourself to believe it. It might sound like sorcery to you," Smee said, choosing to ignore the hard look that Hook gave him. "Black magic, witchcraft, or whatever name you want to put to it. And young Tuck is at the center of it, though I swear, to my belief, that he is just the focus, and not the cause, that he knows naught of it at all."

"What is it?" James asked, trying without success to hide his exasperation at the way the bosun refused to come out and state bald facts.

"You fix our position tomorrow, Jas. Shoot the sun at noon and see where our *Jolly Roger* is. We'll be a hundred leagues off from where we should be, or I'll kiss Bill Jukes full on the lips!"

It seemed an impossibility. The ship shifted a hundred leagues in the blink of an eye and in some fashion done by Tuck or because of him. Yet there were facts that he himself had observed that seemed to agree with what Smee told him: the sudden change in the way the waves struck the *Jolly Roger*, how the storm had dissipated instantly without a trace left behind, and, most of all, the disappearance of two warships that had nearly been within cannon shot a mere moment before.

The sea and sky around them had changed from one moment to the next. Some unknown event had occurred. What Smee suggested seemed as logical an explanation as anything James could conjure up, impossible though it appeared to a logical, educated mind.

The quartermaster would be very interested to see in what position the noon sighting would place them. Hook allowed his lip to curl in a nasty smile as a thought cross his mind. If Smee was wrong in his estimate by so much as a single mile, the quartermaster would see to it that Smee kept the promise he had so rashly made, though what Bill Jukes would think of it was anyone's guess.

"Brimstone and bile, how could any man—" James started to ask.

"Tuck isn't a man; he's only a boy, and I told you, he does not cause this to happen. He is just the focal point when he has bad dreams. Leastways, that's what I think. Cap'n Conner knows what happens even if he doesn't understand it any better than I do. Brute that he is, he's not the one to scruple at terrorizing the boy to give him those nightmares when he wants our *Jolly Roger* to appear in different waters to escape pursuit."

Smee took up his cup and gulped more rum.

"In all truth, my friend, I think it's enjoying such brutality he is."

James Hook absently took up his own tankard and drank, unmindful of the burn the raw rum brought to his throat. Here was a mystery indeed and one worthy of his intellect. Smee spoke of magic and sorcery, and what Hook had witnessed smacked of magic, if not something even stranger.

The first thing to do was keep a close eye on Tuck. He did not think that Smee had misread the young man, for he held the same opinion—that Tuck was an innocent in more than one way and only a victim because of those strange events. Still, there might be some clue to be found in Tuck's actions and mannerisms.

The next angle to attack the mystery was a less pleasant one, for it would require Red Michael to have need to terrorize Tuck once again. Though his instinct for good form revolted at the thought, Hook would have to stand by without remonstration while Tuck was reduced to a sobbing heap once again. Only then could he do what Smee suggested: stay by his side while he slept and listen to what words came from the troubled dreams that presaged the brigantine being whisked hundreds of miles off course.

"Another question or two, Smee," James requested, even though his head was in a jumble already. "What direction will we have gone during this … this … event?"

"Why, Jas, there is no way of telling. No rhyme nor reason to it at all, so far as I have been able to see. No more than there is to the distance we'll be off course by, saving that it has always been well over a hundred leagues."

"Well then, if we have no idea at all where the *Jolly Roger* will end up, would it not be the wiser course to strike all sails until we can at least see the waters around us rather than risk running aground on a reef we might find unexpectedly close to us?"

Smee had been draining the last of his rum when Hook asked that of him. As the impact of what the quartermaster had said worked through the pleasant haze that the rum had formed within his brain, Smee exhaled explosively, spraying rum over the wall and Hook's bunk. The quartermaster himself had thoughtfully moved aside, suspecting just such a reaction would be coming from the Irish bosun.

It showed the difference in the qualities of their minds that James had thought of possible danger the very first time he had an inkling of what had occurred while the bosun had never given a thought to such a menace to the ship at all. It spoke even more about the quality of their captain, who had not even been concerned enough to stay sober or on deck during such an uncanny affair.

Without so much as a by-your-leave, Smee dashed from the cabin, shouting for the jib to be struck and a sea anchor to be heaved over the side. James Hook looked after the bosun, something akin to a satisfied smile quirking the corner of his mouth. The quartermaster gave in to his sense of the dramatic, even though he was the only audience to observe his actions. As it happened, James had long thought that he was the best audience for his performances, so the absence of a larger group to marvel at his style troubled him in no way whatsoever.

Hands raised as claws imploring the heavens dropped to rake through the thick black curls of his hair, tugging at those long locks as if in despair at the sort of men he was forced by unkind fate to live among while he made his evil name and fortune in the world. An artful silent struggle ensued to compose himself in the face of abject idiocy and to remain, as always, the man of calm and reason. He made a final rueful examination of the rivulets of rum that Smee had spewed onto the wall as the implacable logic of his words had moved the bosun to action long overdue. No scene could have been played half so well, by even the most experienced actor on the London stage, if James was any judge.

In truth, he had reason for his inordinate pride in his ability in that regard, as he had reason for all his pride. In the years he spent at that prestigious public school before disaster had forced him to strike out into the world with only his sword, his keen wits, and the name his mother had bequeathed him, James had been the marvel of all students, as well as an object of suspicion and distrust.

When word got around that young James was slated to discourse on a subject before his classmates, the gallery was always full of students from the other houses. Even the professors crowded in to hear him speak on such occasions. It was not just his masterful grasp of the subject—whatever the subject might be—but also the incomparable style with which he presented his dissertation that drew so many to listen to the young man who was otherwise shunned.

When the blow had fallen that ultimately drove him from England, James had toyed with the idea of becoming an actor.

Never one to embrace false modesty, James knew how great his talent was. Had he set out on that career, he could have been the most famous thespian ever to grace the stage in England or the Continent.

If he had felt less justifiable contempt for his peers, he might well have chosen the life of greasepaint and soliloquies, grandiose gestures and improbable plots, as his path to fame and notoriety. It was the venal nature of those he had been born among, those he had been rejected by, that led him to a higher calling on the open seas. It would be on the great stage of the ocean where James Hook would rise to the heights of his craft, with sword in hand, the deck of a swift ship under his feet, and cannons to announce his presence to the world. Instead of having the chance to marvel at his breadth of theatrical ability, the world would learn to tremble at the depth of his rage.

With such a happy thought in mind, James gave a final dramatic expression of suffering through the actions of others before leaving his cabin. The fumes of rum would dissipate by dawn. On his way out, Hook picked up several thin brown cylinders, a new vice he had embraced while in Tortuga with more gold than any man could need.

In his youth, James had disdained the use of snuff as an effete habit among those who did not recognize him as their equal, just as he thought of a pipe as the weakness of lesser men. When he finally condescended to sample tobacco, it was in the form that the Spaniards called *cigarros*. He found the thick, pungent smoke soothing to a troubled mind if not to his throat. It was not long before he found that the ending of any day was improved by indulging in one of the hand-rolled cigarros before he sought repose.

He knew that the men on deck would have their pipes, and he felt that his form of tobacco use would both make him seem companionable to his shipmates and yet mark him as a man of more refined tastes and exotic habits. The spares he took along were for show only, a display of his generosity when offered to sailors who he knew would prefer their pipes to that strange Spanish habit.

Swinging gently in a hammock strung on deck while the *Jolly Roger* rolled on the waves, Hook smoked his cigarro and allowed the soothing quality of the smoke to lull him. Barely able to keep his eyes open, despite the turmoil of that evening, he finally took the smoldering stub from his thin lips and carefully flung the ember of tobacco over the rail to expire in the sea while he surrendered himself to sleep and the old reoccurring dream of a glittering, multicolored star that filled him with longing.

Hook felt some disappointment the next day at noon when his arithmetic showed that Smee had been absolutely correct. The *Jolly Roger* was well over three hundred miles from any point she could have logically reached since yesterday's sighting. Hook checked his figures three times and found that they were far south of Jamaica, where wind and current could not possibly have placed them. The disappointment came from being deprived of the pleasure of reminding the bosun of his promise, not from discovering that the mystery was as deep as Smee had claimed.

The ship's boy had been up early, displaying no ill effects from the beating he had taken the night before or from the nightmares that had followed. From his bright chatter and eagerness to be about his chores, no one would have guessed that he had been unjustly punished by his captain that past evening. It was only the physical marks that reminded Hook of what Red Michael had done.

Tuck's face was bruised where Red Michael had slapped him, and there were several small scabs where the captain's rings had cut the young man's face. James felt an echo of dread in his heart as he remembered his own thick, dark blood smeared across the golden skulls and roses of one of Red Michael's heavy rings.

With the resilience of the very young, Tuck seemed to have completely forgotten his mistreatment. If there was any sign of it at all in his manner, it was shown by his desire to remain close to

Mr. Smee or Hook. When Captain Conner lumbered up on deck, the ship's boy found tasks that required his attention as far from the pirate captain as he could get.

Red Michael was content to leave the fixing of their position to his quartermaster and showed only scanty interest when he was told that the *Jolly Roger* was well south of Jamaica. From his bloodshot eyes and unsteady gait, James deduced that the captain was still suffering the aftereffects of too much rum the night before. It pleased the quartermaster to see Red Michael's misery had far outlasted that of young Tuck.

If there could any downside to what had occurred, it was that Tuck held an even stronger affection for James Hook, who cared nothing for boys and very little for men that he considered lesser than his own self. But the quartermaster had spoken up for Tuck when no one else ever had, and the ship's boy was not about to forget that kindness.

The next three weeks passed with the normal boredom that sailors experienced on their voyages. Having no particular destination in mind, it was in some ways worse aboard the *Jolly Roger*, for there was no definite end to their journey. The crewmen drank and talked, gambled at cards and dice, sang in the cool of the evening, and slept during the heat of the day.

Red Michael came up on deck infrequently and gave no commands at all. It fell to the quartermaster to enforce the daily routine aboard ship, which never amounted to much on a vessel in the sweet trade. With James Hook in charge, there was somewhat less sloth than otherwise would have been found on a ship full of pirates, though that was only a matter of degree.

The watches were kept, the decks scrubbed, and what Hook could find to paint was scraped and painted. With no goal, the only duty that was truly important was that of lookout, and that was one task that Hook oversaw religiously. The primary rule of their trade was simple: no prey, no pay. Considering the paltry return for their efforts thus far on that voyage, all hands were eager for the sight of sails that might signal a fat prize.

Hook had another reason to seek prey besides the wealth it would bring. The mystery that Tuck represented needed to be explored fully. Thus far, the quartermaster had learned all he could from asking artful questions of Smee and the rest of the old hands. What he would need to continue in his endeavor to unravel the mystery was a chance to do as Smee had suggested.

He would need to sit by Tuck's bedside while the youngster suffered through his nightmares. That would require—as unpleasant as it was—that Tuck once again endure unjust punishment at the hands of Red Michael. And for that to occur, they needed to find a ship to loot, preferably one that they could strike at near dusk, as Red Michael preferred.

It did not matter whether Hook looked forward to the lookout's cry or dreaded it for what it would mean. That cry did come, as it had to come.

The Caribbean was always busy with commerce. Ships of many nations sailed its waters, for the nations of Europe were eager markets for what could be harvested from their colonies, be it rum, tobacco, molasses, or gold.

"Looks like we have a fat French hen to pluck," Red Michael said with relish, coming up on deck at last to peer at the distant vessel through his spyglass.

"We are close to Martinique," the quartermaster noted. "It would seem a likely destination for a French merchantman."

"Aye, Mr. Hook," said Conner, sneering the name. "A weary crew and a hold full of goods from Europe. What better prize could we ask for, saving a plump Spaniard heavy with gold? No fight in these Frenchies—we can count on that."

"Perhaps not from that crew, but there might well be ships of the French navy in these waters. Come to that, we are not far from Barbados, and the Royal Navy squadron there would be eager to catch us plucking yon French hen."

Captain Conner took a calculating look at the sinking sun and another long look at the merchantman. Hook knew what he was thinking and had to agree with the captain even before the man spoke what was on his mind.

"We keep the lookout sharp and take this prize fast and neat. Strip her to the bone and be gone. Even if the entire French navy sailed out to greet us, we could lead them on a merry chase into the night. Remember that there be no ship what can catch the *Jolly Roger* once darkness falls."

Red Michael had a wicked grin on his fat face, daring his quartermaster to make a comment about how they would lose any pursuit. James knew better than to give his captain that pleasure. It was bad enough that he would have to stand by and watch. He certainly was not going to say a word in praise or protest.

The Frenchmen took flight as soon as Red Michael ordered the black flag run up. A single glance at the skull and bones was enough for that crew, weary though they might have been, to leap to their duty with an alacrity that would have pleased their captain if he had not just been as terrified as the men under his command.

The pursuit was nowhere near as swift as it should have been. James thought that it had been too long since the brig had been careened and her hull properly scraped. The drag of a foul hull could cost them a prize or worse. On the morrow, he would press Captain Conner to find an isolated island where the crew could clean the hull and take care of other tasks that had been neglected for far too long.

Owing to their slowness in overtaking their prey, the dim, distant shape of Martinique was visible on the horizon when Dietz fired off his first warning shot at the merchantman. The squat master gunner managed an impossible shot, shattering the Frenchman's bowsprit squarely on the first shot. As if to prove that it was no fluke, Dieter decapitated the figurehead with his second shot.

With that demonstration made so starkly, the captain of their prey struck his sails immediately. His crew showed the same haste in bringing down the canvas as they had earlier displayed in hoisting the canvas in their attempt to outrun the *Jolly Roger*. The cheers and jeers from the cutlass-waving crew of the brig encouraged the French seamen to divest themselves of every utensil that might be even considered to be a weapon in the hope of saving themselves from grief at the hands of the brigands who were about to board their vessel.

Hook was surprised to see Red Michael appear on deck, laden with pistols and dirks, with a broad cutlass in one fat, beringed fist. The pirate captain was usually too drunk by that time in a chase to do more than offer inarticulate oaths and profanities.

"What, Mr. Hook, you thinks I be unable to board with the rest of these scurvy dogs?" the captain asked gruffly.

The smell of his breath was like that of a distillery that had suffered a broadside: rum and gunpowder, among other things that did not bear thinking about.

"No, Captain. I merely thought you would still be suffering from the sort of stomach ailment that has afflicted you in the past," the quartermaster replied smoothly.

Though he kept his voice bland, James wondered how long it would be before Red Michael suspected that his quartermaster had accused him of not having the guts to board a prize at the head of his men. Or perhaps, Hook allowed to himself, that should be *if* rather than *when*, given the intellect Red Michael had thus far displayed.

Grappling irons were flung, and the lines tied off. Ropes from the brig's yardarms were dropped down, and Hook led the first wave of boarders across to their prize. Behind them, another score of pirates swung across, including Conner himself.

When James saw his obese captain swing across the stretch of open water on that groaning rope, he offered up a prayer for the first time in many years. If God heard him, the prayer was ignored, for Captain Red Michael Conner arrived on the deck of the French ship safe and sound.

Red Michael, a pistol in each hand, glared around, clearly annoyed that there was no resistance from the crew of the merchant ship. He was, for once, ready for a fight, and there was no one to oblige him. He found it most vexing, though used terms a bit more profane to express himself.

The French crew had already cowered before the swarm of pirates as if confronted by so many rabid wolves. Their captain alone stood apart, and that might have been only because of malodorous nature of his craven crew.

The captain was something of a dandy, garbed in a red coat and matching hat with a long white plume. A lanky fellow, who rivaled James in height, the French captain's morose features held none of the tragic nobility that James Hook believed his own face to display. Still, the man had a sense of style, as his garments so ably attested.

"Un très beau manteau, Capitaine," Hook remarked with sinister pleasantness, displaying his mastery of the French language.

The quartermaster next gestured with the hook in his left hand toward the captain's broad-brimmed hat, a menacing smile spread across his face. That terrible weapon, in the hands of a darkly handsome man with such a smirk on his lips, was doubly unsettling. The French captain reached up with trembling hands, understanding what that gesture meant and eager to comply.

"Bah," snarled Red Michael. "We've no time for such things!"

He fired his left-hand pistol into the captain's stomach and belched a laugh at the man's pained expression.

The French captain cast his eyes at Hook, both of his hands now against his wound, his hat falling to the deck. There was a look of pleading on his face. James could only put on a sad expression and spread his hands in a passable imitation of the Gallic gesture to indicate that things were beyond his control.

The mortally wounded man nodded in glum acceptance. He

stumbled back a few steps until his hip bumped against the star-board rail. Casting his eyes upward to the French flag, or perhaps to the darkening heavens above, the French captain tilted back-ward until he overbalanced and plunged into the sea, wearing the sort of expression of forlorn contempt that only a Frenchman could master.

"Do you feel better for that, Captain?" Hook asked sweetly.

"No, no, I do not," grumbled Red Michael, shoving the spent pistol into his belt.

He let his fingers play across the butts of the other pistols tucked under that wide, straining expanse of leather thoughtfully.

"Well, perhaps a touch better at that."

His eyes roved over the trembling sailors surrounded by the crew of the *Jolly Roger*. There was no fight in that lot, but there might be some entertainment to be had from them. It had been a long time since his crew had sweated anyone. And there was keelhauling to consider, as well as a host of other amusements, including his personal favorite. Perhaps they could spare a few hours.

"Sail ho!" the voice of the lookout echoed from atop the mast of the brig, interrupting the captain's musings. "Two ships, no, three, coming fast from the island!"

"Blown and blasted!" Captain Conner stormed, the pleasant vision of torture ripped apart by the warning cry.

"Strip 'er bare, and make sail!" Smee called from the deck of the *Jolly Roger*. "We must be gone afore those French warships get our range!"

There followed a mad rush to gather up all that could be con-sidered as valuable and get it back to their ship. Hook regretted that the French captain's hat, left behind on the deck, was a size too small and crawling with lice as well. Perhaps he could find something with the same style when they returned to Tortuga.

The mixed cargo was shifted rapidly and with an eye toward value and utility. Fine French pistols, lead ingots, and casks of gunpowder were set aside for the use of the crew, as were several crates filled with carefully padded bottles of fine wine. Kegs of nails, rolls of printed fabric, and other sundries were added to the cargo they had already stolen. The ransacking of the officers' cabins was conducted under the watchful eye of Red Michael himself, with a careful accounting of every coin down to the last silver *écu*. Clothing and other personal items were also included in the booty, haphazard bundles rushed across to the *Jolly Roger*.

Red Michael was not the last man back to his ship. He crossed over while the cargo was still being shifted, unsatisfied by the lone murder he had committed. The next time, aye, the next time, there would be some fun to be had as well as booty. Next time, they would strike when they would have time to entertain themselves for a bit, not merely snatch at wealth and show their heels to those who might pursue.

The vessels that put out from Saint Pierre flew the flag of the king of France, but they were small and lightly armed. Had he wanted to, Red Michael could have fought them and perhaps even sunk all three. It was certain that the *Jolly Roger* had men and guns enough to force the French ships to retreat. What troubled Conner's cautious nature was the possibility of a larger warship that might be making ready to join the pursuit behind those lesser vessels.

Rather than make a fight of it, the pirate captain chose the wiser—which is to say, safer—course, as pirates usually will. There was no profit in a stand-up fight against any navy, even when the odds were in their favor. Gentlemen of fortune, even such disreputable examples as Captain Conner, sought wealth, not conflict.

Red Michael ordered out all sails and a course that took best advantage of the wind. The French, thinking that their puny show of force had frightened the buccaneers, sailed in pursuit, as Captain Conner had expected.

As the gloom of dusk thickened into full night, the brutal

spectacle that James had witnessed once before was repeated. Red Michael demanded Tuck stand before him, and then the pirate struck the boy to the deck while berating him for imagined flaws. The captain roared out a list of nonsensical misdeeds. The brute used the same open-hand slaps as he had on the previous occasion. While he displayed no feelings for Tuck save disdain, Red Michael did not want to risk damaging so valuable a tool as the ship's boy had proven to be.

The quartermaster was certain that only such a consideration kept the captain from using a closed fist to club the lad down in a broken heap. Hook had to keep repeating that thought to himself to prevent acting on his natural impulse to challenge Red Michael then and there. The sheer unfairness of the captain's treatment of Tuck made the thick, purple blood boil in Hook's veins.

When Red Michael ordered the sobbing Tuck taken below and locked in his cabin, it was James who stepped forward and took charge of him. The pirate captain grinned as if in triumph. After what had happened the last time, he was thinking that his quartermaster finally understood without any doubt who commanded the *Jolly Roger.*

If Michael Conner could have known what was passing through the mind of James Hook at that moment, he would have fired a brace of pistols into the man's head in an instant. The fate of many men would have been changed had Red Michael had access to Hook's thoughts that night. It was to his own misfortune that such information was beyond the grasp of the pirate captain.

James took Tuck below as ordered and then disobeyed the order by passing the airless little cubby that was Tuck's berth. That night, Tuck had his nightmares in Hook's small cabin, with the quartermaster looking over him and taking note of both what Tuck said and the varied expressions that passed over his face in his sleep.

James ignored the rising howl of the wind and the tossing of the brigantine as another storm blew up out of a clear night sky.

When the ship suddenly ceased to rock, he ignored that too. On deck, Smee called for all sails to be furled and the anchor to be dropped, finally cautious of the dangers that might await them in unknown waters. The quartermaster paid no attention to any of it, seeking to miss no murmur or twist of Tuck's nightmare-ridden features.

What he saw and what he heard troubled James deeply. The words that Tuck uttered were mysterious and heavy with menace but even more so were the expressions that passed over his face: mocking boyish innocence—such as his own devilish brothers had so often displayed—boyish courage, boyish curiosity, and, most of all, boyish arrogance.

It was not the courage, the feigned innocence, or even the arrogance that disturbed Hook. Rather, it was the entirely *boyish* nature of those expressions that gave James a deep feeling of unease. Tuck had comported himself in such a proper fashion that the quartermaster had nearly forgotten the tender years of the ship's boy. That night, he recalled again that Tuck was as much a *boy* as he was a member of the crew, perhaps even more so.

The words were concerning more from the snatches that they revealed than from any true menace.

"Those marauding Indians," Tuck muttered as he tossed, an odd expression of delight on his sleeping face.

"The hungry bears and the wolves," he said later, as delighted as if discussing a basketful of puppies.

"Ugh, starched collars and waistcoats," the boy moaned in the voice of one undergoing torture of the most dreadful sort.

"Mermaids, fairies, little better than girls," with the air of one who has had far too much experience with such creatures of myth.

"Oh, you vicious cannibals, you *fell* for that false trail once too often," he chortled demonically in his sleep, and Hook felt a tingle of dread as his luxurious black hair attempted to stand upright.

There was a cargo of meaning in the stressed word "fell" that

James knew held a terrible joke hidden away where even Tuck with his waking mind could not find it.

Who was this young man who hid a wild, arrogant *boy* within him? Which adventures were fact and which were mere fantasies? Pixies and mermaids were foolishness, though Indians, cannibals, and wild beasts might hold some truth.

And what of the island he spoke of in brief snatches? Mountains and jungles, deserts and waterfalls, crystal lagoons and noxious swamps. Was there such a place of stark contradictions anywhere in all the wide world?

Tuck stopped tossing and turning, nestling down as the last of the nightmares left him, and he sank into dreamless sleep. One last word passed his lips to puzzle Hook for the rest of the night.

"Neverland."

Chapter 8

Innocent Diversions

Hook felt the sweat dripping down his face as he prepared to meet the next attack. His rapier in his left hand, his rough iron hook in his right, he breathed deeply and evenly despite his exertions. His weight on the balls of his feet, ready to lunge, retreat, or whirl to either side, James was a spring under tension, ready to be released.

Reversing his weapons had proven to be surprisingly easy. The need, at first, had been to give his opponent a sporting chance. It soon proved unnecessary, for he fought against a foe with skill far greater than he had expected. As the combat continued, Hook found that he was at no disadvantage, and thus he had no reason to risk switching hands while the battle went on.

From the corner of his eye, the bulk of the *Jolly Roger* cast her long shadow across the rocky beach as she floated serenely in the lagoon of the nameless islet. Three weeks had passed since they dropped the anchor in that remote place. The brig had been stripped of her cargo and guns. Even the slimy ballast stones had been unloaded to lighten her as much as possible. With much labor, she had been dragged up onto a sandy stretch of the beach so that her hull could be cleaned right down to the keel—scrapped, painted, and caulked with oakum and pitch.

It had been hard work, lubricated with French wine and

Jamaican rum. The port side was scraped and painted properly, like a ship of the line. Then the ship had been shifted so that the starboard side of the hull could receive the same treatment. After that, the *Jolly Roger* was refloated, dragged off the sand with the aid of ropes run across the lagoon to stout palms and brought back to the capstan, where men struggled on the slanted deck to haul their home back to her native element. Their shipmates put their shoulders to the hull itself or threw their weight against other ropes as they waded up to their waists in the warm, clear water of the lagoon.

Each day ashore was a hard day of work, and the reward each night was rum and merriment, music and jigs until exhausted and nature forced the crew to their beds of soft, warm sand. Quartermaster James Hook worked as hard as any man, so he took his reward as they did, adding one of his precious cigarros to the nightly routine before repose. Mr. Smee and young Tuck also did their part to see that the *Jolly Roger* was as fit and as fast as she ever had been, so Smee often fell asleep before finishing his tankard of grog, and Tuck collapsed on the sand still sticky with pitch, close beside the Irishman.

Of all hands aboard, only Red Michael held himself aloof from the hard work involved. It was his thought that, as captain, he should be above such petty labors. The attitude of their captain did not endear him to many of his men, as might be expected. Hook took the opportunity provided to further sow seeds of discontent among the men, which would bear bitter fruit for Red Michael in the weeks to come.

In the meantime, the quartermaster worked the men hard and showed them that he was willing and able to work twice as hard as any of them. Just as he exhibited in his habits of leisure that he was a man apart from the normal run of buccaneers, so too did Hook demonstrate that he was a man to be respected when difficult labor was required. Cecco and Jukes took pride in having their quartermaster show greater stamina than they could muster. Dusk was impressed by the feats of strength that James displayed from time to time, never guessing how close to his limit the cadaverous quartermaster had pushed himself. Even Mr. Smee found further reason to be in awe of James Hook with the quartermaster's demonstration of his abilities and his knowledge of every facet of the chores involved in making their *Jolly Roger* into the same swift vessel she once had been before so many routine tasks had been neglected by their captain and the previous quartermaster.

On the morrow, the ballast stones would be returned to their place, scrubbed clean with fistfuls of sand. Then the guns would be loaded aboard and, lastly, the cargo.

That late afternoon, Hook was reaping the harvest from another project he had been engaged in. The return on his labor was far more than he had expected. For all his expertise with his blade, he found himself matched by an opponent that none would have expected. At least he could be assured that none watching that strenuous bout would think to make unwise comments regarding the foe James faced or the quartermaster's inability to best that foe.

It had been his thought that the youngest among them had never had a chance to learn some of the finer points of the trade practiced aboard the *Jolly Roger*. Red Michael might view Tuck as merely a useful instrument to be protected and an annoyance to be carefully abused, but James Hook saw far more in the young man. While the captain might not want Tuck risking his hide in battle for purely selfish reasons, it seemed to Hook that the ship's boy had the same need to know how to use weapons as the rest of the crew, seeing as they were all pirates together.

To that end, Hook had been instructing Tuck in the finer points of using his knife for defense and offense whenever there was a break in the work. He offered basic techniques at first, though Tuck progressed so rapidly that James suspected the young man had experience from a past that he could not consciously recall. It was as if his body knew what to do, and it only required a reminder for his conscious brain to join in properly.

The mock combat the pair was engaged in that afternoon showed that Tuck had quickly learned all that Hook could teach him. With rapier and hook, the quartermaster could hold his own against Tuck. For all his greater reach, strength, and experience, he could do no more than that.

In part, James felt pride in his pupil for having advanced so quickly. In greater part, he was concerned by the way Tuck skipped from rock to rock in great leaps that brought to mind the muttered snippets about flying Hook had overheard when Tuck was in the throes of his nightmare. As Tuck raced across the sand, he feet so spurned the ground that there was hardly a mark to show his passage, as if he weighed no more than thistledown.

Hook, try as he might, was in no way as swift of foot. It was his reach and the reach of his blade that keep the two of them on equal footing. A strange thing that a mere youth with a knife no longer than his forearm could equal a trained fencer such as James Hook, yet Hook had to acknowledge that it was no more than bare truth. There were depths to Tuck, possibilities that few young men contained despite greater muscles.

With the training that the quartermaster had given him, the ship's boy was good, very good indeed. In time, if Tuck paid close attention and practiced as Hook told him to, he could someday be great. Not just with a knife, but with any blade—perhaps any weapon that came to hand, no matter what it might be.

Just as Hook had proven his ability with the gaff hook, young Tuck might be able, in the fullness of time, to be able to use anything as a weapon.

Before the quartermaster could pursue that thought further, Tuck sprang up from behind the rocks ten yards from where Hook had last seen him. The flashing blade was barely deflected by the rough iron hook in the quartermaster's right hand. The return stroke of the rapier clipped three strands of hair as Tuck sprang away, turned a somersault, and vanished behind another outcropping of gray stone.

Yes, Tuck could become a truly great fighter if Hook continued to train him. That was an enormous "if," given the temperament of James Hook. Some men might view such a pupil as a friend and potential ally. By the events that had shaped him, James could only see the possibility that such a student could someday prove to be a dangerous rival.

The skill that Tuck demonstrated in their next few passes led James to decide that there would be no more lessons. He could still beat the young man if their bout had been in deadly earnest rather than just a test of their respective skills, and he wished to keep things that way.

That edge came from certain dishonorable tricks that Hook knew and Tuck did not. While he despised poor form, he would resort to the most dirty, underhanded behavior to keep his own dark blood in his veins. He was not about to help create the man who might someday best him by teaching Tuck too much.

They stopped their dangerous play when a bellow came echoing across the lagoon from the *Jolly Roger*. It seemed that an enraged bull had somehow found its way onto the brigantine. Either that or Red Michael had run out of rum. Time for Tuck to return to the ship and resume his duties.

Smee and a few of the others who had witnessed the bout congratulated Tuck on his skill with a knife and Hook on his ability as an instructor. For all his unease at how quickly Tuck had mastered his blade, James was in his element when heaped with praise from those he saw as owing him such praise. It was as good as rum or one of his reeking cigars, as he saw it. And like too much rum or too many cigars, it put disquieting thoughts completely out of his head for a time so that his vague suspicions regarding Tuck vanished in the late afternoon air as they all piled into the longboat for the short trip to the *Jolly Roger*.

Three more days passed, and the brig set sail with the tide.

Her hull was clean and smooth, her rigging and sails were in proper repair, and the men of her crew were as hungry as sharks scenting blood in the water. All hands were eager for loot, with their captain being the most eager to sight prey.

Red Michael had developed a desire for the sort of entertainment that could only be found aboard a vessel flying the skull and crossbones. Even under that grim banner, the amusement he sought could be only had after a prize had been taken, when the surviving ship's officers were invited aboard the pirate craft for a "special treatment." Having no patience when it came to his person pleasures, Captain Conner was even more abrasive and cruel than usual while all hands were searching the horizon for the first glimpse of a sail.

The captain almost giggled with delight when at last a vessel was spied on the horizon. It was far from a pleasant sound. Most of the crew bustled about, loading pistols, slipping baldrics over their shoulders, and testing the edges of various knives. Red Michael was pulling on his least stained coat and selecting a garish hat so as to present the properly dashing appearance when he boarded their new prize. He wore a length of canvas over his neck like a stole, loops sewn into the cloth holding half a dozen loaded pistols. Three more were shoved into the belt around his huge belly, along with a couple of wicked knives. In one of his beringed hands, Red Michael clutched a notched old cutlass that had seen a score of battles.

The ship turned out to be a Spaniard—not a grand galleon but a simple merchantman that had the misfortune to sail under the flag of Spain. The captain of that vessel seemed to believe that his crew could fight off undisciplined pirates. That was a belief that he was soon disabused of in a most forceful manner.

Dietz was in good cheer as he first shot away the rudder of the merchantman and then brought the flag of Spain—as well as a goodly length of mast—crashing down on deck. The boarding party was in high spirits as they swung across to engage their foes, this time led by Mr. Smee. The bosun carried Johnny Corkscrew in one fist, the rest of his "family" tucked in his belt so that they could join the fun at a moment's notice.

Of all those aboard *Jolly Roger*, only Tuck did not display a wild joy. That was because Captain Conner had commanded him to remain aboard the brig. Hook, taking command of the small crew left behind, observed the petulant youth muttering about having no interest in engaging in such vicious antics. He disclaimed to no one in particular that there was no honor or adventure in overwhelming a poor, ill-trained crew of frightened Spanish sailors.

Such remarks annoyed the quartermaster. Along with Tuck's sullen pouting, it showed that he had been wrong in his judgment of the ship's boy. Tuck was, as Smee insisted, still only a boy. Not the young and promising man Hook wanted to see but just a boy with the foibles all boys were subject to. It made Hook aware that his own conclusions could sometimes be faulty. That was a realization that James Hook was loath to accept, no matter the evidence before his own eyes.

The sour words muttered by Tuck proved true, for those Spaniards were no match for Red Michael and his men. The pirate captain had done little fighting since James had come aboard the brig. That day, James saw that there was more to Red Michael Conner than bluff, bluster, and a fondness for rum and brutality.

Captain Conner rolled through the press of pirates and desperate sailors like a massive boulder set loose to bring destruction to all in his path. Most of his crew knew him well enough to step back smartly as he passed by, his bloody cutlass in one hand.

One Spanish musketeer, well back from the fray, noted the fine, tattered coat and rightly guessed that he had found the captain of the brigands who had boarded his ship. Raising his long weapon to his shoulder, he took aim and fired. The devil, as has oft been noted, takes care of his own, and the musket ball shattered against one of the pistols holstered on Red Michael's chest.

Stung and enraged, the rotund pirate lurched through the press of fighting men and reached the musketeer as he was frantically trying to reload his weapon. Red Michael snatched the musket from the frightened man's hands and swung it like a club. Wood and bones shattered under the impact, and the long barrel bent sharply as the pirate captain slammed the musket down over the steel morion. The metal of the helmet buckled under the blow, though much less than the bones in the neck and shoulders of the soldier wearing it.

Tossing aside the ruined weapon and turning his back to the wreckage of the man, Red Michael looked for more Spaniards to cut down, only to find that the portly captain of the vessel, along with his officers and the few remaining sailors, had thrown down their weapons and were begging for mercy from the brigands who had captured their ship.

Mercy. The very thought of it caused Red Michael to laugh—and not in any pleasant way. As if those Spanish officers would have offered any mercy to the crew of the *Jolly Roger* had their positions been reversed. Captain Conner knew too well of the mercy that Spain offered English pirates—or any Englishmen, for that matter.

The rope was a kindness to those who fell into the cruel hands of the dons. The lash, the rack, and the thumbscrews, as well as starvation and beatings, were the best an honest pirate could expect, their last years spent in a cold, rat-infested prison or chained to an oar in a galley. If their captors were particularly cruel, such poor souls would be turned over to the Inquisition. The tortures they would undergo at the hands of the black monks in the name of saving their souls were so unspeakable as to make any man long for the embrace of the flame and the release of being burned alive at the stake.

Well, Red Michael could offer the Spaniards hospitality to equal their own and give his crew the entertainment they craved after so many weeks at sea. Of course, he would be merciful and not inflict his guests with torments for months on end. A night of amusement and then there would be an end to it. The pirate captain smiled at the thought of the end he had in mind.

"All right, you swabs," Mr. Smee yelled, only slightly out of breath from the battle. "Get this tub stripped of cargo right quick!"

Johnny Corkscrew had exercised well that day, and Smee was content.

Under the guidance of the Irish bosun, a dozen of the fiercest-looking brigands stood by to guard the remnant of the Spanish crew. The rest of the hands scurried below, some to the cargo hold and others to the captain's cabin and the crew's quarters to search for valuables. Anything that might fetch a copper or that caught the fancy of one of the pirates was taken aboard the *Jolly Roger*. Garments, bottles, casks, chests, and bundles came from the cabins and the cargo hold, all heaped haphazardly amidships on the brig. The bosun had said to strip their prize, and the pirate crew did their best to strip her down to the bare boards.

In short order, everything of value was aboard the pirate ship, including the portly Spanish captain and all his surviving officers. With laughter and jeers, the buccaneers cut loose their lines, and the wind filled the sails of the trim brigantine.

"Dietz, give them Spanish lubbers a salute," Red Michael commanded in a dangerously jovial voice.

The gun captain, understanding Conner completely, fired a rolling broadside aimed at the waterline of the merchantman. As an added insult, Dietz used the gunpowder taken from their prize as a test of its quality. It performed the task well enough to satisfy Trommler when his guns fired.

What remained of the Spanish crew hugged the blood-stained planks of the deck in fear as the thunder of heavy guns smote their ears and made the ship shudder under them. When the first few heads cautiously rose up to peek over the rail, they saw the pirates disappearing in the distance, veiled by clouds of smoke.

Only then did they realize the damage done to their vessel as a last gesture of contempt from Red Michael and his crew of blood-thirsty brigands.

Captain Conner did not even deign to glance at the damage wrought by his master gunner. Instead, he plucked a bottle from among the booty piled on deck and knocked off the neck of the bottle with the blade of his cutlass. Guzzling the fine vintage of Spanish wine as though it was no more potent than cheap ale, the blubbery pirate captain gestured with his blade for his men to eat and drink their fill from the provender newly arrived aboard the *Jolly Roger.*

The Spaniard had been weeks out of her home port, so most of the foodstuffs in her galley were reeking and moldy. That was the common condition of food aboard any ship. It could be even worse on a naval vessel, for corruption among those in charge of procuring supplies was legendary. Only pirates tended to eat well, for they stole only the best for themselves and seldom engaged in long voyages where they would be reduced to the maggoty salt pork and moldy biscuits that were the normal ship's rations.

There were just those special items taken from the captain's cabin that were still capable of arousing the hunger of the crew of the pirate brig. Among that culinary bounty were two wheels of pale and pungent cheese, still sealed in wax, and a wedge remaining of a third such wheel, now wrapped in cloth. Added to that were several crocks of pickled onions and the few dozen shriveled yet flavorful apples. Lastly, there were several strings of thin, dried sausages, so dark that they made James Hook think of his prized cigarros threaded together end to end.

While the captain of the merchantman looked on, the viands that had kept him so plump on the long voyage were devoured by the pirates who had looted his ship. The best of his personal supply of wine was guzzled down and spilled like it was the cheapest new vintage to be found in the lowest dives of a French port. If he had not been justly concerned for his own fate, he might have even shed a tear or two as his personal provisions were consumed to the last crumb and drop by the ravenous cutthroats. One incident brought a fleeting smile to the otherwise fear-filled Spaniard.

Noodler, in search of strong drink, smashed open the end of a cask he discovered among the booty and began guzzling the contents, only to discover that it had been a cask of olive oil. The roar of laughter at Noodler's discomfort that came from the crew of the *Jolly Roger* gave cover to the brief smirk that curled the fat lips of their prisoner. Of all the crew, only one man and one boy saw that flash of a disdainful smile.

Tuck would say nothing, perhaps having some slight sympathy for the captives. The quartermaster would remain mum as well, wanting to see the reaction of his shipmates to the "entertainment" their captain had planned for them. For his purposes, nothing would be gained by giving those lads any reason to hold ill will against their prisoners beyond that which their nationality already aroused in the crew of the *Jolly Roger*.

After the display of gluttony, Red Michael gathered all hands together and spun a tale of woe, the central characters being the Spanish captain and his surviving officers. To hear Captain Conner tell it, those poor men suffered grievously from too much idleness, owing to brawny sailors cruelly doing all their tasks for them.

"What I proposes, so as to help these poor unfortunate souls, is a course of exercise what we oversees," Red Michael finished with an evil grin.

The men of the *Jolly Roger* grinned back at their captain, most of them in full agreement, knowing what their captain really meant.

It was a little practice that was known as *sweating*, a common treatment of captives aboard a vessel sailing under the black flag. The prisoners would be force to run around the deck, urged on by dagger point and sword tip. They would run and run and run some more, until they were drenched with sweat and blood from the shallow wounds that kept them running.

When they dropped from exhaustion so deep that not even cuffs and kicks could bring them to their feet, there would be some other form of torment visited upon them. The quartermaster stood a bit back from all that, observing and planning. He did not enjoy such pointless suffering, yet he was not appalled by it either. It was all a part of man's inhumanity to man, which was what had led most of them to take up the sweet trade in the first place.

It was ironic that Hook did not see the similarities between the casual cruelties that he despised in boys and the entertainments that Captain Conner and the crew of the *Jolly Roger* found in tormenting the captive officers from the Spanish merchantman.

Boys inflicted their malicious attention on frogs, turtles, snakes, mice, birds, and whatever other small animals fell into their uncaring hands. Pirates, with the crew of the *Jolly Roger* as a prime example, indulged their appetite for viciousness on other men, captives taken from various prizes. Yet being men rather than mere boys, James saw their actions as a normal reaction to the floggings and other punishment most pirates had suffered while they were still honest seamen sailing under civilized laws.

Hook did have enough humanity within him to sternly send Tuck below before the sweating became too intense, and it was well that he did so. After the fatigued captives collapsed on the deck, Red Michael made a wry comment that they must be over-heated, at which point the crew tore the tattered garments from the captives until they had only the rags of shredded breeches left to them for their modesty. The next act in that inhuman theater of pain was "the trial," a mockery of justice in which a variety of charges were brought against the Spanish captives.

Captain Michael Conner himself acted as prosecutor, leveling charges of cruelty and debased behavior that many among the crew had themselves experienced before they turned to piracy. Whether such charges were true was of little importance, though

James had to admit to himself that they likely were factual even if there was no evidence to support the accusations. It was the nature of far too many "honest" captains to act as a cruel and merciless God while at sea. The reputation of the noble Spaniards was such as to make the list of fictional torments that Red Michael clamed had been suffered by the common seamen of the captured vessel seem more than just plausible.

Mr. Smee had the unenviable task of defending the prisoners. His attempt was earnest and inept, made laughable by the very intensity and passion of his inadequate words. For all his Irish heritage, Smee lacked the ability that came from "Kissing the Blarney Stone," as his fellow countrymen would have called it.

It was strange, Hook mused as he sat apart from the ludicrous proceedings, for the man had been so persuasive when recruiting a new quartermaster to serve aboard the *Jolly Roger.*

As for Red Michael, he played the part of the incensed prosecutor like a second-rate actor chewing the scenery at a country playhouse. Fat hands clawed the air in mock rage, the rings heavy with rubies making it appear as if those hands were speckled with blood, as they might soon be in actuality. His voice rose in a falsetto that aped the speech of an educated barrister but in a most common fashion, as James Hook viewed it from where he stood some distance from the farce.

The quartermaster was distanced from the proceedings because Red Michael claimed that he wanted him to be alert so that no enemy vessel would be able to come close while the crew was enjoying their little diversion. Given the antipathy Conner had shown toward James from the first, it was no surprise that the pirate captain thought to punish the quartermaster by using that thin excuse to keep him out of the fun. Captain Conner viewed Hook as a man who was too thin and active to be trusted by a corpulent commander such as himself, too efficient and alert to be murdered by stealth, and too skillful to kill in an open duel.

If Hook was any judge, Red Michael also feared that his

quartermaster might suspect the feelings his captain had for him. James allowed a grim smile to play briefly across his handsome features as he mused on how correct Captain Conner was to hold that secret fear. The best the obese pirate captain could do for the moment was to keep Hook removed from the fun by claiming a need for him to remain at his duty.

What Red Michael did not realize was that James Hook preferred to view the sorry affair from a distance. Having a duty that prevented him from participating in Red Michael's amusement was no hardship whatsoever, as far as the quartermaster was concerned. Quite the opposite, in fact, though James gave no points to Red Michael for his inadvertent kindness.

As entertainment went, Hook thought that a good book of sonnets by the immortal bard would be far superior. He did find the theatrics mildly instructive as to the nature of the men he shared the deck with, marking those who took too much enjoyment in the suffering of others against those who seemed only to see the crude humor of the immediate event without looking ahead to the ultimately tragic end that Captain Conner had planned.

While keeping a desultory watch on the open ocean around them as well as the expressions on the face of his shipmates, James almost missed the fact that Red Michael had brought the trial to a close. His final accusations toward the prisoners and exhortation of the jury of grinning pirates had gone unheard by Hook. It was only when that jury roared out their verdict that he realized that the entertainment was entering its terminal act.

"Guilty!" half a hundred voices roared out in a rumbling volley like the broadside of a man-of-war.

"What, me fine members o' the jury, should be the punishment?"

"Death! Death! Death!" was the chant the buccaneers took up.

"Aye, death," murmured Red Michael, rubbing one crimson-speckled hand in the other. "But how shall it be done? Shall we keelhaul these Spanish lubbers and let the barnacles rip their flesh?"

"Er, ah, begging you pardon, Cap'n," Mr. Smee said with a mild helpful air. "We just spent three weeks cleaning, caulking, and painting the bottom of the *Jolly Roger*. Not a barnacle left to her. She's as smooth as a Boston doxy's bottom, so she is, all thanks to Quartermaster Hook."

"Oh, yes. Let us thank Mr. Hook for that," Red Michael growled dangerously. "What punishment, then, for these lubbers? Marooning? Too slow—no amusement in that. Hanging?"

Captain Conner looked around to see many of the crew thoughtfully fingering their own necks, imagining the end that might await any or all of them. No, hanging would be a poor choice, given the unpleasant associations all pirates had with that form of execution. It would be an unfortunate ending to the festivities, and one that would not be recalled fondly by his crew.

"Boiling in oil?" suggested Bill Jukes.

"LaSalle, how much oil do we have aboard?"

"Not enough to fry even the smallest of these Spaniards," the cook said, somewhat sadly, as if deep-fried Spaniard was a dish he enjoyed preparing.

For a moment, they all seemed lost in thought, for the execution could be no common form of death. As with the entire farce, it had to tickle the imagination of the pirate crew and their malicious captain. But what?

"Ah, me fine hearties! I've just the thing," Red Michael said.

He made the announcement with such an air of inspiration that Hook, always one to suspect deeper planning and motives, deduced that the captain had been holding this thought in reserve from the very beginning. All the other suggestions had been but play to build suspense and thus increase the excitement and enjoyment among the crew.

"They shall walk the plank!"

"The plank!" The plank!"

Those words ran in thrilled whispers from man to man among the crew of the *Jolly Roger*. For the life of him, James Hook could not understand what stimulated the bloodthirsty imagination of his shipmates in the thought of the prisoners walking along a board. There must be a deeper meaning to the suggestion of "the plank" than he was aware of, which was a strange thing, as he had been in the sweet trade long enough to know all the tricks commonly used by pirates to rid themselves of unwanted guests.

Ephraim Carver, the carpenter, came forward carrying a long board, easily twelve feet in length, close to a foot wide, and two or three inches thick. Cookson, at the carpenter's direction, loosed a section of railing and set it aside. Ephraim pried up several short planks from the deck and passed lengths of rope through the cavities thus made, under a support beam for the deck and up again. The long board—or plank, as Hook understood it to be—was shoved out so that the greater portion hung out over the open ocean. Cookson and a couple of the other hands stood on the plank while Ephraim tied it tight against the beam.

"All snug and firm, Mr. Carver?" the captain asked jovially.

Turning a baleful eye on the quailing prisoners, Red Michael bestowed upon them a smile that held no emotion save for malice. Quartermaster Hook leaned forward in spite of himself, finding that there was cause for interest at last.

"Guilty ye have been found, an' by a jury as fine as any ever to sail these waters," Conner spat. "Guilty of half a hundred crimes—tormenting and misusing poor honest seamen, greed, gluttony, cruelty, and bein' Spanish chief among your sins. For them crimes an' others we've not even touched on, I have every right and duty to cut ye down without a quiver or qualm; 'stead of that, I gives you your chance to leave this fine company unharmed."

Red Michael drew his cutlass with a flourish and pointed toward the plank and the open sea that lay beyond.

"You'll leave my ship with naught but the clothes you wear

and make your own way in the world as the good Lord sees fit," he announced, mocking piety, the hint of a wicked chuckle incompletely hidden among his words.

The ability to understand English was weak among the captives, but they slowly digested the words of their tormentor and found the flavor not to their liking. At a gesture from Red Michael, one of the prisoners—a lesser officer, if his youth was an indication—was separated from the others and placed on one end of the plank. With a wall of daggers bristling on both sides and Captain Conner's cutlass pressing on a tender place behind him, the young man slid farther along the plank until he had passed the edge of the deck.

Only that bit of wood held the first victim above the waves, and a flimsy platform it was. James felt a grim smile curl his lips as the Spaniard tugged desperately against the ropes that held his wrists bound together. A short walk with bound hands, urged on by sharp blades. A prick or two might draw blood, so he would not resist too strongly the urging of sharpened steel. Everyone knew that a drop of blood in the water would draw sharks. This immediate threat would drive from mind all the little wounds that he had suffered earlier while he had been sweated around the deck of the *Jolly Roger*.

Oh, but to walk to the end of the plank and then into the ocean with bound hands, all without a struggle? Without even a word of protest? The man started to swear in his native tongue, and someone pinked him with a blade by way of bidding him to be silent.

Cruelty this was—and delicious cruelty at that. Black Sam Bellamy had been a hard man, and he had dealt with those who crossed him in a direct and fatal fashion. Blackbeard tended to be more theatrical, showing his genius by twisting burning matches in his beard when boarding a prize or in coolly calculated acts of cruelty directed against both foe and friend. For all their notoriety, neither of those pirate captains had ever conceived of anything nearly as entertaining as making prisoners walk the plank.

If Red Michael had dreamed up such a torment on his own, there were unsuspected depths of evil genius within that corpulent hulk. Just as Hook had discovered the unexpected power that resided within the flabby arms of Red Michael, so too did he see the possibility of wit he had not previously suspected behind those bloodshot eyes. It was good to have such potential revealed before he put his plans into motion, for Hook still lusted to wear that ring of Captain Conner's on his own hand and to take his repose in the cabin that Red Michael had for himself, once he had seen the captain removed from his present position.

The first candidate for the captain's delightful little walk lost his balance and fell before he was half the distance to the end of the plank. Half a curse and a splash marked his descent into the rolling green swells of the ocean. Most of the crew pushed to the rail to watch. Hook, further toward the stern, took a few unhurried strides and peered down in time to see the fading ring of foam drifting astern. The Spaniard did not rise to the surface.

One by one, the rest of the captives took their walk, some wailing and sobbing, some stoic in the face of the inevitable. Only one impressed James Hook.

That fellow, tanned and fair-haired where most of his companions were swarthy, had kept his wits. When his turn came, he strode forward with a careful tread upon the wobbly plank, advancing until he was just beyond the rail. A quick twist of his bound hands, and the ropes fell away. A sidestep to the edge of the plank, a swift grab to snatch a dagger from the lax grip of one of the pirates, and then the man leaped for the end of the board, using the springiness of the plank to catapult him far out over the water in a clean dive that took him from sight.

By the time he surfaced, he was beyond the reach of those few brigands who thought to use their pistols to finish him. With strong strokes, the blond Spaniard swam at an angle away from the *Jolly*

Roger, heading to the south and west where he might find land if he could stay afloat for a few days.

A clever fellow, that one. Hook could almost find heart enough to wish him luck on his long swim. From below, the quartermaster heard a delighted laugh, quickly stifled. Looking straight down, he caught a fleeting glimpse of Tuck pulling back his head from one of the stern windows. The young fellow approved of that escape, hopeless though it seemed. Good form on the part of the lad, which James completely approved of. That proved enough to tip the balance within Hook to an honest desire that their departing guest reach whatever goal he had set for himself. And that was good form on his part, all the more so because he did not even realize it.

With that sudden impulse of goodwill toward the escapee, James nudged a cask over the side with a casual movement of his knee, as if by accident. That barrel had held several gallons of wine until the feast on which Red Michael had led his crew. Only a few cups of liquid were left in the cask when it fell into the ocean, so it floated light as the cork that sealed its bunghole.

Like the clever Spaniard, the cask was soon bobbing in the waves far behind the *Jolly Roger*. That worthy fellow, wisely keeping one eye cast toward the brig in case the pirates should prove to be angry enough to change course and pursue him, saw the keg fall from the stern and ride high in the water as the ship moved off into the distance.

Hook could just barely make out the flash of a strong arm as the man changed his own course to intercept the barrel that would give him a better chance to survive. The quartermaster also heard a faint, suppressed cheer from the stern cabin—Tuck guardedly voicing his approval of whoever had given aid to the Spaniard.

After that, only the pale, sweating captain was left. Twice, that worthy Spaniard stuttered pleas in his native tongue to Red Michael, interspersed with prayers aimed at a more distant power. The pirate captain was unmoved and the other power invoked gave no sign of interest. The Spanish captain wobbled and swayed all the way to the end of the plank, bobbing up and down with his toes holding a firm grip on the rough edge of the wood despite the cheers and jeers from the crew of the *Jolly Roger*.

Red Michael enjoyed the spectacle for a few minutes. In a short time, however, he grew both bored and thirsty. One heavy-booted foot slammed down in the middle of the plank, sending vibrations to the very end. That seemed almost too little to jar the plump Spaniard from his perch, so Red Michael threw his weight into a second stomp on the flexing wood. With an indignant squawk much like a plump chicken, the Spaniard flew awkwardly and, like a chicken, not very well. Up he went, and then down he went, shrieking, to prove that whatever sort of fowl he was, he was certainly no duck.

The frantic efforts he made to stay afloat availed him naught, and he sank from sight despite the blubbery bulk of him. With a sigh, Red Michael turned, the amusement ended for that day.

Chapter 9

Safer Buried

"I can't say how I knows, Mr. Hook," Tuck said solemnly. "I just *knows*. Like I would know my own name if ever someone called me by it."

The ship's boy rapped his knuckles against the side of his head.

"It's all locked in here, that much I am certain of: places I've been, people I've known, things I've seen."

"Things like sea serpents?" the quartermaster asked in quiet amusement.

"No, sir, Mr. Hook. I never said anything about sea serpents. Maybe they are real, and maybe they ain't. I don't know about them."

Once again, he gently rapped his blond-thatched skull.

"Nothing in here about such creatures one way or the other. I might not remember when I saw a thing or where, but I know if I did or if I didn't. I cannot explain it clear, but it is like knowing what was placed in a box without being able to describe the items. I knows that them mermaids that Skylights was talking about are real, 'cause I *knows* that I've seen them, swum with them, and talked with them. I just don't remember when or where or any of the details."

The sky above was a vast dome of sapphire, flawed only by

three wisps of white in the east. The sea below their hull was showing a deep emerald hue that spoke of the ocean bottom being not impossibly far below. Gulls swooped and complained in the wake of the brig as she clove the waves, bound for the only port friendly to a vessel of her nature.

Skylights had been talking about mermaids earlier that morning. How he had seen them more than once, heard their songs, and been lucky enough not to be lured to a watery grave when one of them came hunting for a seaman to carry off to their lair at the bottom of the sea. That led others of the crew to tell tales they had heard from other sea dogs and give voice to their opinions as to the existence of mermaids and other such mysteries of the deep.

The *Jolly Roger* was just hours away from Tortuga. The discussion started by Skylights's tale was just the thing to brighten the generally glum mood of the crew. While the hold was filled with cargo that could be sold for a good bit of coin, the haul was not anywhere near as great as on their previous voyage. Rather than gold and jewels, their treasure was in the form of goods that had to be sold before there was any gold to hold in their hands. There was a lesson in that, and it was one that Hook took to heart.

Red Michael had led them to a fortune, which soon slipped through their fingers as gold so often did. Rather than delight in the memories of that fantastic bit of good luck, most of the crew grumbled that their captain had lost his touch, despite the fact that the voyage would have been considered a success except when measured against their last voyage. A rich prize had to be followed by a still richer prize, for the men only considered the immediate past and the immediate future.

Better to make a smaller haul voyage after voyage than load the hold with a mass of gold and jewels on any voyage except the last voyage. Hook noted that if he were ever to lay hands on such a prize, he would disband his crew when they reached port and were paid off. After living a year or two on the captain's share of such a treasure, then and only then would he gather a new crew and set sail in the sweet trade again—and then with men who only knew the tales of his past successes.

Those who had been given a taste of such wealth would never be satisfied with less glittering booty until they had lived for a time with little more than the lint in the bottom of their purse to sustain them. Red Michael had given his crew a taste of the luxuries that wealth could bring and then took them on a mundane pirate expedition. That left the men hungry for gold and grumbling when they should have been content. It was that dissatisfaction that Hook planned to use to his own advantage—and soon. His picked men were already loyal to him over Red Michael. He just needed the right moment when there were few of the crew willing to stand behind the ogre they called captain.

James stood apart as he always did. In part, it was because of the air he wished to cultivate around himself in the minds of the crew. He also thought it would be bad policy to display the depths of his education in answering the question with regards to the possibilities of mermaids.

While Hook was no naturalist, he had been exposed to enough of the natural sciences in his younger days to understand the anatomical impossibilities of a being that was half fish and half mammal as a mermaid would seem to be from the descriptions always given. The distinct demarcation between the half that was a warm human female and the half that was a cold-blooded scaly ichthyoid argued against the reality of any such creature in the natural world.

Against that was his knowledge of the simple beliefs held by most sailors and how desperately they clung to those beliefs in the face of all contrary opinions. It would not endear him to the men were he to argue authoritatively against mermaids in terms that none of them could dispute. Better to remain aloof from the discussion and let the crew spin out their fantasies as they would.

Tuck had listened to the sailors tell their tales and voice their beliefs for a time before coming to sit beside the quartermaster.

After a few quiet moments, he then declared that mermaids were as real as the seagulls that followed the *Jolly Roger*.

James Hook listened to what Tuck had to say. He did not curl a lip in a sneer as he would have with any other man saying such things or in any way dismiss what the ship's boy said. After Tuck confessed that he *knew* without memory of how he knew, James remained silent for a long moment.

"Does the word *Neverland* hold any meaning to you, Tuck?"

It was a carefully calculated thrust, made in the hope of spurring Tuck's recalcitrant memory. The cadaverous quartermaster kept his eyes on Tuck as he voiced his question, searching for any reaction in the ship's boy at the word that came from his nightmare ramblings.

"Neverland," Tuck repeated slowly, as if tasting the word, getting the feel of the texture of it with his perfect white teeth, trying its fit in his mouth to see if it was properly tailored for his tongue.

"I think I know of it, Mr. Hook," Tuck said, after a moment to savor the word, a tinge of excitement in his voice. "An island, a strange island. That would be where mermaids can be found—and a great many other things as well. Surprising things, even to a man like yourself, Mr. Hook."

Tuck shook his head, as if trying to shake something loose.

"It's in here," he complained, slapping his hand against the side of his head. "I knows it is, just like mermaids and cannibals and great wild beasts. I just can't get at it."

What Hook would have said next was forever lost in the double cries from the lookout above and Bill Jukes at the port rail.

"Land ho! Tortuga ahead to starboard!" was the call from the masthead.

"Warship to port!" the tattooed Jukes shouted from the aft rail. "She be flyin' the French flag, an' her guns be run out!"

The sight of Tortuga was no surprise. A warship of any nation—and one with her guns out and ready for battle—on the other hand, was cause for alarm. Some of the crew reacted without thought, running toward their own guns or grasping cutlasses.

Instinctively, James looked aloft. Relief washed over him as he confirmed that the black flag was not flying to declare their status as outlaw to the world. Unless the French were seeking them in particular for some forgotten crime—or perhaps one they had committed not all that long ago, which was not yet forgotten—there was a good chance that they could bluff their way through whatever was to come.

"Stand easy, men," Hook barked. "No panic and not a hand raised with a weapon in it, or I'll skin the man for my new coat!"

He knew how to make his voice crack like a lash, and men obeyed without thought. Smee, at least, understood what their only chance would be and was herding men below so that the size of the crew would not be apparent to the officers aboard the naval vessel. Tuck darted away without waiting for orders, heading below to tell Captain Conner of the situation.

"Signal flag from the Frenchy, Mr. Hook," Smee yelled. "Says, ah, 'Proceed to Tortuga,' iffen I read them right."

The bosun scratched his head.

"Proceed to Tortuga? We were heading for Tortuga. Why would we change course when we are so close?"

"I think that may be why, Mr. Smee," James said coldly, pointing ahead.

There was a ship aground on the rocks there, a ship that had not been on that reef when they had left that port. The sullen, gray clouds building behind the wreck presented the perfect gloomy frame for such a grim sight.

"Odds bobs, hammer and tongs!" James Hook muttered aloud, deeply unsettled by what he saw. "That is Black Jack Kennedy's *Green Hills*, run aground and smashed by cannon shot!"

"Aye, Jas, and there is Black Jack himself and some of his

crew," Smee said in a small voice, pointing to the dark shapes that swayed among the rigging.

Hook focused his spyglass where Smee pointed. Yes, those dismal dark shapes were the captain and crew of the wrecked pirate ship, hung by the neck and sun dried. Food for the birds and a warning to anyone who followed the sweet trade, clear as could be. No wonder the French warship ordered them to the harbor, for many a ship would avoid a port with such a grisly marker on the rocks outside the harbor.

Things had changed in Tortuga since they had departed. They found another and larger French warship anchored where her guns could control the town and inflict damage on any vessel trying to force a passage into the harbor or trying to flee the port. French marines patrolled the town by the dozen, and many of the merchants had closed their doors to all commerce.

The reason for this sudden show of military force, as they soon came to learn, was a mistake made by Black Jack Kennedy, one that had ended costing the Irish pirate dear.

He had taken a French ship newly arrived in the Caribbean. That was something nearly every buccaneer worth the name had done more than once, but Black Jack had what seemed the good fortune to capture a vessel with a wealthy French landowner aboard, a man traveling with his wife and two daughters.

While the goods aboard a captured vessel could be transferred immediately, ransom for passengers, where they had value, took time to arrange. Some pirate crews did not bother with such a time-consuming process, either leaving the passengers with the crew aboard the stripped prey when they left or killing them with the crew if that was their whim. Black Jack and his men were of a different mind, seeing the gold as easy pay for hosting a few wealthy guests for a time aboard *Green Hills*.

The two daughters, being near to women grown, were lovely to the eye of the pirate captain. Their beauty inspired dishonorable desires in Captain Kennedy. With a careful display of concern for their welfare, Black Jack assured both the girls and their mother that they had nothing to fear from him. He vowed that he would be their protector against any lecherous actions from his ill-mannered crew. Foolish girls and foolish mother, they believed the blarney that came so easily from Irish lips.

While the father had been sent ashore to arrange ransom, first the older of the pair and then the younger had been induced to visit Black Jack in his cabin at night. The wild Irish charm displayed by Captain Kennedy was a powerful lure, so he enjoyed the company of those two lasses during the weeks while waiting for ransom to be paid.

Perhaps the affluent planter, a marquis with friends who were powerful as well as wealthy, suspected something of that nature. He returned with the ransom that was demanded to win the release of his family as well as French warships that were positioned to intercept *Green Hills* as she sailed to Tortuga. The battle that followed was brief, for the wild Irish crew of *Green Hills* were already celebrating their success. Rum-soaked brigands proved to be no match for a pair of French frigates crewed by sailors who expected to fight a shipload of devils out of the nethermost pits of hell itself.

Black Jack survived the fight, as did a round score of his men. The trial was swift, the sentence known before the first man was accused. Their crippled vessel was deliberately run onto the rocks to serve as a platform for execution, and Captain Kennedy and what was left of his crew were rowed over to their own ship and given hemp halters from the spare ropes aboard *Green Hills*. Defeated in battle, beaten by their guards, and stunned by the swiftness of their trial and conviction, Kennedy and his men were not even given a chance to utter their last words.

The bodies were left for the birds, a grisly reminded of the penalty for piracy. Until the bodies were reduced to bones, until the wrecked pirate vessel was broken and scattered by storms, *Green Hills* and her ghastly silent crew would bring a shudder from every sailor who entered the harbor of Tortuga, as was the intent of that gruesome display.

As the brig crept to her usual berth under a slight spread of canvas, James noticed another vessel in the sweet trade was tied to her usual place too. *Walrus* sat with furled sails and empty decks. Before an uncertain feeling of dread could crystallize, the big, bluff figure of her quartermaster stepped into clear sight. The man shaded his eyes as he looked toward the *Jolly Roger*, the distance making his face unreadable.

James Hook felt an unexpected gladness at seeing Barbecue on deck so openly. That meant that the French navy was not just imprisoning or hanging suspected pirates out of hand, as his own countrymen would have done. It also meant that the residents of Tortuga had not betrayed the pirates who brought so much wealth to their island. Their loyalty was to the men who brought booty to Tortuga to be traded for gold that ran through their fingers while they were on the island, not to a distant king who cared nothing about them.

Thanks to the usual laxity of the French navy, before the strutting French lieutenant and a squad of uniformed marines arrived to examine the ship, some of the crew of the *Jolly Roger* were able to leave and mingle with the dockworkers and idlers always found at the waterfront. To have completely abandoned the brig would have aroused suspicion and started a hunt for the crew. To have kept all the men on board would have aroused a different sort of suspicion, since the crew was easily four times the size needed to properly man the ship were she on any legitimate business.

Red Michael, attired in a subdued coat and feathered hat as befit the captain of a merchant ship, along with James Hook and Mr. Smee, remained aboard, as did Tuck and a score of the hands. The ship's boy presented a grimy appearance, for he had cleverly nipped down to the bilge with the black flag wadded in a tight bundle. That incriminating bit of evidence was buried under ballast stones near the stern, where no search was likely to discover it.

It soon became obvious that there was going to be no search for proof of piracy. Those ships of the French navy were in Tortuga to exact revenge on Black Jack Kennedy and his men. Beyond that, they were not going to crush piracy in Tortuga in the fashion that Woodes Rogers had employed in the Bahamas. Bringing French law and justice to Tortuga would be a strenuous and unprofitable exercise. The king would be displeased by the reduction of revenue that would result were all the pirates driven from the little island under the French flag.

Instead, that officer and his men used to opportunity to legally loot the *Jolly Roger* of anything that struck their fancy, under the guise of confiscating possible stolen goods. Those fancy French pistols disappeared, as did some wine, bolts of cloth, and sundry other portable booty. The coins gathered from the prizes they had taken on that voyage also were confiscated, with no excuse given beyond the fact that they had the power to do so. The French lieutenant went so far as to take a ring from Captain Connor's hand—the silver skulls and carnelian ring from Red Michael's right pinky finger.

Such behavior was far more common among the officers of the French navy than the principled actions that Woodes Rogers had performed in New Providence.

After some subtle threats issued with the intention of cowing the rotund captain of the *Jolly Roger*, the French officer haughtily gave them leave to sell their remaining cargo in Tortuga, satisfied with the loot he had acquired. The marines under him marched off the ship burdened with their own share of the good confiscated, laughing at the foolish English merchants that they had so easily robbed.

"Mr., ah, Hook, make certain that Dietz understands that we never again leaves a prize flying the flag of French above the waves," Red Michael growled, once those brigands protected by the king of France were off his ship.

The threats issued by the French lieutenant would have effects in the future for other citizens of France that he never intended. The presence of the French navy also had an immediate detrimental effect on the auction of goods from the *Jolly Roger*. Not only did the armed soldiers put a damper on the spirits of all involved, they bolstered the courage of the merchants who had previously offered fair prices for stolen goods that were in high demand.

With the power of their king prowling about with loaded muskets on their shoulders, the merchants of Tortuga felt free to offer a pittance for cargo that men had died over, knowing that the pirates could ill afford to hold on to merchandise that would not feed them or put rum in their cups.

While it was true that those merchants felt more loyalty to the pirates than their king, their allegiance to their purse was even greater than any fondness they might have for the brigands that enriched them.

Red Michael had no choice but to accept the bids offered. His men were already unhappy and needed their share to buy rum and women to easy their ire. Those dogs would bark and growl, as Captain Conner well knew, over the paltry pay they received for the voyage. It did not trouble him overmuch, for the crew always fretted over how small their share was, except for that last voyage. As he saw it, that bit of cleverness and luck should buy him plenty of respect from his men.

Hook knew differently, especially since he had been working to feed the vague feeling of discontent that followed in the wake of great wealth completely spent and gone. It would only take one more mediocre voyage or a bit of ill luck on the part of Red Michael to put the power behind James Hook rather than Michael Conner. The quartermaster was already doing all he could to ensure that that the crew was dissatisfied with their blubbery blustering captain. He only needed a whim of fate to aid him.

Not that he was willing to wait for Dame Fortune to smile on him. That fickle lady gave or withheld her charms as she so chose. It was true, however, that those who needed her least—because of their own efforts—often received her favor as a reward for their labor and planning. In that respect, James knew that the mistress of fate would never find him lacking.

Except for those assigned by the captain to remain aboard the *Jolly Roger* until relieved, the majority of the crew took their meager share and searched out the various forms of pleasure that they most hungered for. James Hook did not turn his steps toward rum, women, or food. He had a better use for a part of his funds, as well as a task to be completed for a shipmate.

First, there was a visit to the tailor who had earlier that day made such an excellent purchase of cloth from the cargo of the *Jolly Roger*. Among the bolts of cloth had been one of a scarlet hue that strongly reminded James of the coat worn by the unfortunate French merchant captain that Red Michael had killed for no good reason.

A coat of that flamboyant color and stylish cut was something Hook viewed as worth the silver it would cost him. With his command of the French language and his politely sinister manner, the quartermaster soon came to an understanding with the nervous tailor who measured his tall thin customer most carefully.

There had been no threats made, only polite conversation, yet the tailor knew in his bones that it would be a poor policy to deliver anything less than the best for the gentleman who carried an iron hook as a weapon. There were stories aplenty in Tortuga about the crew of the pirate brigantine and the quartermaster who fought with his *crochet de fer*. Of all that fearsome crew, he might well be the most terrible, even more to be feared than the bloody-handed captain.

James Hook was aware of that thinking by some of the merchants of Tortuga. It pleased him greatly. Someday, that reputation would be known the world over.

His next stop was at the small shop of Monsieur Favager. Unlike at the tailor's, James displayed only respect to the merchant of fine blades. The sword seller was an artist with edged weapons both long and short and thus was deserving of proper reverence from even a master fencer like the quartermaster of the *Jolly Roger.*

The mission that brought Hook back to that little shop was a simple one. Oddly pleasurable as well, though the quartermaster gave little thought to why he should feel contented in doing a favor for Tuck. He was there to purchase another blade for the lad.

The ship's boy liked the knife he had bought with the help of James on their last visit to Tortuga. A fine, sturdy thing it was, with a good edge. It was not, however, a fighting blade. After his tutelage under the quartermaster, Tuck wanted a dagger, a real weapon, not a tool that could be used to defend or attack in a pinch. He wanted, in point of fact, a dagger similar to the one that Hook had purchased along with his rapier on their last visit with Monsieur Favager.

As Tuck had been ordered to remain aboard the *Jolly Roger* by Captain Conner, James had been happy to undertake the purchase of a proper fighting blade for his young friend. He did not wonder that he considered the younker as a friend, nor did he muse on how like a boy it was that Tuck would want a "better" blade once he had his first knife.

Without becoming aware of it, Hook was accepting that Tuck was indeed a boy rather than a young man. He was accepting that not all boys were as he had once thought of them, based on his own sad experiences with that species. Tuck was—and it would have surprised James had he actually thought about his feeling regarding the lad—a *good* boy, one worthy of friendship and trust.

The weapon that Monsieur Favager produced upon hearing Hook's requirements was a beautiful dagger with a double-edged tapered blade a foot long. Simple lines, a good grip, solid cross guard, and a strong blade made it the perfect weapon for a boy who moved as swiftly and silently as did Tuck. James knew that his young friend would be pleased.

That the dagger cost a few coins more than Tuck's meager

share from that voyage did not trouble Hook in the least. It was nothing to him to put in what was lacking. Indeed, he viewed it as good form, a sort of payback for all the shares that Tuck had never received from Red Michael. Since Hook planned to replace the captain of the *Jolly Roger* very soon, it seemed only right that he should start paying the debts of the ship even if it was not his to command just yet.

The evening was still young when he completed his tasks. Having stopped at the *Jolly Roger* and delivered the dagger to an excited Tuck, the quartermaster found a few pieces of silver still in his pouch. James turned his steps toward a favored haunt of his, that same Bent Cutlass where he had first met Mr. Smee.

Heavy clouds scudded overhead and built, layer upon layer, as the wind gusted and brought the smell of dust and rain. It would be a raw and stormy night, unless Hook missed his guess. A good night to be under a sturdy roof with rum and good company.

The clientele that night proved to be a mix from the two pirate vessels docked in Tortuga, though the crew of the *Jolly Roger* and Captain Flint's boys took tables on opposite sides of the public room.

Blue-jawed Flint, his bland quartermaster, and a dozen others from the *Walrus* complained about the French navy over tankards of raw rum. Red Michael, Smee, and Dietz, as well as ten other shipmates, added curses for the greedy merchants almost as if the two separate groups were sharing a common conversation. Barney Goodtipple had his barmaids circulating between the two groups with rum and ale aplenty, offering credit to the pirate captains in a show of support to the men who were his very best customers.

One thing that the owner of the Bent Cutlass was certain of was that the good will of the pirates that frequented his establishment while they were in port was worth more in actual coin than any temporary profit he might make when said pirates were suffering hard times because of the French navy being in town. Free grog would be going too far, but allowing spirits to be purchased on credit not only bought him favor from two powerful captains and their crews, it also left coins in the pockets of the men, coins that might be spent on the wenches serving out drinks. There were, after all, empty chambers above the public room and the barmaids paid back a bit of what they earned from dalliances above for the rent of those rooms by the half an hour.

"The best of our cargo stolen on account of them havin' the power to take as they please," growled Red Michael to no one in particular.

"A chest of gold doubloons what good men bled and died for, an' that toad of a French cap'n just has his men hoist it offen my ship, and us not able to so much as protest on account o' bein' under the guns of his ship the whole time," Flint muttered loudly, as if in reply.

Neither captain would speak to the other directly. That animosity motivated their crews as well. Even a common enemy in the form of the French navy did not make them forget their rivalry, though it went a long way toward allowing them to share the tavern without the prospect of violence breaking out. Patrols of French marines passed outside the dingy windows of the Bent Cutlass from time to time, clutching at their hats and leaning into the rising wind. The sort of decidedly unfriendly fight the rival crews might otherwise engage in would be sure to attract marines with muskets, bayonets, and no sense of humor at all. Better for all within the tavern to keep bitter words to a minimum.

"What good is it to snatch a fortune only to have it taken from us in turn?" Red Michael asked the room in general. "How can an honest pirate know it be safe to sail into a friendly port with his booty when the soldiers of one king or another might have decided to make an example of a few of our brethren while we was about our unlawful business?"

"Bury the boodle," stated Flint bluntly, directly answering his brother captain and bitter rival.

"Eh. What's that?" Flint's quartermaster, Barbecue, asked of his captain.

Others in the public room leaned forward, interested to hear the answer.

"Bury the swag. It be safer buried than aboard ship if we was to sail into a harbor that had turned against us. When we is sure we has a safe place to spend the booty, we goes back, digs it up, and shares out according to articles with every man o' us who still be above the waves."

"Aye, bury it, says you," rumbled Red Michael derisively. "An' what if the men of the French king or the English king or the Spanish king—God rot 'em all, says I!—what if they takes and hangs you afore your treasure can be meted out all equal like?"

"Why, that be obvious to so smart a man as yerself, I'm thinkin'," the quartermaster of *Walrus* said with an insincere smile. "The secret goes to the grave as a final laugh on thems as thinks they be better 'an us what engages in piracy for a livin'. I heerd tales aplenty of good men tormented for the location of buried treasure when there weren't no treasure to be had. Gettin' no answer is what all king's men expect anyway, so what better bit of humor at the end than the knowledge that you took what no man will ever get back?"

There was a lack of logic in those thoughts that seemed obvious to James, though he decided not to voice those flaws. If anything, he could see an advantage to having treasure buried at some remote location, especially if only a very few knew exactly where the booty was hidden. Knowledge, as he had long held, was power, and knowledge held by a very few could be even more powerful. The fewest number of people holding a secret that he could think of was one. There were ways to arrive at that number and be certain that only he held such a secret, which would give him a great power over those who might wish him ill.

"Indeed," James Hook added boldly, as if in agreement with his fellow quartermaster. "We are outside all the laws of men, as those laws have made us. Why not take to the grave what we will never spend rather than let it go back to those who oppress the world? Or worse than that, let it fall into the hands of those who lack the courage we have to *take* a livelihood from this sorry world but instead rely on the skill and arms of better men to hound and harass us to a watery grave or a final dance at the end of a hempen leash?"

Hook took up his jack of rum and dashed the contents down his throat in a single gulp. The fiery liquid burned harshly and made his eyes tear, but his voice was firm as he continued.

"Better buried, as Captain Flint has said, whether we ever return for it or not. King's men will steal from us as we steal from others, and the more fools the lot of us if we let it happen because we lack the wit to take precautions!"

Many heads nodded to his words. Those among Flint's crew surreptitiously glanced at each other, many of them including Barbecue in their knowing looks.

Smee, Starkey, and Bill Jukes let a thoughtful gaze rest on their own captain briefly before turning their eyes to their quartermaster. Neither Red Michael nor Flint seemed over pleased with what James Hook had said, though there was naught in his words that could be considered a challenge to either of them.

Across the room, the broad bland face of Flint's quartermaster turned to Hook. For a moment, several emotions flickered on his features like a candle guttering in the breeze. Concern, perhaps even fear, was there, as well as thoughtful plotting. That moment passed so swiftly that James almost wondered if he had seen those expressions when Barbecue allowed a lightning-quick smile and a wink directed for Hook's eyes alone.

Hook knew that they could never be friends. It was unlikely that they would ever be anything but bitterest enemies. Yet there was an understanding between the quartermasters of those two pirate ships that went beyond the knowledge of any of the others gathered in the smoky tavern that night.

Barbecue approved of Hook's bold words. He also knew that making the oft-told myth of buried pirate treasure into a reality would require an element of discretion. Limiting the number of crewmen who knew exactly where the booty was buried would be a necessity. In turn, that necessity could easily lead to betrayal, mutiny, and even murder. A captain could lose his command and his life for keeping such a secret too closely guarded.

It was obvious to James Hook that Barbecue not only relished the thought of supplanting Flint as captain of *Walrus*, he also saw in his enemy a similar desire to take command of the *Jolly Roger* and a willingness to promote a scheme to his captain that would make such an endeavor easier to accomplish. There would always be members of a larcenous crew willing to do dirt to their ship-mates for a bigger share of the bounty they had collected.

No doubt, Flint's quartermaster intended to double-cross his captain before Flint could act against Barbecue. For his part, Hook planned much the same fate for Red Michael Conner. Aye, there was an understanding between those two, without any doubt, and for all that neither thought of the other as anything but a dangerous foe.

James smiled sedately at Barbecue and nodded slightly, raising his refilled tankard to his lips. An agreement of sorts, an acknowledgement from one rogue to another. Yes, he would be happy to run through the quartermaster of *Walrus* on any excuse, perhaps even without an excuse. He knew that the big bland-featured Barbecue felt much the same about him, with a bit of fear thrown into the bargain.

Yet there was a silent agreement between them with regard to the future of the captains they served under. A glance at Red Michael showed the blubbery pirate guzzling down rum directly from a dark bottle. The rings on his fat fingers gleamed in the candlelight, throwing off shafts of scarlet, gold, and silver.

Hook smiled, as much to himself as to his counterpart across the room. Outside, the wind howled as the storm grew in strength. Whatever fate awaited Captain Flint, he was certain that the silver ring of Captain Conner's that he had come to covet would be on one of his own fingers when the *Jolly Roger* returned from her next voyage.

Chapter 10

Too Many Times to the Well

The storm grew through the night though the patrons of the Bent Cutlass took little note of it. Rum, wenches, and a continuing call for the damnation of the French king, as well as all other kings, consumed the hours of darkness in a pleasant fashion. Wind howled harshly through the cracks of the door and the window frames and rain drummed raucously on the roof tiles. Lightning crackled with a brilliant white flash, quickly followed by thunder like a rolling broadside of thirty-six pounders. Palm fronds, branches, and loose tiles swirled by the windows. The fury of the storm attracted little notice from the drink-sodden pirates that Barney Goodtipple and his barmaids served.

It was Hook's own inner sense of time that roused him, for there was no dawn to show that the sun had risen. The common room of the Bent Cutlass looked like a shambles, save that the strewn bodies were victims only of rum, not violence. The common animosity against kings and their lackeys had served to prevent bloodshed between the two rival pirate crews where otherwise there would have been cold stiff bodies scattered around the tavern.

It was rare for James Hook to lose himself in rum. It was even more unusual that he had done so in the company of others.

The severity of the weather, combined with the rum and his own happy thoughts of usurping command of the *Jolly Roger*, had made him loath to venture out into the night. An aching head and gummy eyes set the quartermaster in search of water to wash his face.

His quest to perform his morning ablution led him to the alley door. Upon opening that portal, he received the required water in a mixture of driving rain and salt spray whipped by the wind from the crest of waves pounding against the harbor wall.

The effect was even better than plunging his head into a bucket of water taken from an English stream at the beginning of spring. Shocked out of the last of his lethargy by the stinging water dashed in his face, James snorted and stepped back, fighting the wind to get the door closed and latched. While scrubbing his face with the sleeve of his shirt, he hurried to the window and stared out into the blustery gloom through the bull's-eye glass.

Even that distorted view showed that the powerful storm still held Tortuga in its grip. The first thought Hook had was for the safety of the *Jolly Roger*, not only as a part of his duty as quartermaster but also because he regarded himself as the future captain of that fine vessel. To have it battered into a useless hulk before he could walk the deck as her commander was a thought he could not tolerate.

"Smee!" Hook bellowed. "Blast you for a useless lubber, Smee! Where are you?"

"Aye, Jas, reportin' fer duty," the bosun slurred, a sodden voice from a dark corner.

Two slumbering bodies rolled aside, and the rotund Irishman rose from between them to stand on unsteady legs, blinking owlishly in the dim room, his spectacles balanced precariously on the tip of his round nose.

"What be th' trouble, mate? Why roos … *rouse* a man in th' middle of the night?"

"It is morning, you fool, and there is a full gale blowing! We have to get to the ship and make sure she is battened down properly! Wake up some of these drunken jackanapes, and get them to the ship! You hear me, man? Get some of the hands on their feet, and get to the *Jolly Roger* right away!"

"Eh? What? A gale?" the bosun asked, rubbing his eyes with his palms. "What are you going on about, Jas?" he mumbled, staggering to the door of the tavern.

The rain that washed in when he opened the door had the same effect on Smee as it had had on Hook.

"Saints and stars, Mr. Hook, there is a *hurricane* blowing!" Smee shouted, as if giving the quartermaster news that he was unaware of. "We need to get to the ship—"

"And make sure that she is properly battened down. I know that, Mr. Smee. Wake up some of these layabouts, and follow along sharp-like."

James Hook looked around at the piles of sleeping pirates.

From the far side of the room, Barbecue straightened up and nudged the evil-faced Pew who slumped beside him. Flint was nowhere in sight and neither was Red Michael Conner. The quartermaster of Walrus was already shoving at some of his shipmates to wake them.

"Where has Captain Conner gone to?" James demanded of Smee.

The bosun merely pointed a finger upward. It was too much to hope that Smee meant that Red Michael had been gathered to his eternal reward during the night. That was the wrong direction to point if that had been the case.

"Rosalie, that plump wench with the red hair," Smee added as explanation.

It was better, Hook decided, to leave Conner to whatever pleasure he had found.

"Follow along as quickly as you can," he snapped to Smee, dashing out into the wind and blinding rain.

Behind him, he heard both Smee and Barbecue yelling and

cursing to get members of their respective crews awake and out to their ships. The roaring gusts of the wind quickly drowned out every other sound except the occasional rumble of thunder from the swirling clouds above. Bent nearly double, James Hook forced his way toward the docks as if wading against the current of a waist-deep stream.

The *Jolly Roger* was still there, the men on watch struggling to prepare the brig for the full fury of the storm. With Hook to command them and the half dozen more hands that Smee brought to help, the ship was soon battened down and as ready as she could be for all that the hurricane could throw at her. The *Jolly Roger* was tied tight to the dock and padded with rolls of cloth that had not yet been sold to protect her timbers. Besides that, Smee had managed to get the anchor dropped on the seaward side and snugged tight as well to keep the ship from beating itself to pieces against the dock.

It was a notable blow, which ran on for three dreary days. Thanks to the heroic efforts of Hook and Smee, the *Jolly Roger* weathered the hurricane with only the most minor of damage. Members of the crew worked diligently under the command of their quartermaster and bosun, taking four-hour watches that were constant wet labor under the lash of wind and rain. James Hook and Mr. Smee were the only members of the ship's company that remained on their feet until the fury of the hurricane began to wane.

When the fourth day dawned, the skies were clear of all but a few straggling clouds drifting northward after the main body of the hurricane. The quartermaster—for once unmindful of his thick black curls that had been washed out straight by the constant rain or his filthy garments that he had had on since the night he went to the Bent Cutlass—barely managed to stumble to his tiny cabin before dropping into an exhausted sleep. The bosun made no such effort, the heap of sodden canvas that he collapsed upon being all the bed he needed for the next ten hours.

The town had not weathered the storm nearly as well as the *Jolly Roger*. Roofs had been swept away, trees uprooted and flung through walls, and fences flattened by windswept debris. Whole sheds and shacks had been plucked into the sky, often with their inhabitants, and had vanished into the maw of the hurricane, never to be seen again.

Even the French navy had suffered. The fine frigate anchored in the harbor had dragged her anchors under the influence of the wind until she ran hard aground. The foremast broke off in a tangle of canvas and rigging that carried six French sailors to a watery doom. Heeled over on the sand, cannons on her gun deck tore free from their tackle and careened across the tilted deck to smash into the hull on the opposite side, crushing two gunners to death and maiming a third.

Of the patrols ashore, three marines had died when a fireplace in one large building, undermined by rivulets of rainwater, collapsed, bringing down a two-story chimney in an avalanche of bricks on their heads. Three other men of that squad had suffered cuts, bruises, and broken bones.

An officer from the French squadron was lost, that same lieutenant who had led the inspection of the *Jolly Roger*. He was found in the morning when the storm finally moved off, face down in a puddle of filthy water. Some bit of rubbish caught up by the wind had, it appeared, struck him a hard blow behind the ear, and he had lain unconscious, drowning in four inches of dirty water.

When James awoke near dusk, he took the time to brush out his hair, slip on fresh clothing, and settle a rakish hat over his long curls before stepping out on deck. At that same moment, Captain Conner put his foot on the *Jolly Roger* for the first time since the storm had begun. Red Michael had shown no concern for his ship during the hurricane, leaving the care for the brig in the hands of his quartermaster and bosun. He had, instead, followed his usual routine while in Tortuga, visiting his contacts to see what information they might have for him.

Red Michael told what had befallen the French soldiers with relish. When Hook noted the silver ring with skulls and a drop of blood-red carnelian back on the captain's right pinky, he immediately understood that there had been no accident involved in the death of the French lieutenant. He also suspected that the chimney had not fallen at an opportune moment purely by chance either. These were things that he would ponder on deeply, for they had to be considered in light of his plans for Red Michael Conner. Strength, speed, cunning, and a deep desire for revenge—all these were hidden qualities of the captain of the *Jolly Roger*, disguised under a thick layer of fat, drunkenness, and crass behavior.

"Mr., ah, Hook, be the ship ready to sail?" Red Michael demanded suddenly.

"Well, yes, Captain," the quartermaster said with some surprise. "We can have all the men aboard within an hour, I suspect. LaSalle should have brought rations aboard by now, and there was but minor damage from the storm. Yes, I am certain we can sail with the tide, should you wish to."

He thought a moment and added, "And if the French will let us."

At that, Red Michael roared out with laughter.

"Quartermaster, you have not taken stock of our French friends, have you? Yon frigate be barely seaworthy and in no shape to forbid us from sailing. As for the other ship … well, have you taken a squint at the wreck on the rocks?"

It was unlike Red Michael to be so jovially cryptic. James took up his spyglass and focused on the distant wreck. The broken vessel had been dismasted by the storm, as might be expected. Black Jack Kennedy and his grim hanging crew had been taken down to Davy Jones by the hurricane, no long on display as a warning to those thinking to take up the sweet trade.

The more he studied the wreck, the more wrong it looked. Those were not the lean, rakish lines of *Green Hills*, even allowing for damage from cannon shot and pounding waves. The angle of the late-day sun left the hulk a darkened silhouette, though the color of that hull seemed off from what Hook remembered.

"That is the other French frigate," James Hook said at last.

"Aye, Quartermaster, taking the place of the ship she helped to slay. Back broke, crew feedin' the fishes, and no use savin' as salvage. That be truly a jest from the black-hearted gods of the sea, as I sees it."

Conner snorted laughter through his noise.

"We sails with the tide afore last light, and there be naught the Frenchies can do about it, nor much they can say neither, as we be just an honest merchant ship for all they knows."

And so it was that the *Jolly Roger* sailed just as Red Michael commanded and was well away from Tortuga before the sun dropped behind distant clouds far to the west. The captain of the frigate might have uttered a few memorable French curses to speed the brigantine on her way, but aside from that, his attention was more given to the report he would need to write regarding the loss of half his squadron to a hurricane. English merchants, even if they were pirates more often than not, were secondary to salvaging his career after the debacle in Tortuga.

The captain of the *Jolly Roger* was so happy with their easy departure from Tortuga that he celebrated even more than usual and thus was in no fit state to speak of his plans until the following morning. Of course, come morning, his aching head required a noggin or two—or three—of rum, so no course was set at his command, and the brig sailed first west and then south. Hook laid the course, thinking it best to stay in waters little frequented by legitimate shipping until the captain had told them of his plans for that voyage.

Tuck was kept busy running food and rum to Red Michael. His new dagger remained in his cubbyhole, though he openly and proudly wore his first knife on his belt. Captain Conner might not have noticed that blade before and might be adverse to seeing the ship's boy armed when he finally did take note. It was that thought that led Tuck to wisely keep his new pride and joy safely hidden away until he better knew his captain's temper. Hook understood and approved, though it was in his mind to ensure that Tuck did not suffer from such worries for much longer.

"Mr. Hook," Tuck panted, scampering up from belowdecks, "Cap'n Conner wants you in his cabin, 'long with Mr. Smee, Mr. Starkey, and Mr. Dietz."

"Time and past time," the quartermaster muttered, heading below.

The master of the *Jolly Roger* awaited his officers in typical fashion. Owing to the sultry weather, the cabin windows were open wide to allow in a breeze. Red Michael sat at the chart table, wearing only breeches and an undone waistcoat. One beringed hand scratched at the ginger hairs tangled across his broad pasty chest, dislodging several lice onto the table. Idly, the captain crushed the vermin one by one under his thumb.

Hook, at least, was faintly nauseated by the evidence of filth that was slowly accumulating again in the cabin, despite all his efforts to transform both the ship and her captain. Vinegar and lye would be required in large quantities to rid the *Jolly Roger* of all the vermin aboard. The quartermaster amended that thought, realizing that cold steel and gunpowder would be the key ingredient in removing the largest louse of the lot before a proper cleaning could be undertaken.

"Gentlemen," Red Michael said, with a sneer that James was certain was aimed primarily at him. "I have a worthy prize for us to be snatchin' from the dons. Chests of cut and polished emeralds. Aye, and gold as well, enough to allow every man jack o' us to retire from the sea forever. A bit of courage and a bit of cunning, and we'll all have wealth beyond imaging!"

"A fine prize, sir," Starkey said politely. "But where, might I be asking, are we to find this worthy plum so as to pluck it?"

"Ah, Mr. Starkey, right where the Spaniards will never think to be findin' us," Conner rumbled with a grin that showed off his blackened teeth. "Right back on Isla de Tres Palmas, where we had such a memorable success these months past."

There were questions and objections from Hook, Smee, and Starkey. Dieter Trommler remained phlegmatic, concerned only with what he needed to hit with his cannons and at what range. Captain Conner had an answer for every question and protestation. Once again, James Hook was reminded that there was a dangerous mind behind the slovenly, drunken facade presented by Red Michael Conner.

"Gentlemen," the captain said, stressing the irony of using that word to address men of their low character, "I have made our plans, and it be for you to carry them out!"

* * *

Sergeant Alvarez mopped his forehead with a bit of cloth and surveyed the work his men had done. It had been three weeks since the *huracán* had swept across the island, four months since those accursed *piratas luteranos* had disgraced the comandante and the rest of the garrison with their dishonorable trickery. El comandante, when not cursing the pirates, their mothers, and grandmothers, had ordered a pair of the culverins moved from their place on the fortress walls to new positions on either side of the entrance to the harbor. Camouflaged emplacements had been constructed for the heavy cannons, with huts to store powder and shot for the guns.

That hot afternoon, Alvarez and his men were positioning the second of the heavy bronze culverins so as to command the sea for a long distance from the mouth of the harbor. During such hard labor, Alvarez missed his companion, Pacheco. Fat the man may have been, and a decade older than Alvarez, but he knew all the ways to inspire the ignorant peasants pretending to be soldiers to do their work both properly and swiftly. It had always been Pacheco's way to avoid labor in the afternoon sun as much as possible, and Alvarez copied that tactic of his deceased companion.

A distant rumble caused the sergeant to look to the sky, at first thinking of thunder. Only when he saw the cerulean void above, without a trace of white, did he cast his gaze out over the ocean and spy the vessels racing toward the harbor.

The smaller craft in the lead flew the flag of Spain. Behind her at the edge of cannon range was a brig that displayed a black banner on her masthead. Pirates, boldly trying to take a prize right under the guns of the fortress.

"Prisa, cargar el cañón, tontos!" Sergeant Alvarez roared at the squad of soldiers staring stupidly at the distant ships.

He wanted to fire at those *piratas malditos*; he wanted to sink them or drive them off and rescue those on the small ship. He wanted to strike a blow for his poor friend Pacheco. More than that, he wanted his men to ready and firing their cannon before the men of Lieutenant Chavarria got their gun into action.

The pirates fired their bow chasers again, throwing up spouts of water close to the port side of the racing sloop. Across the gap that was the entrance to the harbor, Alvarez could hear Lieutenant Chavarria exhorting his men to move quicker.

"Sargento Alvarez, we are ready!" one of the men shouted as he stepped back from the long cannon.

"Perros, burros, cerdo ciego!" the sergeant roared in anger. "What are you waiting for? Fire! Fire!"

"At the pirates?"

"Por todos los santos de los idiotas! Of course at the pirates! Fire! Sink them!"

The culverin thundered and leaped back against its tackle. A moment later, the sister gun across the way fired as well. Shading his eyes with his hand, Sergeant Alvarez watched to see where the balls would hit. After a long moment, a fountain rose between the two vessels. Another heartbeat and a second such fountain marked where the second shot had struck, also well clear of either ship.

"Rápidamente, vuelva a cargar!" the sergeant bellowed at the top of his lungs.

From across the expanse of water, he could hear the high-pitched voice of the lieutenant shouting similar orders, interspersed with weak-sounding curses.

The pirate broke off her attack at that demonstration of Spanish gunnery. The cannon that Sergeant Alvarez commanded fired a second time before the brigands were out of range, throwing up a second flume of water close behind the ship. Poor inept Lieutenant Chavarria managed to get his laggardly soldiers to fire again as well, though nearly a minute after the piratas malditos were beyond even the range of the culverins.

The little sloop sailed on into the harbor, dipping her flag in salute as she came into the pier. A dozen soldiers with muskets held at the ready double-timed to meet the ship, a portly captain dashing to keep up with his men.

"La bendición de la Virgen Maria en usted," the captain of the sloop cried out, jumping down to meet the captain of the guard.

Captain Ossa could tell that the man, handsome enough in his way, with the massive arms of a wrestler, hailed from some Italian port originally. The first mate of the tiny crew was busy bandaging another crewman who had both arms terribly injured. A round-bellied fellow, who was clearly an Irishman, knelt near the railing, muttering a prayer of thanksgiving under his breath and kissing the crucifix he wore on a leather thong around his neck as he blinked in near-sighted fashion at the harbor around him.

"Those thrice-damned pirates, they come for us though we have only a cargo of hides, dried fish, and olive oil," the captain of the sloop exclaimed, waving his hands in the typical Italian fashion as he spoke.

"We have had trouble with pirates here before," the captain

of the guard said shortly. "On that account, we must search your vessel and examine and make a record of your cargo."

"Ah, si, si, Capitan más honrado," the Italian said hastily. "I shall have my men make ready immediately!"

He turned to the ship and called to the dark-haired mate.

"Gancho, have the gangplank run out! These good soldiers need to examine our cargo, so be swift!"

The first mate, a gaunt hawkishly handsome fellow with his long black hair pulled back and tied with a bit of twine, was still busy with the wounded man. He spoke slowly and carefully to a huge, blank-faced African standing nearby. No doubt, the sailor was as dull-witted as he appeared, Captain Ossa thought, for it took twice for the meaning of the order to sink in to that ugly skull. The muscular *bobo* finally nodded and picked up the heavy boarding plank by himself and placed it so that the officer and his men could come aboard.

The inspection did not take long. A part of the port rail was gone, shivered into splinters by a cannon ball. No doubt that was where the sailor with the broken arms had received his injuries. From the bloodstains on the deck, Captain Ossa deduced that there had been other members of the crew that had been even less lucky, though they were no longer aboard.

Belowdecks, they found the ancient cook, still so frightened by the brush with the pirates that he could only stutter. In the galley with the cook was another sailor, French from his accent, a bandage around his head and over his left eye, fingering his rosary like a good son of the one true church as he thanked God and all the saints for their deliverance.

As the captain had said, the hold reeked of fresh, uncured hides, and dried fish. Casks of olive oil had been stacked and roped neatly in one section and covered with spare sailcloth for further protection. There was naught else of interest and nothing that appeared suspicious, even though Captain Ossa had been warned by the comandante to be suspicious of everything out of the ordinary. This was merely a merchant vessel that had sought refuge from marauding pirates.

There were too few men aboard to be any threat. Three of them able-bodied, with the rest made up of a cripple without the use of his arms, an imbecile, a half-blind Irishman, and an ancient cook who trembled so that he could barely slice a turnip. The only son of Spain among the entire crew was the mate, Gancho.

No, the men that remained aboard the sloop were hardly enough to properly man her to sail around the harbor, let alone pose any sort of threat.

Even so, he posted a guard to watch the ship, as the coman-dante had ordered. The sailors would not go further than the *taberna* at the end of the dock, of that he was certain. Simple seamen like that, after their close brush with the piratas malditos, would think only of drowning their fear in wine. Gomez would have an easy duty that night.

It was, for Gomez, a very easy duty indeed. The first mate had come ashore and visited the taberna as Captain Ossa had predicted, buying several bottles of wine and returning to the battered sloop carrying them in a basket. The sailors drank deeply and talked quietly, subdued by their close call. The hours passed slowly, until it was nearly midnight. Another hour, perhaps, and the next watch—Jorge or Alvero—would come to relieve Gomez at his post.

The sudden eruption of musket fire in the distance brought the soldier fully awake. He clutched his pike and turned toward the fortress that towered behind him. A greasy smile creased his broad face. Si, el comandante had been correct. Allow the tale of emeralds to be spread, and the piratas malditos would return. Gomez almost wished he could be with the squads that had am-bushed the marauders—but only almost. It was far safer to be watching over timid sailors than facing greedy buccaneers.

"Perdón, sargento," a quiet voice said. "What is going on over there?"

It was the first mate from the sloop, looking toward the sound of guns with wide eyes. His shirt was stained crimson, and he reeked of the wine he had spilled while swilling it. Gomez was amused that the ignorant fellow mistook him for a sergeant rather than recognizing that he was but a common soldier.

"Fear not, amigo. It is just my fellow soldiers greeting some of those piratas in a fashion they will not enjoy," Gomez said, a grin splitting his beard.

"But why would piratas come here, with so many fine soldiers and these great cannons? What could draw them like moths to the flame, to be flattened under the hands of your messmates?"

Gomez gestured to the bottle that the gangly man clutched in one hand. The sailor understood immediately and handed over the jug of wine. Good, thought Gomez, it was nearly full. Not that it would be so for very long. Gomez slaked his thirst with a long gulp before answering.

"Our comandante has tricked these devils, letting out word that there is a fortune of jewels and gold stored here, awaiting a galleon to carry it home to Spain. Being greedy fools, the piratas came to steal it, not knowing that there were six squads of musketeers concealed and waiting for such an attempt, as there have been every night for the last six weeks. It takes patience to catch the wolf, and we have been very patient."

"Ah, and this bait for these wolves, this treasure, that is just a story to get them to come to the trap?"

"Indeed not, my fine friend." Any man who gave Gomez such good wine was a friend, at least as long as the wine lasted. "El comandante knows that these accursed sea bandits have many ways to learn things, and they had to be convinced that there was a fortune in emeralds here to steal or they would never come. In the comandante's office there sits the very chest of emeralds and the sacks of gold that these brigands sought, which they will never see."

"But you could show them to us, could you not?" the first mate asked.

Gomez noted for the first time that there was a second sailor with the first, a fellow who proved to be very good at being inconspicuous when he wanted to be. It was that short, rotund fellow, who now wore a pair of ridiculous glasses perched on his round nose. Gomez also became aware, in a painful fashion, that the second sailor had a dagger in his hand. The needle-sharp point rested just under the lower edge of the steel cuirass the soldier wore, angled for a thrust up into his kidney if the need arose.

"Uh, uh, si. This I can do," Gomez squeaked, losing his grip on the bottle he had nearly emptied.

"As I said, Mr. Smee, it would just require asking in the proper fashion," the cadaverous man said to his shorter companion, not a trace of drunkenness in his voice.

Gomez, made eager to please by the unspoken threat from the smiling Irishman, quickly led the pair of sailors into the heart of the citadel. With the bulk of the garrison either on the walls overlooking the swamp or wading among the mangroves in search of pirates, he had no trouble avoiding the few soldiers still on guard. While it might have gone badly for the two seamen, he was certain that it would have been still worse for himself had an alarm been raised.

"Here, señor. It the office of the comandante, and here is where he has kept the emeralds," Gomez said.

"And here is where you will awake with an aching head," Smee replied without a trace of rancor in his voice as he rapped the soldier smartly behind the right ear with the pommel of his dagger.

The man collapsed forward and Hook—for it was Hook who had played at being the first mate of the sloop—caught him neatly and hauled the unconscious soldier into the room as Smee held open the door. Dropping him unceremoniously in a corner, the pair of them made a short search that uncovered a chest of emeralds and several of canvas sacks full of gold coins.

"Bit smaller than I thought it would be," Smee opined. "Only the one, as well. Red Michael did say 'chests' didn't he, Jas?"

The bosun of the *Jolly Roger* tucked his blade back into its place beside the rest of the family in his belt. Hook grasped the neck of a canvas sack and lifted, judging the weight.

"How much more could you carry by yourself? This is better than ten pounds of doubloons in this one bag, if I am right. There are three more just like it, which is not bad pay for this night's work. If that box is a full as these sacks, we will still each receive a fine share, gold and jewels."

There was no need for further speech. Each man took his burden, and they retraced their steps with silence and caution. They had knowingly entered the lion's den for the prize they carried and had no intention of bringing attention to themselves. Cecco and Dusk, the supposed captain of the sloop and the dull-looking African crewman, had already crept out to the guards by the culverins placed near the entrance to the harbor. Those two would do what they did best, removing a threat to their departure with razor-sharp steel. They would wait for the sloop to sail out in darkness and rejoin their mates as they made their escape.

"Skylights, Noodler, Foggerty, hoist the staysail and jib!" Hook whispered harshly as he came aboard the sloop. He stowed the sacks of doubloons amidships.

A foul odor assailed his nose.

"Sorry, Mr. Hook. We ain't had a chance ter wash off," muttered Bill Jukes, seeing the expression of distaste on the quartermaster's face.

Along with Cookson, Alf Mason, and Ed Teyne, the tattooed Jukes had hidden in the malodorous bilge until well after dark. The Spaniards would have been more suspicious if they had known the true size of the crew the sloop carried. Add in that four of them spoke no Spanish, there was no safer place for them to be than the one place no fastidious Spanish officer would ever think of searching, even if it were the foulest spot on the entire sloop.

They were all Hook's men, loyal to the quartermaster over Red Michael. James had left the rest of his personal crew aboard the *Jolly Roger* to keep a sharp watch over Captain Conner. Of those he had suborned, only Gentleman Starkey was in danger, for he had been placed in charge of the landing party that was to distract the soldiers. From the amount of musket fire, it seemed that those decoys had performed their task in too efficient a manner.

"Quite all right, Mr. Jukes," James replied, breathing only through his mouth because of the remarkable stench coming off the man. "Take the wheel. Mr. Teyne, at the bow, and keep a sharp lookout. Cookson, Mason, space yourselves between Teyne and Jukes and replay the directions that Teyne gives, but keep your voices low. Any man who forgets will put our necks in a noose, but I'll carve his liver before the Spaniards lay hands on us!"

Hook and Smee made quick work of lines holding the sloop to the dock in typical pirate fashion, slashing the rope without thought to future need. The gangplank was treated in the same careless fashion, allowed to drop into the harbor as the sloop silently moved off into the darkness. The slight splash went unheard as another volley of musket fire echoed in the distance.

A moonless night with a partly cloudy sky to veil the light of the stars was the perfect night for the sloop to slip across the harbor and out to the vast ocean beyond the rocky entrance. Even if the attention of all the soldiers had not been on the mangrove swamp, not even the sharpest eye could have seen the little ship sail across the harbor.

El comandante paced the rampart at the rear of the fortress with half a company of soldiers spread out on either side of him. More soldiers moved through the mangrove swamp with lanterns and muskets, seeking the remainder of the raiders who had so foolishly attempted to sneak over the back wall on a second occasion.

El comandante already had many fish that had come to his bait, but he wanted the entire school. None should swim out to sea. Nearly a score of the English piratas malditos had fallen to the muskets of his soldiers already. His men had complained bitterly these past few weeks, spending their nights among the mangrove swamp with the leeches, mosquitoes, and snakes. This night, however, they would sing the praises of their comandante, for his cunning had allowed them to destroy a major force of these piratas luteranos already. When the signal was given, the rest of his trap would close and none of the English dogs would escape!

Thinking on that, the obese commander of Isla de Tres Palmas snapped his fingers, summoning his aid.

"Pedro, it is time," the officer snapped. "To the watchtower, make haste! You know what to do!"

Back on the sloop, Hook and Smee each tossed a small cask, painted white, over the rail, one to port and the other to starboard. Attached to each cask was a line tied tight to the rail. Between the phosphorescence of the foam that swirled around them and their own pale color against the dark sea, each bobbing little barrel should be enough for Cecco and Dusk to locate the ropes they marked. Both men knew that the sloop would not stop if they missed their one chance for escape from the Spanish fortress island.

"Look there, Jas, a skyrocket," Smee said as something rose with a whoosh from the highest tower of the citadel. "Seems strange, don't it, that anyone is lighting off fireworks at this time of night, what with all else going on. I wonder what it is that they are celebrating?"

James Hook looked up, his eyes following the trail of sparks into the starry sky until the rocket burst in a huge flower of glowing red comets. His mind wrestled with facts and speculations, discarding the illogical and winnowing down the possibilities until only one terrible potential answer was left. Before the second rocket climbed halfway along its path, he voiced his conclusion in a voice that mixed dread with a degree of contempt for the clueless bosun.

"They are celebrating our hanging, Mr. Smee."

"Eh, what's that, Ja ... er, Mr. Hook?"

Smee could hear the suppressed anger in the voice of the quartermaster and decided that it was no time to be overly familiar with that mercurial fellow.

"Even though there really was a chest of emeralds and sacks of gold doubloons here, allowing the story of them to be spread was a trap for us," the quartermaster replied as if explaining to a child.

"Aye, that is so, Mr. Hook, but we already knew that it was a trap."

"Indeed we did, Mr. Smee. We knew it would be a trap and came anyway because the bait was real, and we thought we knew how to snatch that bait without springing the trap. The Spaniards, however, knew that we would at least suspect that we were entering a trap and be doubly cautious, so they set a trap around this trap, in the event that we slipped past the first snare."

"Which we did, neat and clean, thanks to you," Smee put in with admiration.

"And that is why they are springing their second layer of defense. Those rockets are to summon Spanish warships posted at some distance from the island. Some will arrive here sooner than others, depending on the winds, but they will all be coming to blow us out of the water."

Smee gulped and turned pale. They had the treasure, and they had the means to escape Isla de Tres Palmas, true enough. Escaping a Spanish squadron was another matter entirely, even if they managed to rendezvous with the *Jolly Roger* first. And there was Gentleman Starkey and the men with him. They had provided the timely distraction and would have retreated to their longboat. Those men, or at least those of them that had escaped the ambush of the Spanish soldiers at any rate, also had to be picked up before they could flee into the night with their prize.

Dusk and Cecco clambered aboard, each man having caught their line. Even before they were over the rail, James ordered all sails hoisted. They had to rendezvous with the *Jolly Roger*, and then the *Jolly Roger* had to pick up the men under Starkey's command before they could flee.

The certain knowledge that Spanish warships would be closing in from every direction inspired haste. The quartermaster wanted to be sure that haste did not turn to panic—that no mistakes were made because his men were in a hurry to escape a threat that had not yet appeared on the horizon.

Even with all the planning their captain had done to slip past the obvious snare, returning to Isla de Tres Palmas had been a serious mistake. James Hook decided that it would be the last mistake made by Red Michael Conner as captain of the *Jolly Roger*.

Chapter 11

The Storm and the Boy

A moonless night with clouds hiding most of the stars made it easy to slip unseen from the harbor of a Spanish fortress. It became even easier to take leave unnoticed when the majority of the men on watch had their attention turned in another direction. The task of locating and rendezvousing with another ship, however, became somewhat more difficult when the night was as black as the inside of a bucket of pitch.

"A blue star!" Skylights called down from atop the mast of the sloop. "Three points to starboard!"

"That is our course, Jukes," James Hook said quietly.

Since they had left Isla de Tres Palmas behind, Billy Jukes and his odorous companions from the bilge had taken the time—at Hook's pointed suggestion—to wash the stench from their clothing and hides. In the private opinion of the quartermaster, none of those brigands had ever smelled better, though that particular bar had been set very low.

Rather than have lanterns lit, red and green, port and starboard, which might draw the attention of unfriendly vessels, the *Jolly Roger* had a single lantern lit, perched at the top of the main mast. A heavy glass shade of deepest indigo allowed only a dim and distinctive blue gleam. Canvas shades permitted that glow to be seen only from astern, which was the direction from which Hook and his men would be sailing. Only someone who knew what to look for would notice the flicker of blue light among the few scattered low stars that were not blotted out by the clouds.

It did not take long to reach the brigantine that lay with all sailed furled. Hook, Smee, and the others quickly transferred from the sloop that they had stolen from Spanish merchants a week earlier, taking the chest and sacks of doubloons with them. The sloop was cast adrift, perhaps to locate her former crew where they had been sent down to Davy Jones by Red Michael and his men.

"Ye have done excellent work, Mr., ah, Hook," Red Michael allowed reluctantly.

The sight of those green gems glittering in their chest softened Captain Conner's mood, if only slightly. The golden gleam of the doubloons helped as well, though James had the suspicion that Red Michael would have been equally happy had the quartermaster failed, if for different reasons.

"Clap on all sail, Mr. Smee. We needs to be underway, and I'll have the hide off any man that don't jump lively. Hear that?"

"What of Mr. Starkey and the men with him?"

"You saw those rockets, d' ye not, Mr., ah, Hook? You know what they means, I hope? There be a Spanish squadron out there, spread t' the four points of the compass, and they all be sailing in this direction, a net spread wide t' catch us. We've no time to waste waiting for dead men!"

Red Michael's foul breath was thick with rum. His speech was slurred with the black drink he so favored. That might be why he chose his words so carelessly. Whatever the reason, it did not sit well with the crew that he intended to abandon that third of the crew that had slipped ashore to act as a diversion for Hook and his men.

There had been casualties among those men, of that they were certain. Such deaths would be mourned properly in Tortuga with rum and willing wenches. A violent end was expected in the life they chose, whether from musket shot, sword's point, or noose. To die in such a fashion was an end they all expected.

Hearing their own captain so callously disregard the loss of their shipmates was something else entirely. Red Michael as much as said that he had sent Starkey and the rest to their deaths and had no concern for any of them who might have survived to try to reach the brig. Those words stirred anger in the men of the *Jolly Roger*. Those were their shipmates out there, struggling to return to the ship after enduring Spanish musket fire as a diversion to enrich them all.

James was more concerned with the bad form displayed by Red Michael than he was with the fate of Starkey and the others with him. He did not consider them to be his friends. Companions, yes. Shipmates, without question. But that did not mean that he held any fondness for them, nor would he mourn any of them who did not return.

That is what he told himself.

There was an unspoken promise made when the captain of the ship sent a portion of the crew into grave danger. It was expected, by one and all, that the ship would be there for them to return to or at least that the *Jolly Roger* would remain a reasonable time waiting for the missing men before departing, no matter what danger threatened.

It was unspeakably bad form to break that guarantee so abruptly, simply from what appeared to be cowardice. To Hook, not only did Red Michael display bad form, he was giving the quartermaster the opportunity he had been waiting for, when the crew would be inclined to support overthrowing Captain Conner because their own passions were inflamed against their blubbery leader.

"Ahoy, *Jolly Roger*!"

The cry was faint and weak, displaying both distance and distress.

"Arr, that be Chauncey, him what went with Frank, Archer, Kent, and the rest along with Starkey," one of the crew said in surprise.

The moment was lost. Hook instantly changed his focus, commanding a sharp lookout, while he bent over the rail and shouted cautiously back in the direction the voice had come from.

"Ahoy, yourself! Is that you, Chauncey? Who is with you?" And then, before an answer could come, to the men around him, "Get some bull's-eye lanterns and cast a light, though be careful. Some of you men stand by with muskets in case this is a trick. Dietz, have you a gun ready? Aye? Stand by as well, in case!"

It was a few minutes before a dim white shape was spotted in the darkness. That shape soon resolved into the triangular sail hoisted on the spindly mast of a longboat. Half a dozen men lolled dispiritedly in the bottom of the boat, with one more man slumped over the tiller.

"Mr. Starkey, is that you?"

"Aye, Mis'er Hook. Permiss'n ter come 'board?"

The quartermaster gave quick orders for one man to get the line from the longboat and another to help the men in her up the ladder to the *Jolly Roger*. Smee dropped down to the boat to help, hoisting first one bloody sailor and then another up to helping hands. At the fourth man, Smee started to lift and then lowered him again, taking off his cap and crossing himself.

"Archer, Mr. Hook. He's past all help in this world."

James Hook took off his own hat and bowed his head. Archer had been a competent seaman with nothing outstanding about him. One pirate among many and no more friend to the quartermaster than any other. It was good form to show respect at the passing of a member of the crew, which Hook made certain to do. Red Michael merely displayed impatience, commenting profanely that Smee should send the poor sod off to Davy Jones and be quick about it.

"Though he deserves better," Hook said, putting weariness

and regret in his voice that seemed sincere, "Captain Conner has it right this time. Deliver our shipmate into the keeping of the sea, and help the rest of these men aboard."

The crew would remember that when the time came: the insensitivity of Red Michael and the sympathy expressed by their quartermaster. Poor form and good form in contrast, a display that would help the crew decide who they would support. James waited the few moments it took for Smee to easy the body over the side of the longboat before placing his hat back on his head.

Red Michael sneered at that bit of sentiment, too gone with rum to realize the mistake he was making.

With the last of his men aboard the *Jolly Roger*, Gentleman Starkey took a moment, aided by Smee, to furl the sail and unstep the mast of the longboat. Once that gear was bundled in the bottom of the little craft, all neat and proper, he slowly climbed the ladder, followed by the bosun. The longboat, stolen like the sloop that had been left adrift when its usefulness was at an end, was allowed to trail behind the brig on its line as the sails were shaken out and took the wind.

"Mr. Hook, those men need tending," Smee said as he followed Starkey aboard. "You are the best we have at that sort of thing."

"As you say, Mr. Smee. Have Tuck fetch the medical chest forward to the crew's quarters."

Among the crew of the *Jolly Roger*, there were many talents to be found, some quite unexpected. The bosun, Smee, as an example, was a surprisingly good hand at darning, sewing, and knitting, often being called upon to mend the garments of his shipmates. One talent that was missing, however, was that of physician.

Ephraim Carver could do passable work with a saw and hot pitch if a mangled limb needed to be removed. LaSalle could pull a rotten tooth, and Smee could sew up cut flesh as easily as he could torn cloth. None of them had any skill at healing beyond those crude abilities. Their quartermaster, being a man of extensive education, excelled all of them combined in his ability to treat wounds for all that he had never aspired to study medicine beyond the common knowledge of men of the station he had come from.

Chauncey was the first subject that he tended to, extracting a musket ball from his shoulder while the man's friend, Edgar, held him down. The other survivors of the diversion party had similar wounds, sometimes carrying two or three Spanish musket balls in various parts of their body. Hook worked with tweezers, scalpel, and probe to clean out the wounds and then irrigated the holes with rum and water mixed equally and bandaged them with clean linen.

In part because of the extravagant use he made of it and in part to spare Tuck from the sight of the wounds, James sent the boy aft to fetch still more rum. Since he gave the whole of his attention to the task at hand and still retained enough rum to finish his work, he did not notice when Tuck failed to return as expected.

He had completed his doctoring and was washing his hands in a basin of water when he heard Tuck cry out in pain. Hook knew immediately what was occurring on deck, something that he had thought to preempt. The requirements of the wounded crewmen had distracted him from other business that needed to be addressed at once.

Dashing on deck, the quartermaster saw Tuck crouched before Red Michael, one hand rubbing the bruise on his cheek. The pirate captain stooped suddenly, grasped the knife shoved under the boy's belt and ripped it free.

"A useless whelp like you ain't got no need for a blade," Red Michael snarled, tossing the knife over the side.

Tuck started to say something and subsided, wisely holding his tongue.

As if he knew what Tuck was going to say, the captain reached under his coat and drew out another blade, the longer dagger that Hook had but recently procured for the ship's boy.

"You got no need for any blade at all, an' you won't have none so long's I be cap'n of the *Jolly Roger*!"

That weapon followed the first over the side, and Red Michael swung up his hand to slap Tuck once again.

With the Spanish trap made plain by those rockets to summon waiting ships, Red Michael was eager to give Tuck the nightmares that would sweep the *Jolly Roger* to another spot on the wide seas before the coming of dawn. Hook had been equally eager to forestall such brutality. Failing in that, he was determined that Red Michael would not strike the boy a single time more.

"Stay your hand, you bilious, blubbery dog!"

Red Michael turned at those words from his quartermaster, a nasty grin etched on his greasy face. It was as if he had been expecting those words from Hook and was ready to counter whatever move the quartermaster made. That smile turned sickly when the dagger that Hook carried seemed to leap into his moving hand. A lunge and slash, followed by icy pain, and the pinky of Conner's left hand was bouncing across the deck, the silver ring still gleaming through the splash of blood.

There was more than brutality in that blow. Having studied Red Michael in preparation for that moment, James was certain that such a physical lost, minor though it was, would throw off the corpulent captain's thoughts and reactions. The quartermaster knew that he would need every advantage of wit and speed to accomplish his goal without giving Conner the opportunity to introduce Hook's insides to the outside world.

Before Red Michael could grasp the pistol in his belt, he found his right hand snagged by the iron tip of the hook James had made into a versatile weapon. A sweep of the razor-shape blade still in Hook's right hand parted Captain Conner's belt, dumping pistols, knives, a knotted length of rope, and sundry other weapons onto the deck. The loss of that belt also made Red Michael pin his sagging breeches to his hip with his left elbow while he clutched at his maimed left hand with his right.

In that situation, the terrible Red Michael Conner, handily disarmed, was in no position to do more than roar orders to his crew. As Hook had won the loyalty of a dozen of the men and Red Michael had squandered the allegiance of the rest, those commands went unanswered save by jeers.

"Aye, ye prancing popinjay," Red Michael snarled. "You have my ship and crew for the moment. What be yer plans fer me?"

The former captain of the *Jolly Roger* was playing for time, as James Hook well knew. It was his intention to play along for a few moments. The answer he gave seemed at first to be what Red Michael hoped to hear.

"Mr. Smee, in what direction lies the island where Red Michael marooned Captain Kendrick? And how far off?"

The bosun gave thought for a moment, knowing their position nearly as well as the quartermaster did. No mean navigator himself, it did not take him long to figure the position of that dreary island or the sailing time it would take to reach the place.

"To the starboard, Jas … er, *Captain* Hook," Smee said, pointing in the correct direction. "Three days if the wind holds good."

Red Michael smiled, thinking that three days would be time enough for him to retake his ship from Hook, Smee, and the other ungrateful swine that stood back and allowed him to be deposed. Ah, and when he was captain again, there would be revenge. The upstart James would rue this day.

"Three days, Mr. Smee? Very good. And how long will it take you to swim the distance, Red Michael?"

While the former captain of the *Jolly Roger* was still puzzling that comment out, Captain Hook gave a low, firm command to *his* men, "Run out the plank on the starboard side."

"Er, ah, Jas … er, that is, *Captain*, what of Tuck?" Smee asked.

James looked to the boy, who sat slumped where Red Michael had dropped him.

A part of Hook thought it would be a good thing for Tuck to see the end of Red Michael Conner, while another part of him argued that the boy would be better off without that vision in his memory. The knowledge that Red Michael would trouble him no more would be a good thing for Tuck to hold on to, but seeing the fat pirate go down to Davy Jones might have an ill effect on the innocent lad.

That gentler part of Hook's nature saw a rare victory.

"See him below, Mr. Smee, and make him comfortable," James Hook said quietly. And then, turning from Smee, "Mr. Jukes, if you would be so kind?"

Hook pointed the tip of his dagger at the severed finger on the deck.

Bill Jukes gingerly picked up the detached digit and held it out to his new captain. James slipped the ring from that finger and waved a hand toward Red Michael. The tattooed pirate then extended his hand toward Conner as if offering a treat to an especially vicious and unpredictable canine. Numbly, Red Michael took back what Hook had removed, his mind still working at lightning speed to discover a way to turn the tables on his quartermaster.

Hook examined the ring for a moment, turning it this way and that, though he never completely took his eyes off Red Michael. Assuring himself that there was no blood on the ring, he slipped in onto the proper finger of his right hand.

"This ring will never leave this hand," Hook declared to his men, fist once again tight around the hilt of his dagger.

"And now," he added, with half a bow toward the former captain, "If you will be so kind as to step this way?"

A broad gesture indicated the waiting plank.

James had exchanged the hook in his left hand for his rapier. At his back stood Dusk, grinning evilly with his needle-sharp teeth; Cecco, with knives in each hand; Skylights, holding his old, notched cutlass; and another score of the crew, weapons in their fists and a desire to see the end of Red Michael Conner in their eyes. Overhead, gathering clouds hid the stars, as if those celestial lights had no wish to see what would transpire next. Lightning flicked weakly among those building billows, each flash stronger than the one before. The wind rose, sighing through the rigging. A black night, perfect for another act of villainy.

"Your choice," Captain Hook said suavely, pointing with his dagger to starboard, "Swim for the island where you marooned Captain Kendrick, or," the rapier swung up, pointing to port, "swim for Isla de Tres Palmas, where the Spaniards will no doubt be eager to greet you in proper fashion."

The smile that crept across the face of James Hook would have given Smee doubts had he seen it. Even Red Michael was cowed by the viciousness displayed on the handsome visage of his former quartermaster at that moment.

"In either case, you will be leaving the *Jolly Roger* in the same fashion you saw so many others leave this vessel—by means of the plank!"

Red Michael was too proud to beg for his life. He also understood, too late, that he would not be able to trick Hook, that the quartermaster had studied him too well to be fooled by any ploy he might advance in the next few minutes. His choice seemed limited to walking the plank or being forced to the end at the point of a sword. It was a crushing thing to realize that he had been outwitted by a man he thought was under his thumb—that the quartermaster who he had so little respect for was the better man by far.

More in futile defiance than out of courage, Conner gripped his breeches in his good hand, gathered what small amount of dignity he had left, and turned his back on James Hook. He ran for the end of the plank, intending to make a graceful dive into the oceans. His grand final gestured was marred by the sturdy plank being unable to support his great weight. The board broke before he reached the last third of its length, dumping him unceremoniously into the ocean, a last, startled vulgarity only partially past his lips before he disappeared under the waves.

A man with that much fat padding his bones should have floated like an empty barrel, bobbing back to the surface after a few moments. Contrary to the very end, Red Michael did not re-appear. Taken by a shark because of his wound, snatched down by Davy Jones by virtue of his wicked nature, or simply pulled into the depths by a perverse current, Red Michael Conner vanished into the sea, never again to be seen by mortal men.

Captain Hook felt vaguely disappointed. He knew that his scheme for dealing with Red Michael had worked perfectly. There was no question that the time needed for theatrics or the bad form of gloating could have provided Conner the moments he needed to think and act, snatching victory from Hook.

Still, it seemed to him that the end of a foe like Red Michael Conner should have had a grander ending than a swift drop into the sea, without even a final useless threat. Perhaps it was just the nascent actor within James that felt the need for recognition and wanted the scene played out in the properly dramatic fashion.

"Mr., er, that is, *Captain* Hook!" the lookout called down from above. "I sees the lights of a ship to the nor'east! Aye, the lightnin' shows her clear! A galleon in the distance!"

The first of the Spanish ships set to trap them. No doubt, there would be others sighted all too soon. Red Michael had done what Hook would never do to trigger whatever magic it was that would send them a hundred leagues away before the dawn came. This final time, it would serve the *Jolly Roger* and her crew well, though never again would Tuck be brutalized for such a base reason.

"Hoist more sail, but keep a sharp eye on the winds," Hook called out. "Make our course east by southeast. And douse that lantern aloft!"

It was unlikely that the Spaniard had spotted the blue glow of the lantern, but there was no reason to take any chances. The crew knew the ship well enough to work her by only the occasional glare of lightning. No point in giving the Spaniards even the slightest flicker of light to track them by.

Hook had seen the storms that came with Tuck's nightmares twice before. This third—and he most fervently hoped the last—time seemed to be far stronger than the previous two events. The waves were already mountains of foam. The wind whirled around and around the *Jolly Roger* in an ever-increasing gale that blew from all directions. Forks of lightning stabbed down from the black and green clouds above, illuminating and framing sections of the churning waters around them in a way that it never had before, filling the crew with fear.

It was what was visible within the momentary frames of lightning that made the men cry out in dread and wonder. There, off to starboard, lightning displayed calm black water where mountains of crystalline ice floated placidly under rippling ribbons of green and scarlet light in the sky. Again, to port, emerald-green breakers rolled ceaselessly against a coral reef, with a beach of golden sand bathed in the bright light of a full moon, though the moon should not have been in the sky at all.

The lightning lit scene after scene, fore and aft, port and starboard, each impossibly there for an instant and then gone, leaving behind a frigid breeze, the scent of jungle rot, or a flurry of yellow and brown leaves that were devoured by the heaving waves all around them.

Mr. Smee clambered up on deck, making his way over to Hook.

"The boy, Smee, it must be the boy!"

"Aye, Cap'n. It's Tuck, sure enough, or what comes with his nightmares. Cap'n Conner aught not have beat him like that."

"It was more than that, Smee. When Red Michael took those knives from Tuck and pitched them overboard, when he told the lad that he would never have any weapons of his own, that wounded Tuck deeper than any slap from that fat, greasy hand."

"The poor lad has the most terrible nightmares as it is."

"Aye, Smee, I know. And you know. We all know what

happens when Tuck has nightmares, but what happens when he has nightmares like *this*?"

As if to emphasize the point, a fork of lightning struck close beside the brig and illuminated massive stone ruins covered with inhuman carvings and half-sunk into a morass of diseased green weed. Ships encrusted with sickly gray moss lay at anchor close to those ruins while strange, unwholesome nightmare shapes flapped overhead on ragged bat-like wings. One such creature seemed to catch sight of the gaping pirates on the deck of the *Jolly Roger* and wheeled toward them. Every hand on deck breathed a sigh of relief as the lightning faded and darkness returned.

"Come, Smee. We must wake Tuck!"

"I don't know if we can," replied Smee, following Hook as he dashed down to the cabin where the boy lay in slumber. "I have tried a time or two, when the nightmares seemed especially bad, and never had a lick of success."

"We still must try, Smee!"

The bosun had laid Tuck on the bed in the cabin that had been given to James. The ship's boy tossed and turned in his sleep, muttering snatches of phrases under his breath. The nightmare that gripped him was a colossal one, filled with terrible visions and events that turned the lad pale with fear and loathing.

"Sunday school," he said quite clearly, shuddering and breaking out in a sweat.

"Tuck, Tuck, wake up!" James said loudly.

There was no response except a mumble that might have been "multiplication tables."

"Up, lad. On your feet," Smee shouted, using the sort of voice a bosun develops to make his orders heard during a gale.

"Polished shoes."

The men bellowed, shook the bed, pulled off the covers, banged the chair, and even splashed water from the pitcher on the nightstand into Tuck's face.

"Starched collars."

"Wake up, blast you!" Hook thundered, raising his hand to strike.

And he froze in that position, unable to even attempt to slap Tuck awake. It was not anything like friendship that stayed his hand, he was quick to tell himself. It was that he would not willingly break his word. Yes, of course. He had promised that he would never strike Tuck when he was captain, and even if that vow had only been to himself, he would not break it. Besides, it would be terribly bad form to strike someone who was asleep, even as a means of waking them.

That is what he told himself.

Smee seemed not to notice, reluctantly reaching down and grasping the skin of the boy's upper arm.

"Sorry, Tuck, but I have to do it," Smee said apologetically.

He pinched Tuck, gently at first and then harder as the boy still did not wake up.

"Reciting lessons," Tuck mumbled as if in agony.

Screwing up his resolve, Smee pinched even harder, digging his thumbnail in until a drop of blood showed. Tuck groaned about conjugating verbs. Smee twisted the skin gripped tight between his thumb and forefinger.

"Not a tie. Please, not a tie."

Smee sobbed and let go.

Tuck sighed, feeling the pain fade even in his deep slumber.

"Neverland," he whispered, delight and wonder in that breath of a word.

"He won't wake up," Smee complained in frustration, self-loathing, and fear.

"Take him up on deck, Mr. Smee," Captain Hook said, racking his brains for what they else they could do. "Perhaps the storm, thunder, and rain will wake him."

The crash of thunder did nothing save to drown out the mumbling that Tuck made in his sleep. Nor did the rain—sometimes warm, sometimes icy, always stinging in its ferocity—draw the boy from the nightmare that gripped him. Some of the men tossed buckets over the side and hauled them back brimming with seawater, with which they drenched Tuck, already soaked to the skin by the driving rain, without even getting a flicker from his eyelids.

The murmurs of superstitious dread became louder, with words like "Jonah," "jinx," and "bewitched" thrown around loosely. With those words, fear spread among the sailors, who were by their nature credulous and illogical. All too soon, they would take some action that they would regret, if Hook did not stop them.

"Smee, we must rid ourselves of this accursed child before he is the death of us all!" Hook declared loudly, seeing the desperate looks on the faces of the crew.

"What, Cap'n? Just kill Tuck in his sleep?" Smee asked, mistakenly thinking his captain was as frightened as the common hands.

Smee would never stand for such a thing, even if Captain Hook would consider it. There were few even in that crew of pirates and murderers who would allow harm to come to the boy under normal circumstances, but that storm was far from normal. There was no telling what a mob of frightened sailors might do if their captain did not lead them along a saner path, so lead them he must.

It would be bad form to do anything less than find a way to save both his ship and Tuck. That was what James Hook told himself, refusing to examine his own feelings for the boy. To be a feared pirate captain, he could have no soft feelings—none at all, at any time. He had to be as hard and cold as the flint in his pistols, as cruel as the rough iron of his hook. He could have no friends and feel no friendship, not even for someone so likeable as the ship's boy.

That is what he told himself.

"Barrels, Smee. Get all the empty barrels we have," Captain Hook exclaimed, inspiration suddenly coming to him when he needed it the most. "Get them sealed and lashed to the gig … no, make that the longboat; it is already in the water. Quickly now, all hands! Make it unsinkable, and tie Tuck in safe and snug so that he won't be tossed out in his sleep, with plenty of food and water for when he awakes!"

The bosun stepped back, horror writ large on his face.

"Put him over the side in a blow like this, Cap'n? And him unconscious and all?"

"This is his best chance, Smee, and ours as well!"

Lightning forked and lit blackness sprinkled with stars that seemed too close. Wind blew into that void with redoubled fury, and the waves were stripped into ribbons of foam that flew into the blackness and froze into gems of ice. The brig lurched sideways, swinging into the star-speckled blackness, which mercifully vanished as the flare of lightning died. The *Jolly Roger* heeled over to her original course with a yard of her bowsprit vanished with the void; they had been that close to falling into it.

"You see, bosun? Did you see? We must have that boy off this ship before something like that or even worse opens in our path! Hurry, man, hurry!"

Smee hurried, and a dozen other of the crew hurried with him. Barrels were swiftly dragged up, sealed with pitch, and lowered over the side into the longboat. Other men shoved some barrels under the thwarts and tied them in place, lashing other barrels to the side of the boat until it would have been difficult for the largest wave to tip the boat and impossible for it to be sunk.

Captain Hook lifted the sleeping Tuck and lowered him down to Smee and Dusk, who placed him on a bundle of sailcloth as gently as a pair of nursemaids laying a babe down to sleep. Quick and sure, they lashed the boy to the bottom of the longboat so that no wave could throw him out, the boy's head pillowed on a hamper of sausages and cheese that LaSalle had provided for his breakfast.

The bosun left the longboat last, casting another anxious

glance at the sleeping boy before scrambling up on deck. Rather than ordering the rope cut, Captain Hook dropped down into the boat to check the work his men had done.

"Dunderheads!" he muttered under his breath, seeing that the knots in the ropes that held Tuck safe also made him a prisoner, for they were all beyond his reach. "They all saw Red Michael toss Tuck's knives over the side—"

A thought came to James suddenly. For a moment, he wrestled with it, forcing it into a shape that he could accept as the proper duty of a pirate captain rather than a gesture of friendship from one person to another.

"One of the last things that cur Red Michael did as captain was steal from one of the crew," he said to himself, thinking of those blades that Conner had thrown overboard to wound Tuck's feelings. "Since I am captain now in his stead, it is my duty to make right the wrong he did."

Only a proper duty, and not feelings of friendship prompted Captain Hook to draw out his sheathed dagger and slip it under Tuck's belt where he could find it upon waking. That fine blade of Toledo steel was worth more than the pair of blades Red Michael had given to the sea, but the cost meant nothing to Hook. Tuck had his blade again, a gesture that was fitting and right.

The new captain of the *Jolly Roger* did not have time to give the lad his share from the treasure they had taken. With the storm around them still increasing in ferocity, that blade would have to suffice until such time as they crossed paths again.

"There, Tuck. A knife, as I promised you," James said softly, placing the boy's hand on the hilt of the weapon.

"Neverland," Tuck breathed, relief evident in every syllable as his hand closed tight around the grip of long blade.

The word was so softly spoken in slumber that Hook only recognized it from seeing Tuck's lips move. An emotion started to form in the chest of James Hook, pirate captain. By force of will, he quickly stifled that feeling before it grew strong enough to be named. What he had done was a duty that was owed, a promise that had to be kept, and proper good form, and there was nothing beyond that in his actions.

That is what he told himself.

As the captain swung up the rope to the deck, forked lightning flared and flared again, striking all around them. Flickering visions of a dozen different strange vistas appeared and disappeared on all sides of the brig as she plowed through massive waves, driven by an increasing wind that threatened to split canvas or pluck the masts right out of the deck.

There was no time for another order. Hook clawed out his rapier with one hand, clutching tight to the rope with the other. A single swipe of that razor-edged blade parted the line holding the longboat, and that boat, with the sleeping Tuck roped safely aboard, rapidly fell behind the *Jolly Roger*.

Lightning flared so brightly that James could see his bones in the hand that held the rapier. The ship was bathed in light brighter than the sun, blue-white and burning. The *Jolly Roger* dropped suddenly, the longboat fading like mist under the morning sun. Tuck was gone, somewhere else in an instant, some strange distant point on the globe. At least, Hook hoped the boy was still on the world he knew. What he had seen in those flickering frames of lightning made him unsure of what lurked beyond.

"Fair winds and following seas, Tuck," he murmured under his breath.

Just one shipmate saying fare-thee-well to another. The common politeness on parting and no other significance than that.

That is what he told himself.

Chapter 12

Cannibal Cove

After Tuck vanished—or perhaps the *Jolly Roger* vanished from the waters where Tuck had been cast adrift—the storm passed quickly, as those nightmare storms were wont to do. James, safe again on the deck of the brig—*his* brig now, with Red Michael gone—considered that his actions might have been too hasty, for all that they had seemed warranted just a few minutes ago.

Well, if that were true, it was too late to change what had been done. As captain, he had to not only live with his decisions, he also had to carry on as if there was no question about the correctness of the orders he gave. To be the sort of captain he aspired to be, any private doubts he had would, of necessity, be firmly quashed within his own mind and never considered again.

It seemed that Smee looked at him with similar doubt in his eyes. The bosun was wise enough to refrain from broaching that subject, especially in front of the rest of the crew. Those cutthroats, at least, regarded their new captain as a hero, having saved them from the briny deep and the clutches of Davy Jones. Some voiced sorrow about Tuck, though many in terms of what a shame it was that the ship's boy turned out to be a Jonah.

"Er, Cap'n, I've had the men strike the sails and put out a sea anchor," Mr. Smee reported unnecessarily. "All hands accounted for, and no damage to the ship."

"Very good, Smee," James said, feeling suddenly weary. "Serve out a ration of grog to all the men, and see to the watch. Keep the lookout sharp, for there is no telling what waters we are in. Make certain that I am awake before the sun rises, I have a feeling that the new day will be a busy one for us all."

Smee had his faults and amusing quirks, but there was no denying that he knew his business. Men were called up for the watch, and the cups were filled with rum and water, mixed very strong as was the custom aboard the *Jolly Roger*. The captain took his own ration and toasted his men before going down to his cabin.

It was still his old cabin, for Red Michael had left behind such an infestation in the stern cabin that it was unusable. James had no interest in fighting the lice and fleas for a good night's sleep, such of the night as there was left. His familiar old bunk would be enough for at least one more night. Hook went to untroubled repose, confident that the bosun would have him awakened if anything untoward occurred during the night.

As he slept, he experienced his old familiar dream again, the star in his dream gleaming brighter and closer than ever before. It almost seemed within his grasp.

Skylights stumbled into the darkened cabin while James was still asleep, the candle in his hand giving insufficient light for the old pirate to find his way without making too much noise.

"Mr. Smee, he says that the sun'll be comin' up soon, Cap'n. Said ye wanted to know," the old pirate mumbled around his few remaining teeth.

Without waiting a reply from his captain, Skylights turned, stumbled, and splashed melted wax on the floor as he left. Hook sat up, a feeling of dislike for the ancient buccaneer washing over him. Someday, he promised himself, glancing at the cruel iron tool that he took his name from—someday.

James stood, stepped in the wax, and slipped back, falling on his bunk. Smee bustled in at that moment, tsk-tsking under his breath.

"Near to dawn, Jas. No time to be lounging in bed, even if you are the captain. A busy day ahead, just as you said. There is something out there, an island I think from the strange smell of the breeze."

There was something strange about the odor on the predawn wind. It was redolent with green growing things in unhealthy abundance. There was also a scent that hinted of exotic animals of many types, more than even the most educated nose could possibly identify. Added in was something that might almost be called the aroma of youth, for it put every man aboard the *Jolly Roger* in mind of his childhood days—a mixture of the smell of worms brought to the surface by summer rain, stolen cake, and damp caves, with a faint hint of fireworks. That unsettling odor called up memories that the men of the *Jolly Roger* had not visited in many long and hard years.

For Hook, the memories were of his brothers and the punishment he always received for their antics. They were the sort of memories to inflame anger in a man like James Hook, recollections that would drive him to deeds so great and terrible that the entire world would shudder at the mere mention of his name.

Other members of the crew, Smee included, seemed to recall events that turned their spines to jelly and their bowels to water. They sweated with a stink of fear, jumped at the slightest unexpected noise, and growled at one another like so many curs crowded together in a trap. That aroma of youth, to them, was the stench of danger, the odor of a threat that they could not understand and feared all the more because it was undefined.

The eastern sky lost the velvety blackness of night, revealing the coming of the sun. With that fading of darkness, a black bulk was revealed, a dark silhouette to the north of their position. At first just a shapeless mass, it slowly resolved into hills, cliffs, and mountains as the eastern sky blushed with the approach of dawn. Orange and yellow overtook the crimson and pink, bringing details of forest, beach, meadow, and jungle to the island. The mountains seemed to quiver and shift until the first rays of the morning sun brought them into sharp focus.

It was an island, though one with strange contrasts: mountains shooting up suddenly, forest and jungle in intermingled patches without rhyme or reason. James could see with his naked eyes two different rivers running from two different lakes, one river meandering from the east to the west, while a second river flowed east from that lake and found its end in the lake where the first river started. It appeared that a noisome swamp was bordered by dry desolation that in turn was framed on the far side by lush, flowering underbrush that spoke eloquently of plentiful water.

"Neverland."

The word was not spoken by Captain Hook, nor was it uttered by Mr. Smee, the two who had heard it from the lips of Tuck while he was in the throes of his nightmares. Instead, it came from Noodler, who spoke that name with a fear-filled awe, as if the syllables had forced their way past his rotting teeth against his will.

Cecco, Dusk, and Jukes echoed that name with whispered trepidation, while others among the crew crossed themselves or made various signs to ward off evil—strange actions from a crew of murderers, thieves, and cutthroats who would cheerfully rob widows of their last copper coin and keelhaul orphans for the sport it might provide.

Such a display of cowardice could not help but annoy James, who feared only one thing in all the world and acknowledged to himself that even that fear was irrational. He had made himself the captain of that vessel to have a band of bold buccaneers at his command, to make him the most feared pirate ever to sail the seas. He had no use for a mob of cringing curs, such as the men appeared all of a sudden to be.

There was naught to be seen to cause such fear as they showed.

It was, after all, just one more island, and men like the brigands that made up the crew of the *Jolly Roger* were well familiar with islands, having either raided them or hidden on them as circumstances required many times in their colorful careers.

With the crew so nervous and snappish, it would have been a poor timing for a new captain to show disdain for his men, no matter how much they deserved his scorn. Instead, Hook decided that his best course would be to ignore the unexplained fear his men were showing. So long as they did their duty and did not balk, he would give no sign of noticing their cowardice.

He put his spyglass to his eye and studied the cliffs on the western side of the island. Smoke rose there in two or three thin streams, separate but close together. Campfires perhaps. The location looked ideally defensible, with the steep cliffs protecting the plateau from the west and south. The distant look of the hills beyond gave Hook cause to think that there were cliffs or steep ground on the north side as well, leaving only one direction of approach.

"I see signs of habitation up there," he remarked. "Smoke from fires and what seem to be the roofs of huts of some kind. We will have to wait to see if they are natives or castaways, friendly or otherwise."

"Aye, a dangerous place, this be," Bill Jukes said nervously, eyeing the distant cliffs. "Red savages live there, I wager, and not friendly to our sort."

"How do you know that?"

The tattoo-covered pirate did not seem to hear his captain's query.

Hook did not press the issue, thinking that Jukes had merely expressed an illogical fear of the sort that all the men seemed to be prone to in those waters. His next words merely directed Smee to bring the brig closer to the island. The bosun knew his work well enough to post a double lookout, for they had no knowledge of what might lurk beneath the calm blue of the ocean surrounding the strange island.

"Mr. Smee, I see what looks to be a bay there ahead. Make for that under light sail. Have a man make soundings as we approach."

Hook studied the calm waters of the inlet. There were some creatures sporting in the water, diving and breaking the surface as if engaged in games. Others of the distant creatures lounged on the rocks, catching the early morning sun. As the *Jolly Roger* drew closer, those swimming things became clearer through the spyglass, showing long tails that ended in graceful flukes, torsos with arms rather than fins, and heads covered in long hair—red, black, brown, and golden yellow. James stared harder through his glass. If he did not know that such things were a complete impossibility, he would have sworn that they were …

"Reef ahead, Mr. Smee!" the lookout cried from aloft.

"Shallow water," was the call from the man with the lead line.

"Steer sharp to starboard, Mr. Murphy," Captain Hook said distractedly, thinking on the impossibility he had seen, something that had to be a trick of the early morning light. "Take in sail, Mr. Smee. I want to study this lagoon for a bit."

"Not a healthy place for men like us, Cap'n," Smee said nervously, squinting toward the creatures that now were watching them. "Mermaids there, and they are not friendly to sailormen, you know."

"No, Smee. I do not know anything about such myths," Hook replied coldly.

What he had seemed to see could not be a reality. There had to be some other explanation for the appearance of female forms with bright, shining hair; long, fishlike tails; delicate shoulders and arms; and round, firm … No, they could not possibly be *mermaids*!

"Odds bobs, hammer and tongs!" James whispered to himself, finally accepting that the impossible was real, at least in that place.

"I knows all about them things," Skylights volunteered to the captain. "Ain't seen 'em often, but they is always trouble and grief fer sailormen like us when they's about. Sweet seemin' they are, and delightful to the eye, but when they offers kisses, there be naught but drownin' and death and a watery grave fer any swab foolish enough to embrace 'em. And most men be that foolish, once they hears the voice of a mermaid. Sweet their song, but deadly, muddlin' the sense of a man 'til he don't know what danger it is to trade a kiss or two with them beautiful devils from deep below."

Skylights looked toward the lagoon with a mixture of longing and loathing on his leathery old face.

"This here be the worst place in all the world to run afoul of mermaids, fer a man don't think right here, 'cause this ain't no place fer men to be droppin' anchor. Neverland ain't no place fer *men* at all."

"How do you know that?" the captain asked with some irritation.

As before, the question seemed to go unheard. Once again, James Hook decided against pressing the matter at that time.

"Smee, we cannot land here with these reefs," Hook said to the bosun. "Make sail, head eastward, and we will see if a safe harbor can be found.

"Aye, Cap'n, as you say," said Smee smartly. And then, with a slight hesitation, he added, "But it might be better if we put this place behind us Cap'n. I … er, the men are not comfortable here, you see."

"No, Mr. Smee. This island intrigues me. It is my decision that we need to explore first. It might well be that this would be an ideal place for the *Jolly Roger* to anchor between voyages. Tortuga to sell our booty and spend our gold. The Spanish Main, the East Indies, the ships of the world to loot and plunder, but here, here in this Neverland, we can rest and plot my, er, *our* future."

James Hook looked at the distant cliffs where Jukes claimed

that red savages had their encampment. He looked at the lagoon where mermaids—yes, he had to admit to himself that they were real and that they were, in fact, mermaids—swam in the water and sunned on the rocks. He glanced ahead, where an arm of the island thrust out to the south, thick with dark jungle.

There was something strange beyond reason about this island, this Neverland. The crew seemed to know it without knowing how. Tuck had spoken the name as if it were a refuge of hope and happiness when he was tormented by his extraordinary nightmares. Even Hook felt there was something about that place beyond the normal and rational world, though he could not, as yet, put a name to what placed the island of Neverland outside the rules of the world he knew.

Beyond that thick stand of jungle was another inlet, two-thirds of a nearly perfect circle that showed the blue of deep water almost to the shore. The lookout atop the mast and the lookout at the bow both indicated clear water and safe passage. Under the command of Hook, Smee brought the brig in slowly and finally had the sail furled and the anchor let go. For a few minutes, all hands on duty secured the ship and made her ready to remain at anchor for so long as Captain Hook thought wise.

"Golden beaches and lush foliage, Mr. Smee. The waters look to teem with fish and the jungle holds fresh fruit that I can see from here. I think we can go ashore and reconnoiter from here in safety, Bosun."

From among the men on deck, a giant figure stepped forward, a worried look in his yellowish eyes.

"No, Cap'n. We not go ashore here," Dusk said in his broken English. "Much bad place. Cannibals, very many. They watch us, wait for us. They have cookpots on the fire, all for us."

Hook looked at the massive African in surprise. Not only because the normally silent giant just spoke more words than he had heard from him since he had come aboard the brig, but because those words seemed tinged with fear. Dusk never showed fear. Hook was not certain that Dusk completely understood the concept of fear. The murderous black recognized that emotion in others, usually just before he did something ugly and fatal to them. He did not have such a weakness in himself at all, or so Captain Hook had thought until that moment.

"I see nothing," the self-made captain of the *Jolly Roger* said, scanning the shoreline again with his spyglass.

"Lookee there, where t'ree palms make arch. Lookee close there. See poles? See skulls?"

The distance was too great to be able to see such things as Dusk described with the naked eye. The massive African could not possibly see what he claimed was in that arch of palms. James trained his spyglass at the point Dusk indicated, straining his eyes.

In the shadows of the palms, he could just make out a dozen or so straight, thin shafts, each about the height of a man, and atop each of those shafts, round, yellowish objects roughly the size of a small melon—or the size of a human skull, he thought with a sick feeling, seeing the regular spacing of two small dark ovals above a triangular splotch of darkness on each on the distant objects.

Skulls they might be, at that. Still, he could not let the crew dictate their course to him. That might be the way some pirate ships were run, with a consensus arrived at before every sail was hoisted. It had not been that way aboard the *Jolly Roger* under Red Michael Conner; it had not been that way under the captains before that tub of rancid lard took command; and it certainly was not going to be that way so long as James Hook was captain of the brigantine.

"Put a boat in the water, Mr. Smee," Hook said coolly. "Pick me ten good men. We shall explore here a bit, to see if there is aught to be concerned about."

"Are you sure, Cap'n?" Smee asked hesitantly. "This is no healthy place for the likes of us, of that I am certain."

"How do you—" Hook started to ask, only to have others of the crew voice warnings of their own.

"Packs of hungry wolves in the forests," Noodler said with a shudder. "Their eyes glow red in the darkness when they hunt you!"

"Lions in the jungles," quavered Ed Teyne. "They hides in the bushes and springs when you don't expect them!"

"Cannibals," Dusk repeated, his eyes round and wild.

"Bears!"

"Pygmies!"

"Tigers!"

"Headhunters!"

"Crocodiles!"

James shuddered at that last word himself, a strange tingle of foreboding striking at his heart.

"Worst ees the ol' Gypsy woman," Cecco avowed. "She knowsa too much. She tells you future—always bad, always right. Alla rest, I not fear like meeting her, si!"

"How do you know all that?" Hook roared loudly enough to silence the rest of the crew.

There was a moment of perfect silence aboard the *Jolly Roger*.

"When I was a younker—"

"There were these dreams I had when—"

"I remember when I would wake up—"

"This was the island—"

"But when I were little, we always won—"

Every man seemed determined to answer the question the captain had asked, all at the exact same moment. James could only understand a snatch of words here and there among the babble of every hand talking at the same time.

"SHUT IT!"

A stunned silence fell. Not merely because their captain demanded it. The manner in which he had roared that order, so crude and direct, came as a surprise to every man among the crew.

James Hook had always shown himself to be a man of education and proper manners, for all that he was also a pirate through and through and never scrupled over getting his hands wet with blood. It took much to reduce him to that angry shout, and every man jack of them understood that and feared to further anger their captain.

Like one of the masters at his school, Hook pointed to first one man and then another, indicating that he should speak. Rather than the rod used by a master, the captain used his rough iron hook, the threat of discipline implied being far more terrible than that of the rod in the hands of one master who had always been quick to strike the lad who failed his recital of lessons.

From their words, Hook slowly built an understanding of what inspired this common fear among the men of the *Jolly Roger*. It was as simple and as unfathomable as the most common of things: dreams.

Or rather, the memory of dreams. The dreams they had had as children, the innocent dreams of hunting, horror, and bloodshed so common to most boys, or so James had come to believe.

For himself, he seldom dreamed, and never of aught save one thing—the scintillating star that he was desperate to find. To be certain, he had never dreamed as other boys did when he had been younger, though his brothers had oft spoken of their own nighttime adventures, striking out to strange lands once they had been tucked into bed with the candle blown out.

Their mother had seemed vaguely troubled that her dark young son never had dreams to confess to her, while the fair-haired boys were full of tales of adventure and danger that had occurred while tucked safely in their beds.

Mr. Smee and Mr. Starkey and Dusk and Cecco and all the others confessed to having just such dreams in their memories. There was little of those dreams that they recalled, save for moments that were terrible to them as men grown, though each of them confessed to having enjoyed the danger as a dreaming boy.

Wolves and crocodiles, bloodthirsty red savages and crafty little cannibals, mermaids and fairy folk, all things a man had the wit to fear and a boy would delight to meet and match wit and cunning against without thought of danger.

Aye, and that was the rub of it: the men were wise enough to understand the danger, where the boys they had once been only saw the adventure. That knowledge brought with it fear of what they were certain prowled and waited on the island, this Neverland.

Hook would have liked to deny all he learned, would have much preferred to believe that it was all coincidence and happenstance, that sections of the island merely reminded his men of those boyhood dreams. Except there were the mermaids, which old Skylights feared, and which could not possibly be real elsewhere in the world. And there were the strange murmurings of Tuck when in his nightmares, naming the same beasts and dangers the crew recalled from their own boyhood days.

There was no denying the strangeness of Neverland and no wisdom in trying to ignore the possibilities of danger. The thing that needed doing, as Hook saw it, was to investigate the truth of what the men believed, and they could easily do that from the cove where the ship was anchored. A well-armed party ashore could search the jungle, with muskets and cannons to provide covering fire from the *Jolly Roger* if the need arose.

"Mr. Smee, chose ten good men and have them man a boat," James Hook ordered. "Mr. Trommler, run out the guns on the port side: three loaded with double canister, the others with double round-shot. Pick the best men with muskets, and have them stand by with loaded weapons, three muskets to the man. Confer with Smee if there is a conflict between the men you want and those he wants."

"Aye, aye, Cap'n," said Smee.

Dieter gave a laconic "Ja" to show he understood.

The bosun caught Hook's eye and tilted his head toward

Dusk. The captain responded with the slightest shake of his head to say no and then looked over at the gun captain and gave a slight nod toward the gigantic African.

"You, Dusk, you vill help mit the gunz," Dietz said brusquely.

Whatever Dusk knew or thought he remembered, he would be useless because of fear in that thick undergrowth. Better to have men who were just nervous and fearful than a man unstrung by panic. Nervous men might fire at shadows whereas one infected with panic might spread that disease to others and doom them all when simple determination and courage could win the day.

"Smee, see to it that every man ashore has at least four pistols loaded and ready. And do we have any grenades aboard?

"Four pistols to a man. Aye, Cap'n. And we took a box full of iron casings from a Frenchy about a year back. They are down in the power room, just waiting to be filled and fused."

"I think a dozen shall suffice, Mr. Smee. You and a few others of the men have your pipes with you and lit."

Come to that, Hook himself would have one of his dwindling supply of cigarros lit and in his mouth, with a few more stashed in the pocket of his coat. If there proved a need to use those iron spheres filled with gunpowder, there would be no fumbling with flint and steel to make fire for the fuses. Nor would any of the men be burdened with a burning slow match. The embers from a pipe or the glowing end of his cigarro would be enough to light the fresh length of fuse stuffed in the small opening of the grenades.

The men assembled under Smee's command, each with a brace of pistols shoved into his belt. Some had the extra pair on a bit of twine or ribbon around their necks while others stuffed their second brace of pistols into the pockets of ragged vests or tied them loosely to their sashes with a bit of cord. Hook himself had a pair of fine French dueling pistols in his belt and a second pair every bit as fine holstered in the ends of a stole slung over his shoulder. Smee, of course, had his friend Little Timmy Thunder as well as Big Tommy Thunder and another pair of matched flintlocks that he called The Thunder Twins all in a row in his belt, loaded, primed, and set on half-cock.

"Carry on, Mr. Smee," Hook commanded.

The bosun ordered the boat over the side. Once it was afloat, he directed Cecco, Jukes, Edgar, Jacob, Noodler, and the others of the landing party into the boat, following after them. As was fitting for his new position, Captain Hook clambered last into the boat, appointing Ed Teyne to command the *Jolly Roger* until his return.

It was only a matter of a few dozen yards to the beach. As the bow of the boat drove up onto the sand, James braced himself. Last to leave the ship, first ashore into danger—that was the privilege and duty of a captain, even a pirate captain. Not that Hook simply stepped onto the sand. A pistol was in one hand, and the other hand held ready to grasp sword or a second pistol, if the need for either arose, as he leaped from the boat onto the golden sand of the beach.

The jungle remained silent save for the calls of birds and the mocking cries of unseen monkeys. Smee and the others came ashore after their captain, with the bosun detailing Smitty and Jeffries to remain with the boat. Those two sailors, one thin to the point of gauntness, the other rotund with heavy, hairy jowls, stood with pistols in their hands, nervously watching the thick greenery a few yards away, while the captain, bosun, and eight of their mates tramped over to the collection of bamboo poles standing on either side of the trail leading into the gloom of the jungle, under an arch formed by three palm trees.

When the anatomist William Cheselden had lectured at the school James was attending, in the years before Cheselden had reached the full flower of his fame, the young man had been in the forefront of the pupils attending. He had closely studied the specimens brought by Cheselden to support that lecture, placing each one on a special shelf in the vast library that was his memory. Hook knew a human skull when he saw one, even one as malformed as those specimens, which had been set on bamboo poles as a warning to trespassers.

Those grisly totems were small in size, falsely suggesting that they had come from children. While not as learned as Dr. Cheselden on the subject, James had remembered enough of that long-ago lecture to recognize those skulls as belonging to adults by the state of the sutures visible to him. The lower jaw in each case was missing, but the teeth still remaining had all been filed to sharp points. The wear on those needlelike teeth suggested that they had seen much use after the dentition had been altered into predatory fangs.

"Come men, naught here but old bones and wood. Nothing to fear," Hook remarked with quiet confidence over his shoulder. "We shall follow this trail and see where it leads. Be silent, for we might find …"

Their captain nodded his head toward the nearest of the poles and its grisly burden. What they might find was obvious to all of them. The men with him needed no further urging to continue their march with all the stealth available to them. Dusk had spoken fearfully of cannibals. Those sun-bleached skulls gave graphic hints of the same terrible beings. It would be best, if such creatures were lurking about, that the men from the *Jolly Roger* saw the cannibals before the cannibals saw or heard them.

James Hook led the way, as was fitting for a captain. In one hand, he still held a pistol, the lock at half-cock. In the other, his rapier was in a firm grip, the ring that had been a recent addition to his right hand glinting and grinning wickedly when a stray shaft of sunlight touched it. James knew how to walk soft and silent, an accomplishment he had learned when he was smaller. It was a talent that had stood him in good stead, and he made the fullest use of it along that twisting jungle trail.

Creepers, lianas, and hanging moss made a tangled rigging on both sides of the narrow trail. Spike-leaf bushes, monstrous toadstools, and ferns fought for every scrap of ground that did not have a tree already growing on it. It was like traveling down a dimly green-lit tunnel that twisted and turned through the thickly overgrown jungle.

After several minutes, a bright glow appeared around the next bend. It was sunlight, unfiltered by a thick canopy of leaves and vines. James slowed his pace, not eager to stumble into the view of hostile eyes. A cautious peek around the bend showed that the jungle opened into a wide clearing. There were dozens of mud and branch structures in the clearing, the rudest sorts of huts, home to a cannibal tribe. The members of the tribe were gathered in a throng toward the center of their village.

They obviously lived a nasty, brutish life. Hook could see no garments on any of them save for loincloths cut from the hide of crocodiles. Each and every man, woman, and child, was coated with dried mud the same pale gray color as that which had been used to plaster their cone-shaped huts. There were weapons aplenty, bamboo spears tipped with stone points, wooden paddles of a shape and size like that of a cricket bat that had been edged with the teeth of sharks, and small, stone-headed clubs that hung from a thong at nearly every waist.

There was only one object of metal to be seen anywhere in the village, and that was the huge iron cauldron that was centrally located among the huts. Where such an artifact had come from was beyond even the imagination of James Hook. A fire burned under that bubbling vat, fed by a wizen, wrinkled form that James took to be the village cook. Besides adding wood to the fire, that repulsive figure sometimes threw handfuls of herbs into the unspeakable broth that simmered in the cauldron or sampled the noxious brew with a long-handled wooden spoon.

Only one man wore more than a coat of grayish mud and a loincloth. He was a grotesquely rotund figure that surpassed even the late Red Michael Conner in blubbery girth. This would be the chief, Hook reasoned, marked both by the rolls of fat that hung down from the massive belly and by the headdress of skulls and bones that hid everything of his head except for beady eyes, a bulbous nose, and thick, drooping lips.

From chieftain to chef, and all those in between, they were as unpleasant a gathering of degenerate humanity as James Hook had ever imaged. While having no fear of those creatures, the captain of the *Jolly Roger* could see no reason to risk the loss of any of his men in an unprofitable battle between corsairs and cannibals.

When Captain Hook turned to give the whispered order to return to the ship as quietly as they had arrived, he was confronted with a curious sight. Mr. Smee was peering through his spectacles at a pair of miniature gray figures, like crude statues formed of dried mud. They were children of the tribe, one with an armload of firewood, the other with a cleaned turtle shell used as a basket, brimming with wild herbs.

In appearance, they were much alike: The same small, misshapen head on sloping shoulders; the same ungainly long arms and spindly, stunted legs; the same large, yellowish eyes, set too far apart to be wholly human. They both wore no more than their coat of dried mud, clumped thickly about the loins. One, if James were to guess, was a boy and the other a girl, brother and sister most likely. They were the most unlovely looking children Hook had ever seen.

Smee slowly smiled at the pair of gargoyle children. After staring at the bosun blankly for a long moment, they smiled back, baring needlelike fangs. The boy dropped his load of firewood suddenly and snatched at Smee's arm, intent on sampling Irish bosun raw. That proved the savagery of those people, for one should never eat an Irishman without cooking him first. Even more uncouth, the cannibal child was willing to take a piece of Smee unwashed, displaying a complete lack on any civilized values at all.

While the boy, if boy he was, showed his savage hunger, the girl, if indeed that creature was female, sprang away, still holding tight to the woven vines that formed the handle for her turtle shell basket and shrieking at a high note that was at the very edge of human hearing.

James grabbed a handful of mud-crusted hair and pulled the boy sharply back as Smee shook free of the grip of those small hands.

"Back to the ship men, and step lively," Hook snapped. "Smee, keep your eyes open for the parents of this ugly imp!"

Captain Hook threw the cannibal boy aside with no more brutality than the act required. The creature landed gracelessly, yet still scrambled to his feet and was gone into the underbrush in a flash. Hook took only a moment to slip the rapier into its scabbard and draw a second pistol. He was at the heels of his bo-sun an instant later, casting glances to the right and left as he ran.

They could hear the shouts of cannibals behind them in hungry pursuit. James cast a glance over his shoulder to see the gargantuan chief bobbing and quivering at the head of a score of his warriors, making surprising speed despite his greasy bulk. A step and spin, and Hook brought up one pistol and fired, another spin and step bringing him just a pace behind Mr. Smee.

That pistol ball had passed closely over the head of the chief, shattering his headdress of bones and skulls. If it had not been for the fact that he had such a low brow, it would have been his skull rather than his headdress that was shattered.

The king of the cannibals might not have understood what a pistol was, but he appreciated the danger that had missed him by so narrow a margin and dropped down to let his warriors pass into the danger zone. What he had not considered was the cloud of dust and bone fragments that blinded the three men directly behind him. Those three went down in a heap atop their leader, with more warriors stumbling and falling over the blockage until the trail was plugged from side to side with cannibals trying to regain their footing. The pirates continued to run, unmindful of the confusion behind them.

It had seemed that the jungle on either side of the trail was completely impassible, making the path they followed the only way to reach the beach. As the pirates fled back to their boat, James saw that such an assumption was erroneous. The apparently impassable tangles of vines actually supported crude pathways of branches that would allow the swiftest of the mud-covered warriors to arrive at the beach ahead of them. With his quick wit and keen eye, Hook also saw a way to delay the cannibals.

It was difficult to spare even a moment in that life-and-death race, but James Hook forced himself to stand and take careful aim, firing his second flintlock at a knot of lianas that supported a long stretch of the wooden path above the jungle floor.

The lead ball, as big around as the end of Hook's thumb, struck that knot and severed it, dumping the branches of the path and a dozen screaming cannibals into a thorny thicket.

"Oh, you vicious cannibals, you fell for that false trail once too often." The words that James had once heard Tuck utter in his sleep came back to him almost as if the ship's boy was at his side.

Without conscious thought, the captain of the *Jolly Roger* muttered a similar phrase, as if compelled to echo words that had been spoken before, perhaps many times.

"You vicious cannibals, you fell for that trick," he said, fighting down the odd impulse to crow in triumph.

Chapter 13

Tangles, Trails, and Mysteries

The return to the *Jolly Roger* had been accomplished without injury to any of the crew. Captain Hook and Mr. Smee had been obliged to fire off their remaining pistols to discourage the ravenous cannibals. Puffing furiously on his cigarro until the end glowed brightly, James had lit the fuse on one of the iron grenades Smee carried in his pockets. The bosun tossed the powder-filled sphere as far as he could back along the trail they had just left, and it rolled almost to the feet of the warriors chasing after them.

Perhaps they had learned caution from their chief's loss of his bony crown, for the mud-covered warriors fell all over themselves in retreating as the sputtering fuse disappeared into the opening of the iron ball. The explosion that followed peppered the jungle with sharp iron fragments, though only a few struck any of the cannibals, leaving bloody streaks on the gray mud that covered them.

As was proper, James Hook was the last man into the boat, seating himself without concern and then deftly plucking a pistol from the belts Cecco and Hannover. As the men bent over the oars with a will, he calmly fired first one flintlock and then the other to keep the savages cowering within the cover of the jungle.

The boat had covered perhaps two-thirds of the distance back to the ship when the cannibals regained their courage. With their chief shouting orders from a spot safely to the rear, the warriors charged screaming after the longboat, running into the sea up to their thighs in futile pursuit. Dietz fired off one of the guns at the shouted command of Hook, placing the pair of cannon balls to raise fountains of water just ahead of the screaming cannibals.

Neverland was such a strange place that Captain Hook decided his best course was to refrain from making permanent enemies on the island until he knew the lay of the ground better. With that thought in mind, he had called for the gunner to merely frighten the savages howling for their blood rather than to slaughter them.

The thunder and smoke from the gun, as well as the seawater that rained down on them, gave the cannibals reason in earnest to scream. Filled with fear, they turned and fought their way back to the beach. Once there, they proceeded to hurl indecipherable epitaphs in their uncouth language until they noticed that the ocean had cleansed their lower bodies of all traces of mud.

As if they had suddenly found themselves collectively in church without their breeches, the entire crew of savages fled back into the jungle with every show of embarrassment and confusion. There was a show of surprisingly pale legs and rumps as they scampered out of sight. There was also a display of a crude and primitive sense of offended decorum that James Hook was surprised to see in such a debased, primitive people. It was, furthermore, something that he would keep in mind when next he faced the warriors of the cannibal tribe.

There was naught to do but haul up the anchor and sail further along the coast of the island. There proved to be another bay after the coast of Neverland curved to the north, again deep enough to safely anchor the *Jolly Roger* a safe distance from the shore.

"Here, Cap'n. Did you see that rock off to the east?" Smee asked while Hook was examining the forested shore through his spyglass.

"Hmmm? What is that, Smee? Where away?"

"There, Cap'n. Two point south of east."

James went to the other rail and trained his glass in the direction Smee had indicated. Aye, there was a rock out in that direction, a round dome rising higher than the masts of the ship, gray and grim without a speck of greenery anywhere about it. Nor was there any beach, just the dark granite rising from the sea. Hollows or caverns in the rock face gave it a spectral, skull-like appearance at that distance. Altogether an unwholesome looking place, the waters around it swirled as if the tide surged over hidden rocks.

"Nothing of interest in that direction, Mr. Smee," Hook said, dismissing the grim islet from his mind.

"Perhaps later then, Cap'n."

"Indeed, Smee. Once we know more about this island, we can explore such places as that Skull Rock."

Hook went back to studying the shore.

"Mr. Smee, have LaSalle gather up some foodstuffs for one man—rum, wine and water enough for three days."

"You sending someone ashore, Cap'n?"

"I shall be going ashore myself, Smee."

"Er, alone, Cap'n?" Smee asked, a slight quaver to his voice.

Hook had proven himself a good quartermaster and had the makings of a great pirate captain. He was, so far as the Irish bosun was concerned, a good friend as well. Oh, he was stiff and stand-offish, true enough. He wore his erudite aloofness like armor, fitted tight around him. It was his protection against the danger of letting others too close to him. For all that, Smee thought of James Hook as the closest thing to a friend he had among the crew of the *Jolly Roger* now that Tuck was gone. While he admired Hook's courage and education, Smee did not want to see harm befall his captain through his own fearlessness or his lack of understanding about what he did not believe to be real.

"Gather the crew, Mr. Smee."

When all the men of the *Jolly Roger* were on deck, their captain invited them to look around the bay and the forest along the shore.

"What memories have you of this place?" their captain asked of them. "What dangers lurk in those woods? What threats are there in these waters? What should a man ashore be prepared to meet?"

The crew looked at the shore and the forest beyond it. Some of them screwed up their faces, engaged in the heavy labor of searching the distant memories of their boyhood dreams

"I remember swimming in the warm waters of this bay," ventured one pirate hesitantly after a few minutes.

"The fish hereabouts tasted might good wrapped in seaweed and cooked over a driftwood fire," another said.

"Apples in the forest are always ripe and sweet."

"The squirrels would throw down nuts for us to eat."

"A hedge of thorns hides a lovely clearing of soft, sweet grass where I could rest safely in the warm sun."

"A spring with drinking water was cold and clear."

The general murmur was a compilation of happy memories, not at all like the last time the crew had dredged up memories of the island. James was surprised and pleased to hear not a single note of dread from all those who held that strange knowledge of Neverland left over from their boyhood days. It was only the handsome Italian who looked troubled and reluctant to speak.

"Well, Cecco, what of you?" Hook asked with a touch of suspicion. "Do you have such cheery memories of this bay and the land beyond it as well?"

"Ah, the land, she's *buono* for the boys that run wild, very much, si. Eet issa up in the hills you mebbe finda the *difficoltà*. Thatsa where I al'ays meet up with wit' *la vecchia zingara* atta her old wagon."

"And what, Cecco, is so fearsome about an old Gypsy woman?"

"Issa not her, but whatta she know. Whatta she mebbe tell you about you'self, whatta mebbe you become, alla you *futuro* that she speak of." The Italian crossed his thick arms and shivered, making the pieces of eight that dangled from his ears jingle faintly. "Whatta she tell me, I don' remember too much no more, but she frighten me verra much, thissa I do remember, si!"

That interested James far more than it frightened him. This Gypsy woman might have answers to explain Neverland. At that moment, answers were something that Captain Hook was willing to risk much for to have in his possession.

In less than half an hour, James was standing on the beach. Mr. Smee plied the oars of the small boat heading back for the brigantine. The final orders his captain had given him still rang in his head.

"Three days, Smee. I shall return by then or I likely shall not return at all. You and Mr. Teyne will be in charge until that time. If, by some mischance, I have not returned by the end of the third day, the pair of you must make your own choice: sail off or send a search party ashore. I will give no commands with regard to that. Keep a sharp watch, for this island has many secrets and, as well you know, many dangers."

Dangers, he says, Smee thought to himself. Yet he was going ashore alone. James was smart as the devil himself and had more courage than any man he could name. It was his common sense Smee wondered about.

Smee feared for his captain, despite Hook's intelligence and courage. All the more so since James seemed entirely lacking in memories of Neverland, though all the crew knew the land, even if they were loath to speak of those memories from childhood. Those long-lost years might almost have belonged to other men, so greatly removed was the crew of the *Jolly Roger* from such carefree and innocent days. It did not seem right or natural for a man like Hook to have such a gap in his knowledge—and quite dangerous too, all things considered.

James patted his gear as he strode into the woods without a glance behind him. Smee and Teyne would guard his ship and crew. He had no doubt about that at all. Smee was too loyal, and Teyne was too new to his post to think about betraying their new captain. There was not another man with the skill or force of personality to stand for captain among the crew, not yet at any rate. Nothing to worry about in that direction.

Nothing to be concerned with about the equipment he carried either. His rapier was at his hip. A brace of pistols were tucked under his belt, along with a flask of powder and a bag containing two dozen lead balls. His trusty and rusty iron hook hung at his other hip. There was a satchel slung over his shoulder containing biscuits, sausages wrapped in paper, a chunk of cheese, and a handful of dried fruit.

Unlike the jungle in the area that James had marked as Cannibal Cove on the chart he was making of Neverland, the forest around this inlet—tentatively penciled in as Buccaneer Bay—was open and offered many paths. Using the sun as his compass, Hook struck off on a northwest course, aiming for the hills that rose beyond the trees.

There were palm trees and other exotic growths mixed in with homey English oaks and apple trees full of ripe red fruit. Some of the bushes were familiar and filled with berries, while others displayed strange fruit, often guarded by wicked thorns. Like any experienced seaman, James harvested what he could of the fresh fruit offered by nature. Munching one apple, which he found to be sweet and tart and juicy, he stuffed several more into his satchel for later consumption. A handful of familiar berries were plucked from thorny vines and popped into his mouth between bites of apple, adding a more pronounced sweetness, while a single cautious experiment with one of the unfamiliar berries produced a cool bitterness that was also surprisingly refreshing.

The thickets of thorn bushes grew denser, crowding in on the path that James was following. He recalled that one of the crew—Cookson, perhaps—had mentioned a hedge of thorns—a place where, in his boyhood dreams, he had slept in safety amid the dangers and wonders of Neverland. It was hard for Hook to grasp the idea of sleeping in a dream, but Neverland had already expanded his notion of what was possible.

With the thought that there might be a hidden clearing close by, the lean pirate kept his gaze sharp, seeking any sign of an entrance to such a place. A good half-hour passed as he paced silently along the path before he saw a clue to such a hiding place.

A dark tunnel burrowed into the tall stand of thorny bushes to his left. Kneeling, he looked into the dark hole. There was a mat of fur within the tunnel, as if it had been lined with curry combs. A careful grasp retrieved a tangle of coarse brownish fur that was distinctly grizzled at the tips.

"A form of *Ursidae*, there can be no doubt," he muttered to himself. "One that I have no familiarity with, however."

The bears that used that hole could not have been very large, for the tunnel was too narrow for even a man of his lean build.

If, in fact, they *were* bears.

Hook saw the marks of many feet going in and out, for the most part too smudged to make out details. In one place, however, a paw had slipped sideways in damp earth, leaving a distinct print in mud under a twist of thorns where it had later dried undisturbed.

Looking closely, James saw good cause to doubt his first thought of small, furry bears. It was not the print of a paw at all, being narrow rather than rounded. Instead of the marks of claws, five indentations marked where five plump toes had slid in the mud, the inside toe larger than the others.

It appeared, in fact, much like the print Hook himself would have left in mud had he trod there unshod, save that it was only about half the length of the captain's own foot.

"The print of a boy," he said under his breath with some wonder.

The crew had spoken of visiting Neverland in their dreams as children. Some vision of this remote island had come to them in their sleep. Coupled with a desire to roam that land, Hook thought that, in reality, it had colored their youthful dreams. Yet here before him was physical evidence of a real and solid boy on Neverland. Given the profusion of smudged tracks, he was inclined to believe that there might have been a number of boys residing on Neverland. The shape of that clear footprint convinced him that the boy who had left that print was no debased cannibal urchin or wayward child from the red savages. His study of anatomy told him it was the foot of a highly evolved youth that left that mark in the mud.

A bit of dirty white in the thorny shadows caught his eye. James crouched down and reached further into the tunnel in the thicket, careful not to scratch himself on the thorns. When he withdrew his hand with the prize he sought, his reward was a tattered and grimy handkerchief, once fine linen, delicately embroidered along the edge and monogrammed with the initials D. J. K. in faded blue thread. It was further proof that children from a civilized location had reached Neverland, for no grown man would be so careless as to lose his handkerchief. That was something only a boy would do while playing and exploring such a place as Neverland.

A puzzle, a mystery, and a most bothersome enigma—James Hook could make nothing of such strange evidence. It annoyed his erudite and logical mind to discover evidence that mixed dreams and reality in the same place. There was also the matter of his vanity having been pricked, for virtually every member of the crew had known something of Neverland while he was completely ignorant of the place. Even young Tuck had spoken the word Neverland in his nightmares to indicate that he had knowledge of the island that Hook lacked.

He would find no answers tramping around in those woods. James tossed the frayed bit of linen into the thorny tunnel and resumed his march, leaving the forest behind a few hundred yards farther along. It was almost as if his desire to be done with the woods had brought them to an end. The rolling hills of the island rose before him, dotted here and there with massive old trees, for the most part, more of the familiar English oaks.

As he continued along, the captain of the *Jolly Roger* idly noticed a sight that would have been common in the land of his birth. So common, in fact, that he did not think of the strangeness to see it there until he was almost upon it.

It was simply a perfectly normal grave, or it would have been, if it had been in an English churchyard. As it was, the rounded gray marker and stone-outlined grave on that Neverland hillside seemed quite bizarre. James took a few steps closer until he could read the inscription.

Rather than a name, dates of birth and death, and a final sentiment about whoever lay beneath the sod in that lonely place, the weathered old marker bore a single strange sentence: "Don't worry, this will be perfectly safe." Nothing more than that, carved deep into the stone in fine lettering.

After thinking over that epitaph for a moment, James Hook smiled. It was far from a nice smile. Sinister was the best word for it, and even Hook knew it. Had Smee been with him, the Irish bosun would have been disturbed, even worried that his captain could smile in such a fashion.

That smile was the result of a thought Hook had. That weathered stone might mark the last resting place of the moldering bones of some adventuresome fool or it might merely be an ancient prank placed by someone with as twisted a sense of the humorous as James Hook. Whatever the truth—and James had neither the time nor the inclination to seek to learn if bones did indeed reside beneath the stone—the idea that the sentence on the grave marker was the last words of an unlucky and imprudent someone otherwise unknown tickled him no end.

Leaving that lonely grave behind, Hook continued on, crossing the first rise and descending into a shaded valley, a beautiful and strange vale, thick with flowers and budding trees, the air redolent with the mingled scents of a thousand varied blossoms. Though the sun still had an hour or more before touching the western horizon, higher hills cast long shadows on the valley, and fireflies already danced in the deeper areas of gloom.

Or were those fireflies? The thought that they danced came naturally to Hook, for it was a poetic metaphor to describe that mating instincts of insects that was in common usage. It seemed, however, that those patterns shown by the flying specks of light were too precise, that the flickering on and off was too perfectly timed, sometimes together and sometimes in counterpoint to each other, to merely be the prenuptial display of a luminescent form of *Coleoptera*.

Some of the tiny creatures near the edge of the darker shadows appeared to take notice of him, for their lights suddenly streaked away in all directions, some vanishing among the bushes below or the branches above. Others sped into the open, where the rays of the low sun banished their own feeble light, which made it hard even for Hook's sharp eyes to trace their paths through the air.

One in particular, rather than fleeing, flew right at his face, stopping at the last instant before darting aside, up, and over the stupefied pirate captain. What had appeared before his eyes in that very brief moment could not be possible but a trick of light and shadow.

Just as those shapes he had seen sporting in the water of Mermaid Lagoon could not have been mermaids, James chided himself. If he could no longer depend on his own keen senses, what in all the world could he depend on?

Those flitting lights were no variety of beetle. No type of in-sect at all, in fact. The creature that had paused so briefly before his eyes had been in the form of a female, a woman, for all that she was no more than perhaps two inches tall. A garment made from a leaf was only barely adequate for the demands of modesty and did nothing at all to hide a shape that would have been very desirable had the … the … *fairy* … been the size of a normal woman. The sound that followed after her was like tiny silver bells, though James understood words in that ringing, as well as laughter of a truly feminine nature.

She was calling to him, inviting him to join in some sort of game. There was promise in those chiming words, some form of companionship, a suggestion of a friendship that would bind them together for as long as they lived.

He turned and strode away, while the tinkling of tiny bells renewed behind him. Her entreaties were almost enough to make him turn. Only thoughts of his steadfast goal in life gave him the strength to put one foot ahead of the other as the tiny winged temptress chimed and wailed disconsolately behind him.

James hurried on, numbed by that latest revelation of Neverland. Red savages or cannibals were not wildly unexpected. But fairies? Mermaids? What else from the realm of myth and legend might be found on that strange, marvelous island?

He gave thought to the old Gypsy Cecco so feared. What else and *who* else?

The trail he chose out of the Vale of Fairies—that name was one he would remember for his map of the island—led through thickets of flowering bushes that had attracted hordes of brilliantly colored butterflies with wings larger than his hand. Stepping through the cloud of bright creatures was like stepping from an enchanted land back into the mundane world. The oaks and tall grass seemed dull compared to what lay behind him, and the stones poking up here and there seemed drab and gray. The common honeybees and dragonflies were just monotonous annoyances after the flowers, butterflies, and fairies of the magical valley.

Only his iron will kept James from looking back at the Vale of Fairies. His goal lay deeper in the island, higher among the hills. What was behind him would only add questions and distractions he did not need. The captain of the *Jolly Roger* marched on. Behind the cloud of butterflies, a tiny bell seemed to chime, low and mournful.

Up a slope and down another, only to climb the next, higher slope. The sun dropped lower in the west, casting longer shadows across the island. Somewhere among the trees already in the gloom of dusk, a wolf howled in anticipation of night, quickly joined by another and then a third. Hook realized that he would need to seek a safe place to make camp before all light was lost. He increased his pace, his eyes sharp for a place where he could spend the night in safety.

James moved through a small grove of straight beech trees rather than waste time going around. Pushing aside a slender branch thick with leaves, he came out on the far side of the grove and found himself on the edge of a road.

It was little more than a pair of wheel ruts leading up into the hills, the other direction curving around the grove of beeches and lost from sight. James pondered the mystery of that road for a moment, for he had seen no indication of it on the other side of the copse of trees.

"Neverland," he muttered under his breath in disgust.

He had no time to follow the road back around the stand of trees. In all truth, Hook was not certain that he wanted to know if the road suddenly began just out of his sight or if it now ran to some destination that he had not seen before. The island was a strange place. He felt certain that any possible answers would be ahead of him and that there was danger in turning aside from the course he had set for himself.

A road, no matter how mysterious, had to run *to* someplace, he reasoned to himself. Perhaps the very reason that the road existed on the island was to lead to something. Further thought reminded Hook that Cecco had said something about the old Gypsy woman and her wagon.

A Gypsy wagon would need a road to roll along. At the very least, such a caravan would be expected to be found beside a road, even if the road ran from nowhere to nowhere. Slender logic, true enough, James had to admit to himself. Still, it was enough to base his next course of action on.

He set off walking at a brisk pace between the ruts, heading higher into the hills. The wolves howled again, and Hook laid one hand on a pistol. The howling from off to his left was answered by an unearthly scream from a different direction.

It was the cry of a creature he had never heard before. From the treatises he had read regarding the exploration of the wild lands of Africa, Asia, and South America, James thought that it was perhaps the hunting cry of some great cat. Like the wolves, such a beast would view him as prey, though the presence of such hereditary foes as canines and felines made it seem likely that neither wolf pack nor hunting cat would seek prey while they knew a greater enemy was about.

Still, it behooved him to find a defensible place where he could spend the hours of darkness. Hook kept to his pace, knowing that an appearance of fear might act as a lure to any predators that were lurking in the thickening gloom. He also kept a hand on a pistol, in case such a hypothetical predator might be more hungry than cautious.

The sun was nothing more than a shrinking crimson crescent on the western horizon, matched by a huge orange crescent swelling in the east—the moon, coming up as the sun went down though there should have been no moon visible according to the calendar. At the most, if Hook's calculations were off by a few days, there should have been no more than the thinnest sickle of a new moon in the east, rather than that huge golden doubloon of a moon rising slowly into view.

"Neverland," James uttered with heartfelt loathing.

Up ahead, in the dusk, he could see a stand of trees to the left side of the road. The white boles of the trees rose out of a wide circle of bushes. The circle of trees and bushes was back against a heap of boulders that thrust up from the soil at odd angles about thirty yards back from the mysterious road. It seemed likely that James would be able to find shelter and safety there for the night.

Two things occurred almost simultaneously. First was the appearance of a lantern among the bushes, a mellow amber light held by an unseen hand. That was closely followed by the howling of a hunting wolf that could have been no more than a few hundred feet behind him.

The lantern held a promise of safety, while the wolf promised something more dire. Hook quickened his pace, not breaking into an undignified run, but still moving along far brisker than was his wont. Behind him, he could hear the thud of several sets of paws, one sounding louder than the others.

"Trage pistolul!" a husky female voice commanded.

James did not recognize the language, though one word sounded familiar. Without turning to take aim, he angled the flintlock in his hand behind him and pulled the trigger. The roar of the pistol was followed by a frightened yelp as the lead wolf was startled by the noise and bright flash. While it had not been hurt, the sudden blast of the pistol shot made the beast break off its charge for a vital moment.

Hook's long stride took him to the edge of the bushes, which he noted were covered in roses that were protected by unusually long and vicious thorns. The cloaked shape that held the battered old lantern had a gnarled staff in her other hand, pushing back a section of rosebush to create an opening that Hook slipped through with only a few threads snagged from his coat.

"Vino, acest fel," the cloaked woman said, waving her lantern toward a dilapidated old wagon. A low fire burned there, and an iron kettle hung over the fire on a blackened metal tripod.

The growls of several wolves showed that they had followed Hook right up to the thorny bushes. He tucked his spent pistol into his belt and drew forth the second one. The cloaked woman reached out a hand and touched the arm that held the weapon, forcing his arm down with surprising strength.

"Asta nu este necesara," she said with clear meaning. And then, looking into the darkness beyond the roses, "Dispari, puii!"

She added a gesture with her staff to her command. The wolves beyond the rosebushes crouched whimpered for a moment and then raced away, seeking their evening meal elsewhere. Without another word, the cloaked woman gestured to Captain Hook to proceed toward the fire, which he did, tucking his loaded pistol into his belt.

By the fire, James saw two stools and a low table already set with two bowls and a pair of mismatched spoons. Again, the woman gestured silently, inviting the pirate captain to seat himself. Hanging her lantern on an iron rod that protruded from the side of the old wagon, she drove the butt of her staff into the ground so that it stood like a branchless sapling and grasped the hood of her cloak with both hands.

"Be welcome, James ... Hook," she said in heavily accented English, and threw back the hood that had hidden her face.

Chapter 14

Second to the Right

Cecco had spoken of the old Gypsy woman in such tones that Hook had been expecting a hideously aged and bent crone, wrinkled and shrunken by the passage of too many years, frightful to the eye. He should have considered that the Italian had been but a lad when last the "old Gypsy woman" had been in his dreams. As such, he would have looked on any mature adult as old, even ancient. When the Gypsy threw back her cloak, James saw that while she had at least a score of years on him, she was in no way so ancient as he had expected.

A tall, lithe figure, she would have been stunningly beautiful in her prime. As a matron who had seen fifty years or more, the woman was handsome, even striking, with long black hair marked by a streak of pure silver three fingers wide on the left side of her head. Her eyes were bright and sharp, like a pair of brilliant emeralds, like the eyes of a hunting cat. The typically tattered Gypsy finery in which she was arrayed did nothing to hide slender curves that were still pleasing to the eye, despite her years.

Rather than a hag, she had the appearance of a Gypsy queen. James had already heard the regal command of her voice. As she turned and hung her cloak on another spike protruding from the wagon, he could see a queenly grace in her every movement.

"I am known as Madame Vadoma," she said in her deep, husky voice, a strange accent lending a touch of the exotic to her words. "A name that denotes one who *knows*." There was a stress laid on that last word that was freighted with deep meaning and mystery. "And you are the captain of the brigantine that is at anchor in the bay."

She gestured toward the east, languid and yet oddly specific. James had the impression that a compass bearing off her hand would have shown the true course straight back to the *Jolly Roger*.

"Indeed; you are correct—" Hook started to say, only to have her interrupt.

"Yes, you are James … Agamemnon."

Hook laid a hand to the hilt of his rapier, sudden fury mottling his face.

Madame Vadoma broke off what she was about to say and laughed.

"It would be *bad form* to murder a woman for merely speaking the truth of your name," she chided without any evidence of fear.

The captain slowly relaxed his hand and let his face drop back into an emotionless mask. This woman did indeed know much, perhaps too much. James needed to learn what he could from her, not frighten her with threats. And she was entirely correct; it would have been bad form to murder a woman out of pride and anger.

"Come, sit. There is goulash in the kettle, and you are hungry. Bring out your wine; we shall eat, and you shall learn much, Jas," she murmured, gesturing to one of the stools.

The invitation held a note of royal command. Despite an instinct to rebel at that hint of an order, James pulled two bottles from his satchel and placed them on the table before sitting on the stool she indicated. This Gypsy might carry herself as a queen, but she was obviously not his equal in breeding or lineage, no matter that he had discarded his family name and the history that went with it.

"Be not so proud, pirate," Madame Vadoma said sharply, as if his every thought was open to her. "Your ancestry is something you cannot claim because of the facts of your birth."

James scowled, and she laughed at him again, though her manner was friendly rather than harsh.

"What you suspect is true, though your mother was blameless, for what could she do as protest against the will of a king? And the man you called father knew what his cousin had done. Being unable to publicly lay blame, he took his smoldering anger out on you. It is all as you have long suspected, boy."

"How can you know such things?"

"Did not my dear little Cecco tell you about me? Did he not say that I knew his future and revealed much of it to him? I know as I knew that Cecco would return someday in the body of a man, though still much a child. I know as I know that you use 'Jas' not as a short form of 'James' but as your true initials. I know as I know why your middle name is Agamemnon."

She smiled, taking years off her face, and winked.

"I am a Gypsy and a seer, and knowing is as natural to me as slicing a man's throat with your sword is to you, Captain Hook."

"Then you must also know—"

"That you would understand this Neverland you find yourself on? Of course I know that. Come; eat. Open a bottle, and we shall drink. I will tell you what I can, though it answers fewer questions than you would like. Much I know, but this land holds a magic that no one but a child can truly understand in full."

James took her at her word and opened both bottles of wine, pushing the better vintage across to Madame Vadoma. She smiled and nodded at the gesture and ladled the thick, spicy stew into the bowls, sliding the one heavy with meat to Hook's side of the little table. Taking up her bottle, Madame Vadoma inclined the neck toward her guest. In his turn, he lifted his own bottle and clinked the neck of his bottle against hers, and they drank before tasting the goulash.

While they ate, Madame Vadoma spoke of Neverland and what she knew of it. James was uncertain as to how much of what she said was truth and how much was Gypsy superstition, though the entire tale seemed to hang together with a kind of logic.

Neverland had been born of the dreams of children, she told him, a creation of imagination and the purest magic. It was a land somewhere between the waking world and that of dreams, yet touching on both, connected in a physical fashion so that one could step from either the world of dreams or the dreary world of mundane reality onto the sandy shore of Neverland. It was a place where the youthful dreamer could visit from the safety of his bed, yet also an island where boys—and, to a lesser degree, girls—could actually visit and stay until they felt the need to grow up.

The red savages made their home on Neverland, as did the cannibals. There had been a Gypsy tribe as well for a time, though Madame Vadoma was that last of her people on the island. There had been other dangerous folk residing there in the past, and there would be others in the future, as the focus and nature of adventurous dreams changed. That Hook and his ship were there proved that the imagination of children had seized on pirates to be the villains in their dreams and thus had reshaped the nature of Neverland again, as Neverland was constantly reshaped by imagination.

"I am more than a figment of some child's imagination," Hook said hotly.

"Just as I am more than that too. Once we Gypsies were as much a scourge in Neverland as the cannibals. Today? I tell fortunes when the rare boy dreams of the adventure of visiting the Gypsy witch. The rest of my people? Poof! Gone, one by one, when there were no dreams spun into magic to sustain them. It has been so long since anyone has come to me, I begin to think that I shall be gone too, very soon."

A sudden melancholy fell on Madame Vadoma, and she drank heavily, as someone weighed down by sorrow and regret might to drown the memories that tormented her.

"But," she added, putting her black mood behind her, "in you, there is a difference. You are not like the other boys who have come before, and you are not like the chiefs of the red savages or the leaders of the cannibals who were drawn in by the magic spun out by a thousand, thousand dreamers. You are a different sort of boy, completely new to Neverland, whereas they had visited here in their own dreams long before they returned with their people, drawn by magic and illusion even as my *neam* were long years ago."

"Perhaps you have been here alone too long, Madame, for you should be able to see that I am no boy," James said with some heat.

"You would punish all the world because of rejection from the man who was not your true father and the casual cruelty of boys who were only half-brothers to you. You have decided to be a villain because you think you could never rise to fame by your own merit. You would make the name you adopted infamous because you scorn the name you were born to. You aspire to be the pirate whose very mention strikes terror wherever he is spoken of. Is that the ambition of a man?"

She smiled, and there was unexpected kindness in her eyes.

"It is not a bad thing to remain a boy within," she said in a soothing voice. "There is no shame in it. The greatest men of history have held within them the heart of a boy, the memories of a boy, the instincts of a boy. It is what makes a man into a great hero or a great villain. To a boy, there is little difference between the two."

Like a conjurer, Madame Vadoma produced a small loaf of crusty dark bread and broke it in half, tossing the larger portion to Hook.

"You are a boy within, despite your size, your skills, and the experiences and learning that you have gathered over the years.

A handsome boy, a clever boy, and perhaps the boy to change Neverland, if you are clever enough, if you can find your way here a second time, unaided."

"If you know so much as you claim, you know that I have accomplished in my life what no mere boy could accomplish!"

The Gypsy continued to give James the reasons she considered him a boy, though she admitted that many a man was every bit as much a boy as he was. Chief among those charges was his treatment of women. Aside from his mother and one other that she wisely left unnamed, James had little regard for the fairer sex, as they had naught to do with the great goal he had set for his life and thus were of little interest to him.

Madame Vadoma made her argument with calm and reasoned logic, as well as a total lack of rancor. There might have been a touch of pity in her words, though James was not certain of that. If anything, her insistence that he was a boy was tinged with a bit of wistful envy.

James gave thought to the saying that girls grew up much faster than boys. It might also be true that women grew up more completely than men as well, becoming far more distant from the girls they had once been. What he saw in Madame Vadoma was a longing to touch the girl she had once been while believing that Hook was still on companionable terms with the boy that was his past.

"No, young James, you have sought to win at games only a boy would think of playing," Madame Vadoma replied, still smiling gently. "You have played well at being a pirate; you have won at the game time and again until you are a captain of those children you call your crew. Yet, for all that, you remain a boy and show only the cleverness of a boy rather than the wisdom of a man. Only a boy would ignore what was offered from the Fae Folk and think himself virtuous,"

"What do you say?"

Madame Vadoma ladled more the of spicy stew into her bowl,

her gnarled hand shaking, and added more to Hook's bowl also. He had eaten well, for all that his mind was on her words and not the food she offered him. After hanging the scoop on the wall of the wagon beside her, the Gypsy queen answered in a thin voice.

"One of the Fae Folk offered companionship, and you ignored her. Not your fault, for you could not have known. Despite that ignorance, there will be consequences for what you did, or rather, did not do. That little *zân* will be gone by daybreak, and her kin will blame you. They are not ones to quickly forget nor forgive."

She shook her head sadly.

"The path you tread will be difficult enough without the enmity of the Fae Folk."

"Eh? What do you mean by that?"

"When a *zân* offers as that one did, she binds herself to the boy. Being rejected makes her *inim* break, and her light, it goes."

Madame Vadoma made a gesture with her left hand, as of something bursting into fragments. Her dull green eyes turned sad.

"That little one, she will be no more when the sun comes up again. Not your fault, boy. Not wisely done either—the pride of a boy instead of the wisdom of a man. You rejected what seemed worthless to you without caring what value it might have or what effect your rejection might have. The other Fae Folk will not forgive you."

Either her words or the wine was making Hook's head spin.

"Should I fear them?"

"This I tell you for truth, and you may remember it always: If you find your way back to Neverland a second time, you will never need fear any man, nor any creature with fur or feathers. No *zân* will harm you, even though none will ever aid you either."

She smiled sadly and shook her head.

"Only one need you fear among the tribe of man, and he is boy—yet more than boy. The king of Neverland and the slave to the dreamers whose magic keeps him young forever. Master of all things in Neverland and the winner of all games played on the island, he is gone now on a great adventure, trying to escape what he is fated to be."

The Gypsy upended her bottle and drank deep.

"Neverland needs a leader for the boys. Sometimes he becomes tired of who he is, what he is. Then he goes on an adventure beyond Neverland, pretending very hard to be someone else. Sometimes so hard that he forgets even his name. Always, he is drawn back. Neverland calls to him when he is unhappy at that play, trying to bring him back where he belongs. He cannot escape Neverland's hold on him."

Neverland calls to him when he is unhappy, Hook thought. As when Red Michael beat him. That was what took the *Jolly Roger* so far from her course at such times. Neverland was trying to bring this leader of boys back to the island when his misery made him vulnerable to the magic of the place.

Madame Vadoma eyed James Hook with speculation.

"Except perhaps this time the magic will find a new boy to focus on. Someone to be a leader of boys, a captain of a crew even more ruthless than pirates, for who is more ruthless and cruel than an innocent boy? When boys come, either in their dreams or in reality, they will need someone to lead them, with the ageless boy now gone."

The Gypsy yawned, her gray hair hanging in her eyes, hiding the wrinkles that had grown on her face as she spoke.

"Gone, yes," she continued, "but he will return. He will be drawn to reclaim his crown and his chains, and then you two shall match your skills."

"Aye? And what will be the outcome of such a contest?" James asked, grasping his own bottle of wine.

"Ah? Who shall win? There you have found a question I cannot answer."

She emptied the bottle and tossed it aside with a wrinkled, crooked hand.

"I know much, yet some things are denied even to me. That

meeting itself is hazy, dependent on your actions and your cunning. First, you must be able to find Neverland once you leave it. That test is something I cannot help you with."

Withered lips stretched in a dry smile that showed yellowed teeth with many gaps.

"Two things I can still tell you: The first is that you are a special boy, unlike any other in Neverland. The second, which you must remember and find understanding to, is a simple phrase that means nothing to me. 'Second to the right.' Nothing more than that. 'Second to the right.'"

Madame Vadoma stood, small, hunched, and wrinkled, one eye milky and blind, the other a faded green.

"I must rest, boy. I don't think I will see you in the morning."

She turned and hobbled to the steps at the rear of the wagon, climbing them slowly. The moonlight made the thin white hair on her head glow, save for the black streak shot through with gray, three fingers wide on the right side of her head.

James felt suddenly sleepy and noted with some surprise that his own bottle was as empty as the one Madame Vadoma had discarded.

"Yes, it is time for sleep," she rasped as a shaking hand opened the door of the caravan. "You by the fire, and I in my wagon. There is no need to fear the wolves or other predators of Neverland. Even the cannibals fear to come near, and the wolves are far wiser about such things than the cannibals."

Hook was too drowsy to do more than stumble from his stool and spread his sea cloak near the fire. It was only the instinct of long lawless years that made him stab his sword into the ground where it would be close at hand in case of need. Too tired even to load his spent pistol, he barely heard the Gypsy croak out, "Good night, boy," before he was asleep. On his first night ashore in Neverland, no dreams disturbed his slumber.

The sun was well above the horizon and sending spears of painfully bright light through the trees when James awoke in the morning. Before opening his eyes, he listened closely for any hostile sound while gathering his wits. The floor beneath him did not sway, so he was not on a ship. He did not hear breathing or the mutterings of voices, familiar or strange, so he was not ashore with a raiding party. The scent of roses and the warble of songbirds helped him place where he was. An island, a strange island, aye, that was it. Neverland, yes. And in the camp of the old Gypsy woman.

Hook sprang to his feet, his right hand closing with practiced ease over the hilt of his rapier, his left touching the butt of his loaded pistol even as his eyes scanned the clearing around him. No one in sight, no threat to be seen.

Nor was there the smell of cooking food, as might be expected, for Madame Vadoma should surely be awake by that hour and preparing to break her night fast, even if she had nothing on the fire for him. Come to that, the fire was dead and cold.

Too cold to have been burning under the kettle of Gypsy stew as it was last night. And the kettle was not as he remembered either, being a rusted and useless hulk with the bottom eaten out of it, hanging on a time-worn tripod that had bent under the weight of that burden many years ago.

That was strange, very strange indeed. Hook turned toward the wagon, seeing it bound by rose vines until it seemed furred with thorns and red blossoms. Surely, the paint had not been so faded; surely, the wooden roof had not been so gray and weathered. The bright colors that had shown in the firelight were all gone, mere ghosts of the glory he had seen the night before.

And what of the Gypsy seer? James had vague memories of her tall, straight, and beautiful, yet also he could see her as an ancient, half-blind crone in her last days.

Magic, she had said—the island reeked of the stuff. It could destroy as easily as it could preserve. Madame Vadoma had spoken of the dragons and other creatures of myth that had faded while the mermaids and fairies remained. Might the last of the

Gypsies, the Queen of the Gypsies, have finally had her last night in Neverland?

James Hook cleaned the tip of the blade on his cloak, thrust his sword back into its scabbard, and hastened to the rear of the caravan. Vines and creepers had formed a web that barred him from reaching the door Madame Vadoma had used the night before. He reached out and pulled a liana free with some difficulty, then dropped a hand to the hilt of his blade.

No, no, he would not cut his way in. He might find the moldering skeleton of the woman he had dined with the night before. He might find something worse, something more mysterious, perhaps something deadly dangerous.

Another thought came to Hook. What if he had not slept through the night but, instead, slept through the years? Given his knowledge of tropical botany, James estimated that at least two years would have been needed to tangle the old Gypsy wagon in the rose vines and other creepers that enveloped it. What if Smee and Teyne had long ago given him up as lost and sailed away?

He glanced at where the two empty wine bottles lay in the grass. Both looked as if they had been used and discarded the night before, just as his memory indicated. The sight of them did nothing to put his mind at ease. If he was right, it was only the morning of the day after he left the *Jolly Roger*, and the first mate and bosun would not even consider a course of action until evening of the next day. But if he was wrong, if he was wrong and the evidence of the Gypsy wagon was the truth...

Hook slashed an opening through the entwined hedge of roses hiding the way to the road and struggled through the gap. Barbed thorns at clutched him as if to hold him there until he was as old and faded as the wagon. Sharp steel defeated the thorns, though tufts of fabric were left behind as trophies for the roses.

The road still ran as it had the night before, unchanged from how he remembered it. That was not reassurance enough, for dusk had cloaked that part of the island when he had seen it. He had to return to Buccaneer Bay and see the *Jolly Roger* safe at anchor, see the crew waiting for his return.

James Hook was not so unmanned by his thoughts that he ran unheedingly down the road. If some foul magic of Neverland had robbed him of several years while he slept, there was no need to hurry, for the brig would be long gone. On the other hand, if, as seemed more reasonable—if reason had aught to do with Neverland—he had passed only a single night on the island, his ship and crew would be there as he expected.

In either case, there was nothing to be gained by throwing caution to the wind and running blindly toward whatever he would find when he reached the bay or toward whatever danger might be found along that path. His return to the *Jolly Roger* would be a deliberate thing, returning along the path he had followed the day before.

With a thought to possible dangers, Hook reloaded his spent pistol and checked the priming on the flintlock he had not discharged. Satisfied that his weapons were in order, he marched downhill, matching his stride to the marks his shoes had left in the dirt of the road the evening before.

Returning to the bay proved easy until he reached the edge of the Vale of Fairies. When he had left there, butterflies had marked the boundary. As he approached from the west, a low buzzing filled the air. Tiny dark specks patrolled the area, specks that resolved into bees, wasps, and hornets as he drew closer. The insects buzzed with anger, darting toward the pirate captain several times in a threatening display until he halted in his tracks.

The words of Madame Vadoma regarding the fate of the fairy that had approached him gave James a clue as to why the valley had turned hostile. Rather than force the issue and risk an assault by those tiny stinging beasts, which he had no means to combat, he chose to circle around the vale. It would delay him more than he liked, but Hook knew the wisdom of discretion and was not too proud to use it, at least when there was no one to witness him doing so.

The new route chosen by James Hook led along a brush-covered ridge before descending into a dark forested valley festooned with hanging curtains of gray-beard moss and enormous cobwebs. The skeletal limbs of dead trees reached out like the grasping hands of drowning men. Owls hooted mournfully in the gloom, and chittering bats fluttered overhead even though it was bright morning elsewhere in Neverland. Pools of black water gurgled and grudgingly loosed bubbles that burst with a fetid odor.

If the Vale of Fairies was a place of light and magic, the Gloomy Forest was in every way the opposite. Even Hook, who feared only the sight of his own blood, felt chills down his spine more than once as unwholesome sounds echoed dismally from the inky shadows on either side of the twisting path he followed.

Though he saw nothing and heard only the croak of frogs and the moan of the wind, he became convinced that several *things* were padding along in the murk just out of sight—hostile things, creatures that were trying to decide if he would be able to defend himself against them. With such suspicions, he slid along as silently as he could, sword and pistol in hand, stopping suddenly now and again to whirl about, trying to catch a glimpse of any beings following close astern.

Besides the concern for his own safety, the Gloomy Forest inspired Hook to brood upon some of the things the old Gypsy had said the night before. Her insistence that he was but a boy, despite his years of education and experience in the wide troubled world was a canker on his pride.

"What mere boy could ever aspire to what I shall achieve?" he muttered to himself, eyes darting from side to side as he looked for a sign of the beasts that must be stalking him.

A darker smudge of shadow in the somber gloom faded back as Hook glanced toward it, and he stepped from his path, raising his pistol to fire. There was no target to be seen, so he advanced further into the Gloomy Forest, taking another pace away from the vague path he had been following. What danger he might have found had he pursued shadows into that haunted valley will never be known, for the rolling thunder of a distant cannon shot drew his attention back in the direction he had been heading.

A signal gun from the *Jolly Roger* fired at the moment Captain Hook was most in danger of losing himself to the phantoms of the dismal woods. His suspicions of shadows and brooding thoughts were replaced by a clear recollection of his goal and a lively curiosity about why Teyne or Smee had fired a cannon to summon him back to the ship.

Hook no longer felt concern that the weird magic of Neverland might have keep him asleep while years passed. He knew every gun aboard his ship by its bark and was certain that the shot he had heard was from French cannon that Dietz called "Philippe."

James advanced with caution, still retaining his sword and pistol in his hands. The end of the Gloomy Forest was at hand, the valley opening into a flower-bedecked meadow, with healthy stands of oak, fir, and birch trees further off toward the bay where the *Jolly Roger* was obviously still at anchor. It took a moment for his eyes to adjust to the brilliant light beyond the limits of the Gloomy Forest, and when they did, he was glad that he had moved with such care and silence.

An unexpected tableau had been frozen in place by the shot from the ship. A magnificent stag and three does stood motionless, heads up and staring toward Buccaneer Bay. A score of yards from them, crouched in the tall grass, were three other figures clutching bows, half drawn, arrows at the ready.

Red savages they were, the very sort that Bill Jukes had so feared. A hunting party, from their look. James could see that all three wore breeches of leather worked with beads and a sort of soft leather slipper that allowed them to move silently. Beyond that, they wore only leather bands about their foreheads that supported upright feathers at the back of their heads and bands of fringed leather about their upper arms.

Knives hung at each hip, supported by belts of woven grass. The eldest of the three, who hung back from his companions, also carried a kind of short hatchet. Its blade was of chipped flint, just like the knives. Across each shoulder was another woven-grass belt that held a birch-bark quiver of stone-tipped arrows.

They were a primitive people, straight-limbed, stern-faced, handsome, and noble in bearing. The two younger men had hair as black as the curls on Hook's head, though theirs was straight and braided into two plaits that hung down their backs. The older hunter had streaks of iron-gray in his braids and deep lines of age across his copper-colored face.

It might be thought strange that Hook did not look upon the savages as lesser men, merely as less civilized men, and he thought the better of them for that. It should be remembered that James Hook looked on nearly all men as lesser than he was, so to him the difference between the noble savages and his own crew were vanishingly small. If anything, he viewed the hunters as an example of the purity and nobility of the natural man when compared to the sloth, greed, and venality of such civilized examples as could be found aboard the *Jolly Roger*.

Remaining in a crouched position, as motionless as the hunters, James watched as the stag flicked one ear in the direction of the bay and suddenly bolted northward, the does trailing swiftly after their lord and master in leaps that covered a dozen feet at a time. The red savages remained as if statues cast from copper as their quarry fled beyond the reach of their arrows. The eldest hunter, obviously the leader of the band, gave a whispered command and a sharp jerk of his head in the direction the rumble had come from. In an instant, all three sped silently from the meadow nearly as swiftly as the deer, going in search of the source of that strange thunder.

While he had no fear of them, Hook could see nothing to be

gained by confronting the savages while they were on the hunt. From his extensive education, he understood that such primitives had strong, simple rules for life—laws and taboos that they never strayed from. They often viewed chance strangers in their land as deadly foes. James Hook had no desire to begin his association with such a people by being forced to kill three of their hunters. It would not have been good form.

As he trotted along once more, he thought of how the savages would react to boys from beyond Neverland in their hunting grounds. From what he knew of boys, he understood that whether in Neverland only as part of a dream or in the flesh, any lad worth the appellation "boy" would relish fighting with red savages just as they would enjoy combat with cannibals.

Would they occasionally lose in their murderous play? Was that why children sometimes died in their sleep? Because they failed in the deadly games they played in Neverland?

Such thoughts made James very glad he had never dreamed of this island with its bizarre magic and wonder. If it had been within his nature, he would have felt pity for men like Cecco and Jukes, Smee and Dusk, who had visited Neverland in their childhood dreams and still carried enough memories to fear the island.

And what of the leader that Madame Vadoma had mentioned? The boy, currently absent, that she had called king and slave? What she said put Hook in mind of Tuck. Not merely because of those nightmares that had eventually drawn the *Jolly Roger* to Neverland but also for other, less obvious, reasons.

Boys usually grew like weeds, yet in the months that James had known the boy, Tuck had not grown a fraction of an inch. Unlike other boys his age, he never lost a tooth. Tuck never even had one that was loose and wiggly in the way that boys so enjoy showing off. All his teeth were still the small, even pearls of first teeth.

Only someone who knew of Neverland, who understood what the place was—even as imperfectly as Hook understood it—could possibly recognize and believe the impossibility of what Tuck was. He was not growing up, not aging. He remained a boy, the same boy that Captain Kendrick had pulled from the sea, unchanged in any fashion.

"He goes on an adventure beyond Neverland, pretending very hard to be someone else," James muttered to himself, remembering what the Gypsy had said. "Sometimes so hard that he forgets even his name."

Tuck did not know his own name, though the lad had said that he was sure he would recognize his name if ever he heard it spoken. Hook was not certain if he should be glad or dismayed that Madame Vadoma had not gotten around to speaking the name of the eternal leader of the boys on Neverland. He was certain that he would search for Tuck once they were away from Neverland though. King or slave, Tuck deserved to remember who and what he was.

But first, Captain James Hook needed to prove himself, if what Madame Vadoma had said was true. Not to himself or to his crew. He had to prove himself to Neverland. He had to sail away from the island and find it again. To that end, he wanted to reach the ship before noon so that he could fix their position.

Yes, he could take the noon sighting the following day if he missed his chance that day, but Hook was too impatient to wait another day if he could avoid it. The prize was more than an island where he could bury his treasure and hide from the navies of the world after he committed a particularly memorable act of piracy that put his name on every lip. There was what the old Gypsy had prophesized, that he had no need to ever again fear man or beast if he could find Neverland once he left it. No man to fear in all the world, save for one particular boy, and Hook was certain he knew who that boy was.

Tuck would never be a person that James Hook feared, for he had taken the measure of the lad and understood Tuck very well. The former ship's boy was a *good* boy in every sense of the word, without the casual cruelty that was a part of most boys as much as their hands and feet. He would never fight in earnest against his old shipmate James, so the only person that the Gypsy said he had to fear was one of the very few people that he felt he could trust.

If he misjudged Tuck, no matter. It had been Hook who taught Tuck to fight with a blade. Hook knew every trick he taught the lad, and he knew what tricks Tuck had not been taught as well. He had no fear of the outcome of such a fight, should it come to that.

Moving quickly, yet with all the caution he possessed, Captain Hook headed downhill toward Buccaneer Bay, choosing a different route than the one employed by the hunting party of red savages. A glance at the position of the sun assured the captain of the *Jolly Roger* that he would reach his ship before it was time to take the noon sighting.

Chapter 15

The Neverstar

Smee and Teyne, bosun and first mate, stood by, fidgeting while their captain took a sun sighting and then a second and a third, muttering under his breath with evident dissatisfaction. James was an experienced navigator and used to finding latitude quickly and with perfect precision. The sightings he took on Neverland that day came out wrong every time. None matched the other sightings and not one was even close to any other.

"Brimstone and gall," he stormed finally, "I will have to discover another way!"

"Er, Cap'n," the acting first mate ventured hesitantly.

"Yes, man. What is it?" Hook snapped peevishly.

"Well, sir, you ain't inquired yet as to why we set off a gun ter call ye back."

Hook's piercing blue eyes aimed at Teyne like a pair of pistol barrels.

"It were on a-a-a … c-c-c-count o … of th-th-th … the savages." the mate stuttered, unnerved by the intensity of his captain's stare.

"Aye, that's right, Cap'n," Smee added helpfully, hoping to defuse Hook's anger. "Red savages, just like Bill Jukes said there would be. A dozen of them came around the tip of the bay, gathering shellfish in the shallows until they saw the old *Jolly Roger*."

"More of the savages?"

"Aye, Cap'n," Ed replied eagerly.

He missed that Hook seemed familiar with the natives, but Smee did not.

"Have you met with them already, Cap'n?"

"Aye, Mr. Smee. I saw a hunting party of the redskins on the island, though they did not see me. I was concerned when your signal drew them to the bay. It seems, however, that you acted properly after all, since their fellows had already found out that we are anchored here."

Captain Hook said that in such an offhand way that Smee almost missed the hint that Hook might have viewed the firing of the cannon as something worthy of punishment rather than praise. Looking closely at his captain and still seeing the signs of agitation on his face, the Irish bosun was glad to have pleased Hook rather than angered him. He would have to explain to Teyne at some later time how careful they would have to be to stay on good side of their new captain.

"Mr. Smee, get my ship ready to sail," Hook commanded. "Mr. Teyne, have those men not on duty assembled with muskets and pistols to be ready should the savages return in a hostile mood. Have Mr. Trommler stand by the landward guns as well."

It took some time to get the *Jolly Roger* ready to sail, for they had to wait for the tide to turn. Bill Jukes did not mind standing near the rail with a musket in his hand, for the thought of redskins troubled him mightily. His shipmates tended to grumble after a while, standing idle when they could be rolling dice or playing cards or passing time in any of a dozen more pleasant ways.

To most of the crew, it seemed that their new captain was overly cautious and timid. It seemed that way until a score of narrow boats filled with red savages rounded the southern point of the bay and a dozen more canoes filled with redskins glided

down from the north. Then it seemed like their captain was pre-
scient beyond the ability of normal men and thus to be respected
and feared all the more.

As Hook had supposed, the culture of the savages was one
that viewed those outside their tribe as foreign invaders to be
repulsed at the earliest opportunity.

To that end, every warrior available had been turned out
along with every one of the birch-bark boats that were able to
carry them. Spears with flaked-flint heads as sharp as razors were
shaken in the air along with stone-headed hatchets, a promise of
what was to come. Bows were strung with deer-gut thongs and
feathered shafts with stone heads like needles were ready at hand.
Copper-colored faces were streaked with war paint, stripes of red
and black, circles of blue and ocher, and green slashes like lightning bolts masked the features of every warrior.

Each slender boat had a champion at the bow, eager to be first
to slay one of the invaders. Knobby wooden clubs, flint knives,
and stone axes were clutched in the hands of those leaders as they
screamed defiance and insults that no one aboard the *Jolly Roger*
could understand.

Most of the crew caught the gist of those shouts even if the
words were unintelligible, and they shouted back insults that were
every bit as indecipherable to the red savages. The words, at any
rate, were beyond the understanding of the attacking warriors.
The intent was as clear to the savages as their insults had been to
the seasoned hands aboard the *Jolly Roger.*

Captain Hook watched the approaching canoes with a practiced eye, judging when the proper moment had arrived.

"Gunner, sink me that lead boat, if you will," he said calmly
to Dietz.

The gun captain complied with alacrity, finding that those
howling savages stirred a long-dormant fear within him. Like Bill
Jukes, Dieter knew the redskins from childhood dreams, though

his memories were more faded than those of the much-tattooed English sailor.

The six-pound cannon ball skipped twice across the water before striking the first canoe dead on and ripping through the fragile birch bark and branches from end to end. The war chief was thrown high into the air and fell back to sink without a sound into churning waves, killed instantly. The rest of his men struggled in the water, some badly injured, other merely shocked at the ease with which these invaders had destroyed their canoe from more than three arrow flights away.

"And now the same to those coming from the north," Captain Hook said with a trace of wicked glee.

The phlegmatic master gunner complied, shattering another canoe into splinters and leaving half a dozen savages swimming away from an equal number of their slain companions. The crew of the *Jolly Roger* roared with approval and merriment, cheered by the ease with which they had bested the redskins.

What they did not notice, but Hook did, was the massive scaly back, low in the water, making for one of the slain savages. Something huge and reptilian swimming in the bay had scented an easy meal. That gray-green back sank from sight a few yards from one of the bodies. A splash and gleam of wicked jaws lined with jagged yellow teeth and the beast was gone along with one of the floating corpses.

"Mr. Trommler, I want a very near miss on the closest remaining boats both to the north and south," Hook declared.

He did not want to provide more provender for that creature than was already adrift in Buccaneer Bay. Primitive monster though it was, that giant saltwater crocodile might come to associate the area with food and remain, which was something that James Hook did not want.

"We will lay claim to this bay with a demonstration of what we can do."

"Er, begging you pardon, Cap'n, but why not just blow a few

more boatloads of those red savages out of the water?" Smee asked in confusion.

Smee was not a bloodthirsty man by nature any more than he was a deep thinker. It just seemed to him that the most practical thing in the world would be to kill as many of their enemies as they could while the opportunity presented itself. Letting so many of the hostile savages live while firing close beside them seemed a waste of powder.

"Mr. Smee, I foresee a great many possibilities if we have a safe haven on Neverland. A slaughter of these savages now could not possibly be complete and would leave us with deadly enemies that would stop at nothing to gain revenge."

Dietz fired a gun to the port side and one to starboard, sending up geysers of water that almost swamped the canoe in the lead of each group of redskins. Shouted commands from the champions in each boat had them reversing their course in the hopes of getting beyond the range of the guns aboard the pirate brig.

"Keep firing close behind them, Dietz," Hook commanded. "Cease fire when they pass beyond the points of the bay."

And then to Smee, "The savages will recognize our claim to Buccaneer Bay and the lands around it because we have demonstrated our ability to hold these lands. Thus, they will not be constantly trying to murder us every time we go ashore nor shall they attempt to sneak aboard during the night and cut our throats, as would be the case if I had ordered the slaughter of those we could kill before the rest of them escaped our guns. They will give us peace here, expecting us to keep from their hunting grounds in return. No doubt there has been a similar arrangement worked out between the redskins and the cannibals."

"Oh, er, I see," Smee said with some confusion.

"No matter, Mr. Smee," Hook said tiredly.

The bosun was good at his job. He had an easy way with the crew and was generally liked by all hands. He did not, however, think far beyond the moment. It had been remarkable that Smee had had the forethought to bring James to the *Jolly Roger* when the ship was so desperate for a new quartermaster.

It seemed to James that it would forever be a waste of time to explain the finer points of his schemes to the Irishman. He sighed to himself again, knowing that it was in his nature to try even when success was so unlikely. Besides, it tickled his vanity to have someone he could display his brilliance to, even if that man did not fully understand.

"Come, Smee; the tide will be turning soon. Up anchor, and prepare to make sail!"

The men of the *Jolly Roger* worked with a will to get underway, for none of them had been comfortable anchored off Neverland. Unlike their captain, they had had dreams when they were young and still remembered enough of those dreams to know the dangers of the island. Moreover, they recalled something that no one had mentioned, that none of them spoke of even among themselves: the boys.

A gang of boys roamed the island, having adventures under a leader who was bold, daring, and reckless. With their leader to guide them, those boys fought redskins and cannibals, slew bears and wolves for their skins, and dared anything for excitement. That band of boys that disdained all things of the adult world would view the crew of the *Jolly Roger* as just another group of foes to fight and kill, for the boys reckoned as nothing the cost of a life and saw only a glorious exploit in bloodshed and slaughter.

Rough, lawless pirates that they were, the crew of the *Jolly Roger* felt relief at being away from the island. They had seen neither hide nor hair of the boys—and for that they were thankful. Red savages and cannibals were something they could deal with. A pack of wild boys, unrestrained by civilized rules, was far too dangerous for honest buccaneers to face. Their captain may have been fearless, but the crew displayed a more practical turn of mind. Gold meant nothing to dead men.

The *Jolly Roger* sailed before the wind until the island had dropped below the horizon. Unsatisfied with the calculations he had made, Hook did not want to sail too far from Neverland before returning to it. Within a turn of the glass after the last peak had disappeared below the horizon, the captain ordered the brig brought hard about and stood beside Murphy, the helmsman, directing him to follow along a direct compass bearing back to Neverland.

But they sailed for two hours without sighting so much as a smudge on the horizon. Hook checked and rechecked his charts and the bearings he had taken. He ordered the five sharpest sets of eyes aloft to scan the horizon in all directions in search for the slightest hint of land, each man with a spyglass and the promise of the captain's share of their next prize. He had the course reversed again for another two turns of the glass and then sailed perpendicular to their previous course for half an hour before turning ninety degrees and sailing for another hour.

Hook was becoming frustrated by his inability to find the island. Neverland was not so small a speck of land that it could have gone unnoticed by the many lookouts crowding the mastheads. His melancholy blues cye began to burn with a demonic fury as his aggravation grew more intense. That frustration was vented on those of the crew around him, with many harsh words being fired at Smee and the others like broadsides from a man-of-war, though to little effect.

Erudite as he was, the insults he chose flew over the heads of his intended targets. Men like Jukes, Cecco, and Smee could only marvel at their captain in his rage. They were enthralled by his use of invectives, which once again demonstrated to them that James Hook was superior to any other captain who sailed under the skull and crossbones. While impressed by the skill that Captain Hook displayed, none took offense, for none among the crew understood the tirade, only the emotion behind it.

Up and down sailed the *Jolly Roger*, back and forth as well, quartering the waters around where the island should have been found. Yet never was land sighted, nor was there the slightest sign that any land might be near. The watch changed, and Murphy was replaced at the wheel by One-Eared Jacob. Smee brought up a platter from the galley for Hook, though the captain only picked at LaSalle's best effort while brooding over his inability to perform such a simple task as navigating back to an island they had but recently left.

By that time, the tropical night had fully fallen. Rather than sail on in the darkness and possibly miss sighting Neverland, James Hook ordered the sails furled. His crew eagerly performed the task under Smee's supervision. Once that was completed, most of the men went below for rum and their bunks, exhausted by a long day with too much work in it for their taste. Only Hook, Smee, Jacob, and a couple of hands on watch remained on deck.

It had been a full and active day for James as well, even more so than for any of the crew. Unconsciously rubbing his thumb across the silver ring that he wore on his right hand, he dozed where he stood near the wheel, almost asleep on his feet. As he hovered between wakefulness and sleep, while he was in that place where dreams are born, he saw Neverland again.

It was his old dream but with more depth and breadth than ever before. First, he saw a vast array of glimmering stars, and chief among them was the one that shifted hues like a tiny diamond throwing out its rays of light. That old familiar star threw its light on an island that he knew was Neverland, which he saw from the viewpoint of a bird circling high above. And close to that old familiar star, to its right once removed, was another, smaller star, one that had never been in his dream before, one that stood directly over the central peak of Neverland.

As he wheeled like a bird in the sky, that new star remained stationary over the island, marking its position clearly in the night sky. Hook suddenly knew the meaning of the phrase that Madame Vadoma had spoken to him; he understood the meaning that she herself had not.

"Second *star* to the right," he said aloud and, in speaking, woke himself.

For it had been a dream, come to James Hook, who never dreamed except that one dream. He—who had never seen Neverland in his sleep as a child, who had never fought cannibals or explored exotic jungles, who had never experienced any of the thousand different adventures most children have in Neverland after they shut their eyes for the night—finally had a dream of Neverland. Waking from that dream, Hook knew what must be done.

The bosun was smoking his pipe, quite content even though he knew his captain was upset over his failure to find Neverland again. He kept a drowsy eye on Hook, who stood nearby, asleep on his feet. Rest was just what the captain needed, Smee thought to himself. In the morning, Hook would come to terms with being unable to return to Neverland, which would be best for all hands. After that, they would return to the Spanish Main and the proper business of piracy. Or perhaps the *Jolly Roger* would sail for the East Indies. There were plenty of rich cargoes to be snatched there as well.

Smee was close to sleep himself and did not notice when Captain Hook suddenly straightened where he stood.

"That star, Smee—do you see it?" Hook demanded of the drowsy bosun, pointing to the one star in the heavens that matched the star in his dream.

"Eh? Star?" Smee babbled, startled to full wakefulness. "You mean the Neverstar, Cap'n?"

Realizing what he had said, Smee clapped his hands over his mouth as if to capture the words, but it was too late. They had made good their escape and scurried into Hook's ear, telling him more than the Irish bosun guessed.

"The Neverstar, eh, Smee? A fitting name. You know it, I see," Hook said with an extreme display of politeness.

Smee already understood that Captain Hook was at his most

dangerous when he was the most polite. That unholy light was beginning to flicker in Hook's blue eyes once again. Smee knew that he would need to choose his words with care, lest his friend do something both he and Smee would regret.

At least Smee hoped that James would regret any rash action on later reflection.

"Aye, Cap'n. I recalled just now that we named it such in the dreams I had of this place as a lad," Smee replied cautiously. "I have not seen such a sight since I was a wee fellow and had forgotten it until you pointed it out to me."

If not the complete truth, there was a kernel of fact in his words, and that appeared to be enough to satisfy Hook for the nonce. Smee hid the sigh of relief he felt when his captain turned away to gaze at the stars again.

"And that other star, Smee, second to the right from the Neverstar—do you know it as well?"

"Er, ah, well, I can't say as I do, Cap'n. It does not seem much special to me, not like the Neverstar."

"No, Smee, not remarkable to the eye, is it?" Hook's soft voice suddenly rose to a bellow. "Get all hands on deck, Mr. Smee! Teyne, where are you, you sot? Shake out all sails! Double the lookout aloft! We make for Neverland, or we'll never set foot on any other land!"

Rum and weariness made the men clumsy when James wanted swift and sure action. There was a prize at stake that none of those common sailors could begin to understand. It took all of Hook's self-control not to lash out when Skylights stumbled into him yet again or when Noodler let a line slip through his clumsy, twisted hands.

"Control and good form, James," he muttered to himself as the canvas finally belled with the weight of the wind. "Control and good form always."

"Stand aside, Jacob," Hook ordered, taking the wheel in his

own two hands. "I have our course, and I will guide us back to Neverland!"

The captain of the *Jolly Roger* did not see the shudder that passed through every man on deck who heard his words.

James Hook was certain he had glimpsed the key to finding Neverland. It could not be found by day, only by night, at the edge of sleep. In that twilight place, between the waking world and dreams, there the Neverstar could be found, and second to the right from the Neverstar was the celestial marker he needed to guide him back to the strange and wonderful island. He could almost taste the prize that awaited him when his ship was able to drop anchor in Buccaneer Bay once again.

As he brought the *Jolly Roger* around onto the course he wanted, Hook saw a brief sparkle to the water ahead as the ship pointed directly toward that second star. The bowsprit swung over a touch too far, and the magical flicker vanished. Aye, Hook exulted silently; he had it now. A delicate adjustment brought the ship onto the proper line, and that elusive ribbon of rainbow light stretched out ahead of them once more.

He could trust none of the men with this task. Standing at the wheel and correcting their course to keep the second star ahead of them, James smoked one of his dwindling supply of cigarros. The silver skull ring he had taken from Red Michael seemed to laugh and wink in the starlight as he adjusted the rudder to keep on the slender road that sparkled and flickered on the starlit water. Excitement kept him on his feet when his exhausted nature demanded that he sleep. Smee had suggested that Jacob or Murphy take the wheel, but Hook would not have it. Neverland lay ahead, and he would not rest until the island was in sight.

Dawn came, and the last of the starlit sea road flickered and vanished. At the same moment, the lookout sang, "Land ho!"

Hook gave the wheel over to Murphy and staggered to the bow, Smee hovering at his arm. Aye, that was Neverland, no mistaking it. The *Jolly Roger* was approaching from the same point where she had approached the island the first time. Drunk with fatigue, James entertained the bizarre fantasy that Neverland could only be approached from one point, no matter what the compass said. He knew the secret; he had the key. That was all that mattered at that moment.

"Aye, Cap'n. You have brought us back to Neverland," Smee said with false joviality in his voice. "Now, you should take a nice rest before anything else."

"Rest? Aye, Smee. Have LaSalle prepare me tea and scones, and wake me for the noon sighting."

Weaving from side to side, Captain Hook made his way below with a worried Smee still at his elbow.

"While you were ashore, we cleaned up the stern cabin for you and moved your belongings, Cap'n. Hope it pleases you."

Pleasing Hook with the state of his new quarters was not what had the bosun worried, however. They were back to Neverland, where he had hoped never again to find himself. With the captain having discovered the way, Smee was unhappily certain that they would return whenever Hook had the notion to do so. There would only be trouble ahead from that—no mistake.

The bosun hurried ahead and flung open the heavy windows to let in fresh air. The room was thick with the odor of vinegar and lye, proving that the room had been cleaned in the proper fashion. Fresh bedding called to Hook with a seductive whisper that he could not possibly ignore. Fumbling with his coat, the captain of the *Jolly Roger* fell across his new bed and was instantly asleep, not even stirring as Smee drew off his shoes and picked up the coat he had dropped without a thought.

"You will be wanting things neat and tidy, I wager," Smee whispered fondly to his captain as he hung the coat on a hook and arranged the shoes on the planks under the coat. "This ship will run a good sight better than when Red Michael was captain."

The Irishman looked out the stern window, catching a glimpse of the escarpment where the red savages had their village.

"And we'll be a good sight better off once we are away from this terrible place."

Nature insisted that James Hook needed sleep. Yet his active mind would allow only so much time to be wasted in idle slumber before it roused him again.

It was a few minutes before noon when Hook was on his feet. Even before Starkey could knock, Hook was at the door, coat and shoes back in their accustomed place, his navigation instruments in his hands.

"Fetch Mr. Smee, Starkey," Hook commanded briskly. "We still have work to do before the sun sets."

As before, the sun sighting he took proved to be very unsatisfactory.

"Neverland," he muttered under his breath, in part fondly and in part with disgust.

The magic of that island meant that there was no way to fix its position on the chart. That also meant that there would never be a map that could lead a foe to Hook's secret retreat from the mundane world either. Bad and good together—which might be the hallmark of Neverland for Captain Hook and his crew.

"You wanted to see me, Cap'n?"

"Smee, do you recall the discussion at the Bent Cutlass regarding burying the treasure we gather rather than risk it falling into the hands of the authorities?"

"Aye, Cap'n, that I do. Though I must confess, I think it better to keep our gold where we can lay hands—"

Hook interrupted his bosun. "I have decided that the gold and emeralds we took on our last visit to Isla de Tres Palmas should be safely hidden away here until after we have ascertained conditions on Tortuga, Mr. Smee. To that end, I need you and eight good men to take me to that grim rock out there along with the booty so that we might see it safely hidden away until we return to claim it."

James could see that Smee was puzzled by the need to bury their ill-gotten gold. No wonder in that, for it made more sense to have coin where they could spend it. Their experience with the French navy on Tortuga, however, had given Hook an idea. Treasure had a great power if hidden away, especially if only one man could lead the way to where it was hidden. It would not matter if the entire crew knew where their booty had been buried if only Hook alone could navigate their way back to Neverland.

Smee at the tiller and Captain Hook at the bow were the only ones who had a good view of the massive gray dome of rock glowering under the late afternoon sun. Cecco and Skylights, Dusk and Noodler, Starkey and Jukes, Cookson and Mullins—all pulled at the oars in pairs, their backs to the bare hump of rock that Smee guided the longboat toward. It was just as well, for capricious nature—or perhaps some greater power than natural chance—had fashioned that sullen heap of stone into a semblance of a misshapen human skull sitting in the shallow, reef-strewn waters east of Neverland.

None of those hard-bitten brigands of the *Jolly Roger*'s crew would have been pleased to see their destination. By the time Smee called for them to ship oars, they were already drifting into the cavern that made the mouth of Skull Rock, and it was too late to voice any objections.

Under Hook's direction, the nervous buccaneers hauled the chest of emeralds and most of the gold onto a ledge of stone within Skull Rock while their captain poked about, seeking the ideal place to conceal the treasure. In less than half an hour, a hollow below the opening that formed the left eye of the massive skull had received the chest and sacks of gold. Loose stones of great weight had been shoved over the hollow and more stones arranged over the slabs until Hook was satisfied that the hand of man could not easily be seen.

By the time the longboat returned to the *Jolly Roger*, the western sky was a riot of orange and red clouds marking the setting sun.

"Break out the rum, Mr. Smee, and see that all hands have a proper share," Hook declared with satisfaction. "Have the cook send dinner to my cabin. It has been a long day, and I feel the need for rest."

Captain James Hook looked around at his ship and his crew, his blue eyes for once displaying happiness rather than melancholy. He absently brushed back the thick, hanging curl of black hair over his right ear.

"Eat well and drink well, my fine gentlemen; you have earned your ease."

Hook looked again at Smee.

"Bosun, have everything ready to sail with the morning tide. Make certain that Mr. Teyne posts an alert watch, in case those red savages have not yet learned that Buccaneer Bay belongs to the men of the *Jolly Roger* alone."

Captain Hook bestowed a smile on all the men on deck. It was a rare thing, a smile from James Hook that denoted genuine pleasure at the efforts of others. Smee had seen it only twice before that he could recall, both times when Tuck had performed remarkably well at defense and offense under the tutelage of Hook. To see the entire crew of the *Jolly Roger* receive that approbation was a rare treat indeed.

The night passed peacefully. There was no sign that the red savages planned another foray against the pirates. The dawn sun was only a few degrees above the eastern horizon when Captain Hook stepped on deck, attired in his finest coat and feathered hat. His normal dreamless sleep had left him feeling refreshed and ready to meet the day and take on the world.

The smile Hook displayed at that thought was in no way as wholesome as the one he had graced his crew with the night before. Take on the world, indeed. That was precisely what Captain James Hook would do—take on the entire world. Neverland would be his retreat, his stronghold. From there, he could sail forth and make the world fear the name of Hook.

"The tide is turning, Cap'n," reported the bosun.

"Mr. Smee, we need remain here no longer," Captain Hook

said to the one man aboard who might almost be considered a friend. "Prepare to make sail."

"What course, Cap'n?" the bosun asked, eager to be away and about their proper piratical business.

"We sail for the Spanish Main, Mr. Smee. We have business there that remains incomplete."

Smee looked puzzled.

"What business, Jas … er, Cap'n?

Hook smiled, a cruel and frightful smile that brought cheer to the Irishman. Whatever had been troubling his captain, Hook had put it behind him. James Hook was back to his old self, no mistaking that.

"The comandante of Isla de Tres Palmas laid a trap for us and thinks he has bested the crew of the *Jolly Roger*. He killed more than a dozen of our shipmates from ambush. Thus, to my mind, he owes us a debt of blood, and never let it be said that Captain Hook failed either to pay a debt or to collect a debt owed."

Yes, Smee thought to himself, whatever had been troubling the captain was behind him. Off to the Spanish Main on a voyage of revenge. After that, there were ships to plunder and treasure to stow in the hold of the *Jolly Roger*. It was the life of a pirate, and a merry one—nor likely to be a short one with a man like Captain James Hook to chart their course.

"Oh, Mr. Smee, when we have reduced the fortress on Isla de Tres Palmas to rubble, remind me to leave a few of the Spaniards alive."

"Eh? Why's that, Jas … er, Cap'n?"

The sinister smile on Hook's gaunt, handsome face grew wider.

"Someone must carry the tale, Mr. Smee. How will the world learn to fear us if we leave no one alive to carry the tale of what it means to cross Captain Hook and the men of the *Jolly Roger*?"

The End

Definitions

Beakhead: Protruding forward part of a sailing vessel which served as a working platform to attend to the sails on the bowsprit.

Binnacle: Wooden stand that holds the ship's compass.

Bowsprit: Forward-pointing mast of a sailing vessel, which carry the spritsails.

Brigantine: A two-masted sailing ship with the foremast square-rigged and the mainmast rigged with both a fore-and-aft mainsail and square-rigged topsail. Light, nimble and of shallow draft, this craft was ideal for piracy.

Culverin: A large, long-barreled cannon that fired a 5 ½ inch ball weighing more than 17 pounds.

Forecastle: Raised forward section of the ship that also contains the quarters for the common seamen.

Galleon: Large sailing ship having three or even four mast. Multi-decked, with a large crew and heavily armed. Well-known for transporting treasure for the Spanish crown.

Hempen Jig: Pirate term for being hung as punishment for their crimes.

Keel: The central beam running from bow to stern along the bottom of the ship, around which the rest of the hull is built.

Keelhauling: A punishment where a rope is passed under the ship and the victim tied by his hands to one end and then pulled over the side, under the ship and back up again on the opposite side. The barnacles and other growth common on a ship's bottom inflict deep cuts and scrapes to the victim.

Ketch: A sailing vessel with two masts, a large mainmast and a smaller mizzen mast behind it, square-rigged. Commonly used to haul cargo.

Linstock: Short staff that held a lit slow-match used to fire a cannon.

Poop deck: Aft elevated deck of a ship that also forms the roof of the stern cabin.

Slop chest: Aboard a pirate vessel, a store of miscellaneous garments and other small personal items gathered from stolen cargo for the use of the crewmen.

Sweating: A form of punishment used by pirates for entertainment. Prisoners would be forced to run a circular gauntlet on deck under the hot sun until completely exhausted, urged on by the fists, clubs and dirks of the pirate crew.

Waist: That part of a ship between the forecastle and the poop deck.

Printed in Great Britain
by Amazon